# THE SOLACE OF SILENCE

# THE SOLACE OF SILENCE

# KIM MURRAY

Cover design and typesetting by Luke Harris
www.workingtype.com.au

Published in Australia by Australian Inspiration 2022
www.australianinspiration.com.au

ISBN: 978-0-6453926-2-3

*For Jock, Coquette, Penny, Beaver, Bella,*
*Dame Patsy Cline and Wee Geordie McKay*

**Among a blaze of lights ...**
*Siegfried Sassoon (1886-1967)*

*When I'm among a blaze of lights,*
*With tawdry music and cigars*
*And women dawdling through delights,*
*And officers in cocktail bars,*
*Sometimes I think of garden nights*
*And elm trees nodding at the stars.*
*I dream of a small firelit room*
*With yellow candles burning straight,*
*And glowing pictures in the gloom,*
*And kindly books that hold me late.*
*Of things like these I choose to think*
*When I can never be alone:*
*Then someone says 'Another drink?'*
*And turns my living heart to stone.*

# PART ONE:
## SYDNEY, 1979

# THE HONOURABLE SIR ELLERY KENDALL QC MP

'Another drink?'

No, I didn't want another drink. If anything turned my heart to stone it was the prospect of sharing conviviality with this over-dressed old fag beside me. I was bored with the noisy, chattering crowd and it irritated me that I was forced to be in their company, feigning good-will and friendship. Normally, I enjoyed my wife's charity affairs because I liked being near her, and, besides, they were always well-organised and brought in millions of dollars for her favourite causes. Tonight, though, I was in no mood for false pleasantries, the attention of over-scented women who wanted to embrace me, or men who wanted political favours. I was restless and weary. Anxious.

I wished myself a long way from this room, even if it was one of the finest venues in Sydney, overlooking the harbour and its twinkling evening lights. How did that Siegfried Sassoon poem go? 'When I'm among a blaze of lights, with tawdry music and cigars ...' Not that there was anything tawdry about this occasion, I thought, glancing around the hotel banquet room with its chandeliers, fine furniture and carpeting, exotic flowers. The men were like magpies in their bespoke black dinner suits and bow ties, the women shimmering like jewels in their couture satins and taffetas. Bankers, politicians, actors, musicians, professors, corporate executives, diplomats: they were all there, the imagined crème of Sydney society, vying to be photographed for the social pages of newspapers and magazines. As always, my wife Anna Maria was the brightest and most beautiful.

'I said, another drink, Ellery?' There was a waspish edge to the voice with the distinct Italian accent beside me, and I reluctantly turned towards the annoying pest. His smile was forced because he knew I had avoided him all evening. And we hated each other. 'You're a million miles away, my friend. No doubt in your world of politics. That legislation you're hell-bent on rushing through …' I took the glass of fine malt whisky from a passing waiter, and gave my determined tormenter my public relations smile, the one the friendly press described as urbane and deceptive. The less friendly described it as akin to a smiling barracuda. It amused me to think of the many epithets used to cover my career in law and politics. But not tonight. My present concern was to untangle myself from this loathsome man who, I hoped, would be out of my life forever in a few days.

'You are a man who always win, no?' Was I mistaken, or was he nervous? I hoped so, because he had every reason to be. It repulsed me to be in his company. 'How do you do it, Ellery?'

I stared at him: Maurizio Stopelli, just recently returned from yet another visit to Italy, a former minor Italian diplomat who discovered that selling drugs provided a more lucrative income. How can *you* do it, I wanted to ask. How can you kill young lives and not give a damn? The room darkened as I thought of my son Robbie, now buried in a remote part of Ireland. He would have been twenty-four this week. Years ago my gentle, talented boy had asked for money to travel to Ireland to take up a scholarship at Dublin University to study his favourite war-time poets, and I was delighted to see him pursue his dream. Money was never a problem in my family, but finding one's dreams a little more elusive. I sighed. It was always the same when I was tired. Guilt and grief moved in to remind me they were a just a pin-prick away.

Only Anna Maria could dim the memory of a pathetic creature lying dead in a Dublin morgue, one year after he had arrived in Ireland, a lifeless body scarcely recognisable as my handsome, athletic son. 'He'll be buried in Ireland,' a skinny, pale-faced girl with an Irish accent had told me. Certainly not, I had protested; Robbie was coming home to Australia for burial. 'But you can't take him away, Mr Kendall,' she had persisted with that soft voice and glazed eyes, this girl who once was pretty, before the alcohol and drugs took over. 'Robbie and I were married .... Did he not tell you?' No, he had not. After the first few letters when he arrived, telling me he was settled in his flat and the generous bank account I had set up for him was organised, I heard very little from him. My phone calls were rarely answered, but he assured me he was happy and busy writing his thesis. All lies.

I remember standing in the rain in a green and picturesque country cemetery, seeing nothing, hearing nothing, unable to offer comfort to anyone, least of all to my son's mother. We were robbed of our only child, and when I threw the black Irish soil on his coffin, I declared war on illegal drugs and those who dealt in them.

Stopelli had been talking now for some minutes, but because I was lost in the past I hadn't heard a word. Now I tuned in, because I wanted to see him squirm. There was sweat on his upper lip, and I knew that soon he would have to patch up his make-up. He looked grotesque, even in an expensive Savile Row dinner suit; short, thick-set, balding hair slicked over to imitate abundance. And evil. Make the most of your freedom, I wanted to tell him.

'You are a lucky man,' he said, 'a beautiful wife, political power ... but such a vendetta, this thing of yours ... will it work?'

'The government's anti-crime legislation, you mean? Oh, yes.' I spoke slowly for emphasis. 'Stringent laws to put behind bars any criminal involved in the illegal drug trade in New South Wales, *and* the rest of Australia if the States follow us? That will give the police greater powers? Working with the Federal police to patrol our coast-line? Powers to investigate sudden and unexplained wealth? Beefing up police facilities and a new drugs unit with unprecedented powers of surveillance? That one you mean?' Stopelli was now drinking fast. Almost gulping his vodka. 'Of course it will go through. My colleagues have been lobbied hard by some sections of the community who are not sympathetic to our policies, and keen to water them down. And, of course, there's been opposition from civil rights groups, who seem more interested in the rights of criminals and victims. No, we have the entire parliament behind us.' Well, eventually. Not without some bitter, hard-won fights. 'And you'd be surprised who crawled out of the woodwork with information in return for favours.'

'Well done, Ellery. If you succeed ...'

'Not if, but *when.*' I felt compelled to sharply interrupt and correct him, because my first prize would be this swine and his vile trade. For far too long he had been protected by powerful sources. I laughed out loud, but without humour and several people, including Anna Maria, turned in my direction. She broke away from a smiling group where she was obviously telling an amusing story, and hurried towards me, lifting up the long skirt of her black strapless gown which had arrived that morning from her favourite Milanese couturier. I drained my glass before she reached me.

Stopelli was pale as I continued to speak in forced but pleasant tones. 'Many people in this town don't want these laws see the light of day. Threats ...' I let the words hang in the air as Anna Maria was almost upon us now, smiling her wide, wonderful smile. Thank God I could now leave this odious man. It was dangerous to be seen with him. I left him with one last parting shot. 'Let's just say, Mr Stopelli, I vowed years ago that I'd clean up the illegal drug trade in this city. That was a personal promise. As Attorney General sworn to uphold the State's interests, it's my duty.'

'I wish you luck, Mr Attorney-General. You may need it. You have a saying in English, no? Don't count your chickens before they are hatched. Goodnight.' His smile was grim as he turned on his heel and headed for the exit.

What an evil bastard. I turned to Anna Maria and kissed her warm, pink cheek. She took my arm and pressed close to me. She looked, felt, and smelt, soft, warm and beautiful. If the bodice of her gown showed too much breast, I consoled myself that I was the one she would sleep with tonight. She belonged to me; not completely, but enough ...

'Come on, darling, circulate. I need you to charm our guests into parting with wads of cash for an excellent cause.' Only Anna Maria could be so attractively blatant about taking people's money. She nodded briefly at Stopelli's departing figure. 'I have no idea how that man got here. He's hateful,' she whispered once he was out of earshot. I felt her round little breasts press against my jacket. 'But the good news is that we've raised half a million dollars so far.'

'You're a wizard, Anna Maria Kendall.' And you're driving me insane with desire, I wanted to add. It was true on both counts. People willingly handed over cash or signed huge cheques for her drug rehabilitation projects, or clamoured for the expensive pleasure of attending her balls, dinners, or cocktail parties.

'What on earth were you saying to that shit?' she asked, shivering with distaste and pressing even closer. My dear wife, glossy and gorgeous, but still the plain-speaking country Italian girl. She greeted a former Governor General and kissed him on his aged, wrinkled cheek. 'Sir William, how lovely to see you ...' She swept passed and dropped her voice. 'I couldn't believe it when I heard you laughing with Mr Stopelli. We never invite him, you know, but he's hard to keep out. Diplomacy, and all that. Plus he donates.'

'A guilty conscience, my dear.'

There was much that Anna Maria didn't know. We slipped into a balcony overlooking the new Opera House and the harbour in all its brightly-lit glory on a warm summer evening. It was good to be away from the noise and the warm crowded room for a few moments, to hold her close, brush her hair with my lips. She was tiny, and, without a high school certificate or university degree to her name, one of the smartest people I knew. I had been attracted to Anna Maria Peroni the moment I saw her behind the cosmetic counter of a city department store ten years ago. Now I loved her with all my heart.

She married me for my money, but I didn't care then, or now. I would have married her under any circumstances. She was then barely twenty, a child, and my friends and family ridiculed my infatuation and begged me to drop her, to stop making a fool of myself, but I ignored them. At forty-five, I wasn't too old to make Anna Maria happy. After Robbie's death, my huge house in Vaucluse was a mausoleum, and, like me, empty and miserable. My young wife brought laughter back into my world by coaxing me away from my desk and to the pleasures of our bedroom. I loved watching her dressing, hearing her sing, as she moved about the house and garden. She had a lovely voice, and I encouraged her to take singing lessons. Opening nights at the opera were special occasions for her, when she was at her most vivacious and yet lost in her own musical world. It wasn't long before she established a trust to raise money for music students.

She was the only one who could make me forget how I had lost my son and my previous wife, both by drugs. One by accidental overdose, the other by her own hand. No wonder I hated the damned stuff.

I tell myself that this beautiful Italian immigrant girl learnt to love me in the years we've been together, but I'm never sure. I worry that one day I will come home and find her gone. Yet I do trust her. Anna Maria has an integrity that I rarely find in political life; she was loyal and in her simple, pragmatic way she had entered into a contract that she would not dishonour. Well, I told myself that. I offered her the life she craved, and if I could not offer her youthful passion in bed, I could hold her and keep her safe. I hoped it would always be enough.

She accepted jewellery, clothes and property with grace and not an ounce of greed, and when I was knighted in the Queen's Honours list for 'special contributions to the justice system' – essentially for doing my job – she was thrilled that my work was recognised and she was now a 'lady'. Yet no matter how cleverly she hid it, there was a shadow, a secret, between us. She wanted children, and that was the one thing my wealth and family name couldn't provide. I didn't want to share her with children, but when she told me three years ago that she was pregnant, I went along with the charade. At least I knew, and liked, the father.

I felt a nudge at my elbow and I was jolted into the present with Anna Maria now beside me on a quiet balcony in a five-star hotel, tables heaped with exquisite food, with the background noise of elegant orchestral music and lively chatter from a room ablaze with lights. She adjusted my bow tie. I smiled down at my lovely, pragmatic wife and whispered how much I loved her. Instead of the usual tossing back of long black hair, her expression became serious as she tightened the grip on my jacket sleeve.

'I know,' she said softly. 'And I love you too.' Do you, Anna Maria, I wondered. Do you really? I wish I believed you. No man had a more delightful companion, a more endearing lover, or a greater supporter of my work, but her heart did not belong to me. Not exclusively. That no longer hurt me. When I spent long hours in parliament house, I didn't enquire where she spent her time; she was always home when I needed her. We had a good marriage. I had my work, she had her committees and ran our homes to perfection. And we had Annabelle. I told myself throughout her pregnancy that I would accept the child without recriminations, but when she arrived I loved her instantly. It helped that she looked like Anna Maria.

We turned back towards the crowd who were becoming drunk and generous. Undoubtedly, it was going to be one of Anna Maria's greatest successes. She deserved it; she had worked hard to be accepted by my friends and family, to find a useful place in Sydney where she could do good work. If my brothers and sisters still refused to accept my Catholic, immigrant wife, it mattered little to me.

To her credit, she had won over my mother, Coralyn, who was a difficult, domineering but practical woman. After a frosty start following the wedding, Coralyn warmed to my new wife and drew her into her own privileged Sydney world. Shrewdly, Coralyn recognised that while her daughter-in-law loved fine possessions and luxury, she was a good organiser, and talented at extracting money from potential donors. Nor was she worried by hard work; not always was she in couture gowns and luxurious venues, but frequently seen in jeans and tee-shirt scrubbing tables or cooking food in homeless shelters. At her request, we never spoke of her family. I knew of them only as market gardeners who ran their business within a whisker of the law.

A waiter interrupted to say there was a telephone call for me. He indicated a private room nearby, and I kissed Anna Maria's hand as she left to rejoin her guests. Once alone, I welcomed the silence and privacy. When I picked up the phone, I was surprised to hear the voice of Police Superintendent James Duffield – 'Duffy' – who had just resigned from my staff, and whom I had earlier in the evening farewelled and thanked for his services. He had been a brilliant adviser, always with his ear to the ground and a mine of information about Sydney's criminals and their activities; he had a sharp mind and a crude, always accurate summary of any given situation. I was sceptical about him when he was seconded from Homicide to work through the anti-drug legislation, but it didn't take me long to appreciate his talents. True, some of his methods were highly irregular, but he got the job done. He drank too much and his vocabulary was blistering, but he was a good, clever cop. Now that our work was finished–or at least now waited to be turned into law – he was back at his old desk at police headquarters, and, I suspect, pleased to be in his natural habitat with his old mates.

Duffy and my parliamentary chief-of-staff, Roland Perritt, were a good team who made my work much easier because of their persistence and skill. While Duffy understood the law, and picked up the protocols and compromises of parliament, he never disguised his distaste for the media or parliamentarians. He hated the laborious committee work, and the 'duchessing' of opponents towards a particular viewpoint, was a tough negotiator with a hot temper, but usually with a hidden card up his sleeve. Yet he often surprised by occasionally adopting a softer, more devious approach to win a point. Above all, he was a man who knew too much. He cared. Cared too much, in fact. That could have been awkward, but it had worked out.

Duffield never wasted time on irrelevant telephone calls or chit-chat. I sighed deeply with a tiredness that was bone-deep. I knew what was coming.

'Yes, Duffy? I'm guessing you're about to say we've got some problems? More threats?'

'My contacts inside Homicide say this one involves you *and* Lady Kendall, sir.' The slide into formality was deliberate. My grip on the phone tightened, and I opened the door slightly to watch Anna Maria standing within a group of admirers, her head tossed back at some joke or compliment.

'Do what's necessary, but keep it discreet. I don't want my wife worried.'

'Any change to who's at your home now?

'No. Just Annabelle. Her nanny, the housekeeper, and the

gate-keeper. You know that house, Duffy; it's as safe as modern tech-nology can make it. God knows we've been through this often enough.'

'I've seen the guest list, but anything unusual about your guests tonight?'

'Well, I see your police mates dotted about, looking uncomfort-able in dinner suits. Tell them next time to do something about their shoes. Stopelli's here, but he seems a bit strange. Issued some kind of warning ....'

'We're keeping an eye on him.'

'God, I hate all this security.' I meant it. It had been a tedious, perpetual problem since I began my anti-drugs campaign a year ago, and I wanted it to end. I changed the subject. 'I appreciate all you've done, Duffy. I wouldn't have got this far without you and Roland ...'

'Not true, Ellery. This is yours. Good luck for tomorrow. I'll be in the Chamber. Any chance the Opposition will retract their support?'

'You never know with that lot, but I doubt it. We've agreed to a few last-minute amendments, but nothing significant. More a question of letting them appear to have contributed when they've done nothing for years.' Why bother telling Duffy? He knew the fight better than anyone. I was wearier than I thought, and definitely anxious. I took a deep breath. 'No, all going well, it'll pass through both Chambers by this time tomorrow night, and law once the Governor signs it off.'

It was stupid to feel uneasy about tomorrow. Everyone, from the Premier to the Cabinet and the backbenchers, were behind me. Even the Opposition, always ready for a fight, had eventually agreed. It hadn't been an overnight demonstration of support, but rather a reali-zation that crime was an election issue for both sides of parliament. The increasing reports of deaths by drug overdose and gangland killings in Sydney could no longer be avoided. Once our powers were legally extended and consolidated, I wasn't naïve enough to think we could stop drug crimes entirely, but by God we would disrupt their profiteers' cess-pits. Perhaps then I could let my son sleep in peace.

'Ellery?' I had been silent for too long, and Duffy was prodding me into action. 'I'll have Stopelli followed when he leaves. When are you due home?'

'About midnight.' I glanced at my watch. Once home, Anna Maria would be high-spirited and fuss about me getting a good sleep, but then chatter about the evening and insist on a final glass of champagne.

'You'll be well-covered, Ellery. But be careful. And goodnight.'

'I have every faith in you, Duffy.'

As I hung up, the door slid open behind me, and even before I turned to see who it was, I knew it would be Anna Maria. Her trademark perfume of *Joy* filled the tiny space.

'What is it, Ellery? Another wretched threat?' Her voice was husky with concern. I felt her fingernails dig into my jacket sleeve, the sharpness almost painful. 'Whatever that phone call was about, nothing must stop you now. Nothing.' Her deep brown eyes were almost black with intensity.

I assured her it was simply a check on security arrangements for our departure, but she raised her eyebrows and I knew she didn't believe me. Her body was stiff against mine, but she gradually relaxed and pretended to adjust my jacket, smiling up at me. I was struck yet again by how fresh and young she was. At thirty-one, she still had that glow, that freshness, that first captured me.

When I first saw her, I wondered whether she was Greek or Italian. She was small and slim, dressed in smart, but obviously home-made clothes and always wore impossibly high heels. Her skin was the colour of light milk chocolate, and her brown eyes were huge and ringed with long, long lashes. It didn't take me long to find the steel behind the gentle gaze. I was excruciatingly clumsy when eventually I found the courage to stop one day at her counter to ask her out. She was embarrassed, blushed pink, and said no to my invitation.

I couldn't help myself. I eventually wore her down, and we had lunch in a harbour restaurant on a lovely sunny afternoon. A week later we had dinner in a fine hotel. Each time I found her lovelier, more interesting and desirable. Very soon I asked her to marry me. She didn't look surprised, but promised to think about it. She did, and as soon as she turned twenty-one, she left home and moved into my house with a small suitcase; we were married in the garden a week later in a short ceremony attended by few people. I opened accounts for her in department stores, European couture houses, and urged her to buy as many dresses, shoes and handbags as she wanted. Jewellery I lavished on her. She accepted everything, but never made demands. In truth, she didn't have to.

'Don't worry,' I said now, and pulled her even closer. Within the welcome privacy of that small space, I wanted her to myself before she was swallowed up by her guests and protection officers. 'I won't give up.' My heart thumped too fast, a reminder that I was more exhausted than I cared to admit. The months, the years, of gruelling parliamentary grind were taking their toll, and, as my doctor reminded me, I wasn't a young man. 'Everything will be fine. Duffy's in charge.'

"Good. You are a great, brave man,' she whispered, clearly troubled. 'You work hard, against such odds, fighting so many people ...'

'My dear, what's wrong?'

She was silent for some moments, but then her words came out slowly, reluctantly. 'My father, the Peroni family, would never harm us, I know, but he has heard of new threats against our lives. That's all he knows, but he is worried.'

I heard laughter above the music, and wanted to end this conversation. To take away the troubled look in my wife's eyes, have her home and safe. Amongst our beautiful possessions and flower-filled garden. Far from the grim reality of poor odds of fighting crime in a big city. I resolved then to retire, take her away on a long holiday as soon as possible. Show her every European opera house. Just her and Annabelle.

14

'We're safe, Anna Maria. I wouldn't let anything happen to you or ... our child. And Duffy has everything under control.'

'I know, my darling, I know. Forgive me ...' She trembled slightly. 'It is just that today, when my father telephoned, I was frightened. I felt that enemies had entered our world ... wanted to destroy us ... tear down the beautiful life you have given me and our baby.' There were tears in her eyes, but she blinked them away. 'We must be brave.'

She is a gifted actress. Within seconds, she flung back her hair and laughed as I took her elbow and guided her towards her guests. Heads turned in our direction and she was swept away with a smile and a glass of champagne held high. I was again alone in my blaze of lights, and my heart felt like a living stone. Especially when I saw Stopelli leave the room, a backward glance at me and a curious, dreadful smile on his face.

\* \* \*

### A Bird in a Gilded Cage

*(Arthur J Lamb and Harry von Tilzer, 1900)*

*The ballroom was filled with fashion's throng*
*It shone with a thousand lights*
*And there was a woman who passed along*
*The fairest of all the sights ...*
*There's riches at her command.*
*But she married for wealth, not for love ...*
*Though she lives in a mansion grand.*
*She's only a bird in a gilded cage*
*A beautiful sight to see*
*You may think she's happy and free from care,*
*She's not, though she seems to be.*

# LADY KENDALL (ANNA MARIA)

Thank God someone handed me a glass of champagne. I could hide my feelings behind a smile and no-one saw my hand shake when I raised the glass to my mouth. People crowded around me, chattering and laughing, but I was barely aware of them. I glanced at Ellery and saw how worried he looked. He had learnt to hide behind a smile, but he could hide nothing from me. Like me, he pretended to shrug off threats and almost believe we were safe behind security gates, minders and policemen. Tonight was different, though. I could tell.

Around me my guests laughed, embraced, chatted above the music, made plans and promises, established contacts; they filled the coffers of the Kendall Trust Fund for destitute young people, and I was grateful for that. Everything was perfect: the room was beautiful with flowers, perfume, music and crystal lighting, the atmosphere one of goodwill and affluence, but I felt creepily watched, followed, trapped. And I hated it. Why couldn't I shake it off? Surely we were secure? Ellery and I were so *privileged*.

Ellery, poor darling, was exhausted. He worked too hard in a hard, horrible world, and he was not a young man. His bad memories still tore at him, no matter how hard I tried to make him happy. I glanced around the room and saw him staring at me. I wasn't surprised; his eyes rarely left me. I smiled back and shrugged sympathetically. Soon we can leave, I silently signalled to him, safely at home and in bed. There we are safe.

I loved my life with Ellery, and who would not? He was my husband, lover, bodyguard and banker. I loved his money and his title, his homes and apartments. I loved my beautiful clothes and jewellery, our overseas holidays, our servants and limitless credit cards. I knew his love for me was a desperate, possessive thing, and he feared I would leave him. But I would never do that.

If ever I felt like a caged bird, I worked harder at making our marriage a good one. He deserved that. At home I fussed over Ellery, poured his drinks and listened to his problems, his frustrations, how duplicitous the world of politics was. How much he loved me. He was an easy, generous man to live with, a careful lover and a thoughtful friend. To the outside world he was important, imperious, patrician, but a kind and loyal soul to those he cared about. When we married, his mother, Coralyn, objected to her favourite son marrying a poor immigrant shop girl with a murky family background, but when she saw that nothing shifted his resolve, and realised only I could bring her son back to life, she accepted me. She extracted her price, but I could live with that. Only then did she invite me into her circle of rich society matrons and committees devoted to raising funds for anti-drug campaigns and rehabilitative shelters. Of expensive lunches and pooled gossip. I shared the hatred she and Ellery had of illegal drugs; I didn't want my daughter to die the way his son had died.

Why was I so nostalgic tonight, I wondered, as I sipped champagne and laughed at an unfunny joke. People were so silly after a few glasses of wine, but it opened their cheque books. I nodded, asked questions, flirted, flattered, and then heard myself being introduced as 'Tonight's wonderful hostess, Lady Anna Maria Kendall, our shining, much-loved star ...' and then I stepped onto a podium to thank everyone for coming along, and for their generous support ... and so on. Blah, blah. I spoke for only a few moments because it was still a trial to speak in public, conscious of my slight accent. Even if Ellery thinks it's cute, to me it's a constant reminder that I am a migrant, a stranger in this land.

Ellery stood at the back of the room, leaning slightly against the wall, tall, elegant, distinguished in his perfectly-tailored dinner suit. Showing his age, but still a handsome man. He is so proud of his Italian shopgirl, I thought, despite what his family and friends think. It was easy to have him fall in love with me; poor man, so lonely, heart-sick, almost crippled with remorse about his son's death and his wife's suicide. I knew I would marry him. Or someone equally as rich. It was my destiny; from the age of twelve I vowed to escape the dust and dull-ness of poverty and shabby clothes, the shame of being called names at school because of my skin colour and the lunches of salami sandwiches. Or my family's *difference,* their lack of English and their hard-scrabble work in paddocks. I never saw myself as a gold-digger, or whatever word people used to describe me. In my own way, I love Ellery and I owe him loyalty and companionship.

Stepping down to applause, I glanced at my watch. One more hour and we could go home. It was unusual for Ellery to wait for me, and it was an indication of his concern. Usually he was content to leave my functions after a quick, professional, thorough tour of the room, a handshake there, a quick word here, an enquiry after someone's health, a whisper to someone useful, a flattering comment to a political supporter. A promise to me that he would be home waiting up with a nightcap. Tonight he was just as charming, just as amusing, but his eyes were dark with concern.

Thank God Ellery was not a jealous man. Would any other man have sat motionless behind his desk as his wife told him she was pregnant by another man? Only the sweat on his upper lip and the trembling of his hand as the fountain pen almost snapped gave him away. No anger, no accusations, merely an acceptance that I wanted this child. If he had kicked me out of his office, beaten me, called me a whore, I would have understood. I would have gone. But he had listened quietly and nodded.

'I'll always look after you, Anna Maria, because I cannot bear to lose you,' he had said. 'Trust me with your child.' There were tears behind his fading grey eyes, but his voice was strong and determined. I believed him, for I had always trusted Ellery.

But I loved James Duffield. He owned my heart. All my houses and diamonds, titles and designer clothes couldn't replace that. I had fallen in love with him many years ago when he was a junior but ambitious cop investigating my family for growing tomatoes to sell without a trading licence. He was so very tall, dark-haired, with a beautiful, strong body and blue, blue eyes. He broke every rule, and laughed while doing it. He wasn't interested in my family's minor infringements, but rather in getting me to meet him when he was off-duty. And I was just as keen. Knowing my family would object, we had to meet secretly. Sometimes we took the ferry to somewhere, or walked in the city parks and shared food from cheap cafés and restaurants, but whatever we did, it was fun. He made me laugh. We were both young and inexperienced, both migrants, and shared the memory of children uprooted from one country to live in another and always feeling misplaced.

It was so easy to share his bed and learn to love his body. I knew he was a tough man when crossed, and he had seen things in his work he wouldn't share, but when he was with me he was the kindest, most tender man in love. When he held me, I felt the world was a safe place; I still do.

He was as poor as I was. He cared little about money, happy so long as he had enough to buy our lunch and a glass of wine. He was smart and over the years he won promotions within the police force, but he would never be a rich man. I silenced him when he talked about the future. He wanted to marry, have children, build a future together, and always be happy, in love. When he was working or I couldn't escape my family, I used to lie on my bed and talk to my sister about the life of a policeman's wife: night shifts, poor pay, the fear of him being injured, or worse, never coming home. Yet you love him, she would say. Yes, I do, I would sigh.

I knew my flaws. As much as I loved James, I could not rid myself of wanting *more* from life. More material things; a different life from that of my poor, shabby family. I wanted to shed the burden of being an immigrant girl in a country that wasn't mine. Only with money and possessions could I see myself secure and respected. Marriage to a rich man was the only way I could see that happening. Of course, if I let my dreams wander I knew it would in the world of opera, but who would accept me and train me? I had no money, no contacts. All I knew was that at work I had seen wealthy women in their expensive designer clothes, an aura of confidence encircling them as they bought dresses and handbags without checking the price. That was the life I could have. Even if I had to pay the price.

It broke James' heart when I told him I would marry Ellery Kendall once I turned twenty-one, and was free to escape my family. I only had a few months to go. James was hurt, and disbelieving. And explosive with rage. I couldn't blame him. For the first time I saw the fierce temper for which he was both famed and feared. He begged and argued non-stop, then walked away but came back three days later, hung-over and exhausted, to continue the argument that I was wasting my life with an old man, had betrayed his trust and thrown his love in his face.

We cried together, but James never understood. How could he? I asked the impossible from him. How could he accept that even when I married Ellery, I wanted – no, needed – him in my life? When I told him that that, he had again exploded in fury; how could I expect him to share! And on and on it went. Even on my wedding day, I secretly met James to tell him I loved him, and always would. Again, we cried. I am ashamed when I think back on those days, and how driven I was to shape my world the way I wanted it. How selfish I was. How cruel. Yet I couldn't let him go.

For nearly a year we stayed apart. Without Ellery knowing, I bought a tiny house in Potts Point overlooking the harbour, shrouded in trees and set back from the street. It was in a quiet but busy street and no-one noticed when I came and went. I begged James to see me again. For weeks he refused, but we couldn't stay away from each other. We were soon meeting regularly, and with his training, he was a master of slipping inside without detection. We never mentioned Ellery. James was still wounded and angry, sometimes bitter, but he mellowed over the years and returned to the fun, gentle boy I knew and loved. He still made me laugh with his playful antics and funny stories. We were still so in love.

When Annabelle was born, he refused to see me again. His anger was spent; now he was deeply depressed at the thought of his child being brought up by another man, and who could blame him? That separation lasted six months, but soon we were meeting again in our sanctuary. I longed to share our child, but that was impossible. Not for the first time, I realised the cruel consequences of my actions. I learnt the bitter truth that there are many things that money cannot buy.

I now know how wrong I was, James. So very wrong. God forgive me, but I wish I had not abandoned my family. I wish I hadn't hurt you, and forced you to share me with another man. Ellery is a fine man, and I cannot leave him. I will not abandon him. But how I long to go home with you tonight and share your future with our child. I cannot undo the past, no matter how much I pray I could. Nor can I forgive myself for the damage I have done to your life. I hate the compromises I forced us both to make. It's true, as the English say, if you make your bed you must now lie in it.

But I am frightened, James. Tonight why do I wish it all could – should–have been so different? And why, my darling James, do I have this terrible feeling I'm going to lose you?

\* \* \*

***To a mouse ...***
*Robert Burns (1759-1796)*

*The best-laid schemes o' Mice an' Men,*
*Gang aft a'gley,*
*And' lea'e us nought but grief and pain,*
*For promis'd joy.*

# SUPERINTENDENT JAMES DUFFIELD (DUFFY)

'Oh, Jesus. Fuck.' My head was in my hands. This had to be a nightmare. It was two in the morning, and there were more than a few celebratory drinks cluttering my desk to mark the end of a long and complicated project with the Attorney General. I was crammed into my old Homicide office with Ellery's chief of staff, Roland Perritt, and Bob Connolly, my sergeant and good mate, and the beers were cold and welcome. It felt good to be back with the old team; at home, where I belonged.

What we had just heard couldn't be right. Surely nothing could have gone wrong? I had earlier checked on the Kendall security arrangements, and was assured the couple were safely escorted home with armed officers; there were duty cops at the house itself; every patrol car in the vicinity was on alert, security guards in the hotel's ballroom and parliament house had checked every inch of the place. I could relax, enjoy the beers ... but the impossible had happened. Surely it was a joke, or a mistake? I scrabbled around in my jacket for a cigarette until Bob held one out for me. My hands shook, and only after a few attempts got it lit.

Bob and Roland had got the gist of my conversation with the Chief

Superintendent. It took that one phone call to interrupt a bawdy story I was telling and for us to realise our celebrations were over. I was now in charge of an investigation into the murder of the State's Attorney General and his wife, managed, apparently without any struggle or difficulty, and in their own home. Dear God, how did this happen, despite all our checks, double-checks, high security?

'You OK, boss?' Bob's face was creased with concern. No, I wasn't OK, I wanted to say. Roland sat stunned, white-faced and unable to speak, still staring at the telephone. Please God, let this not be possible, I thought. Surely someone was taking the piss. Perhaps it was a return-to-duty joke. That was it. None of the boys liked it when you were singled out for parliamentary work, no matter how good it looked on paper when you were after promotion.

'Is this a fucking joke?'

'Hardly, boss.'

It was hard to believe, yet I knew from the Chief's tone that this nightmare was very real. I dropped my head onto my hands again, and struggled with the realisation of what this meant. But surely Anna Maria couldn't be dead? It wasn't possible that someone would harm her, let alone extinguish her life. Ellery? Sure, he was always a target ...

'Boss ... the car's waiting downstairs.' I could hardly blame Bob for staring at me. He had never seen me react like this, though we'd been through a lot together – drunken sprees, stake-outs, pay-backs, pranks, high-speed car chases, murders, suicides, mangled bodies, road accidents and kids dead from deadly drugs. There wasn't much we hadn't seen or heard. We were the hard blokes, objective, cynical, tough and efficient. We had trained ourselves to be untouched by horror, lies and bastardry. Most things were fixed with a piss-up at the local boozer. But this was different. I felt sick and it wasn't the booze. I swallowed hard. The bright lights outside my window were blurred, and I wondered why. I wiped my eyes, and smashed my fist on the desk. Inside my head there was a roar, no, no, no ...

'Boss, maybe we should go ... all hell's broken loose.'

As Head of Homicide a couple of dead people had never bothered me, but this time I was shattered, forced to pull myself together, pretend to Bob and everyone else around me this was just another routine case. Your average cock-up. I crushed out my cigarette and stood up. I barely acknowledged Roland, who was still motionless and sitting, a glass of beer in his hand, his eyes glazed. Obviously what was happening here was different from his usual parliamentary pencil pushing, point-scoring and circular arguments; this had blood and guts and too close to home written all over it. I slipped into the role of Superintendent James Duffield as best I could: in charge, hard-headed, the best drinker in the Force, the smartest, the fastest up the greasy pole; James Duff-ield, Duffy to his friends, the one who never let anything worry him and who kept his secrets to himself. Who knew that all I wanted to do was find a corner and howl like an injured animal?

The Chief Super had said it looked like a professional assassination. Instinct and training kicked in, and, as if in a trance, I made a call to Terry O'Brien, my mate in the Federal police and asked him to get his guys to look out for any strange activity at Sydney airport and the docks. Earlier that night I'd been told Stopelli had gone straight home from Anna Maria's function and the lights in his apartment had gone out half an hour later, but my guts told me that he was involved. What had Ellery said about Stopelli muttering some kind of threat?

Bob and I were stony-faced and silent as we drove to what we would now call the 'crime scene'. We let the sirens fill the void. The traffic was light, and I drove fast. Too fast, but I snapped out instructions to Bob. When we arrived, the Kendall mansion in the wealthy suburb of Vaucluse was ablaze with flashing police lights, and when I saw journalists and television cameras outside the high gates, my stomach churned with fury. I clenched my fists. Christ, trust those mongrels to have faster radio connections than we did. Granted, for them this was a sensational 'breaking news' story; it wasn't every day an Attorney General and his wife were murdered in their own home, while a child slept upstairs and live-in staff quietly watched television in their private quarters. I elbowed aside a television journalist and cameraman who blocked my path, and told them to fuck off or have their limbs torn off, one by one.

Hope remained even as I entered the house and was shown through to the sitting room that this couldn't be true, but seconds later I knew the truth. This was no joke. The time for kidding myself was over. Anna Maria had been shot through the heart at close range and Ellery had a neat bullet hole through his forehead. Either the shock or the blast had thrown them both back onto the sofa. I couldn't help focussing on Anna Maria. Even with the purple bruise and open wound on her cheek, she was still beautiful. Her dark eyes were closed, and her right arm was flung across Ellery's chest. There was only a hint of blood on her dress while blood and splinters of brain had burst from the back of Ellery's head and spilled down his white shirt. Powder burns to his forehead showed how close the killer had been.

Again, only the sheer force of training and instinct forced me to absorb the whole scene. I tried to reconstruct the events leading to the deaths, but my mind wasn't functioning clearly. I felt panic; well almost. I had to calm down and work out how this could have happened. How had two people been shot without any alarm being raised? How had the police on duty around the house missed this? I forced myself to be objective and impersonal: the intruder – if not one of the household staff – had entered the house unchecked, found this room without being intercepted, then surprised two people having a glass of wine before going to bed. Anna Maria had been struck on the face, possibly made unconscious, while Ellery was shot in the forehead through a cushion to blur the noise, hence the flurry of feathers around the room and on the bodies. She had then been shot through the same cushion. The kind of pistol would later be verified, but it looked like a small calibre. From experience, I recognised the execution. A gangland warning.

The room was hot, crowded, and smelt of blood. I acknowledged the police forensic pathologist and a team of specialists gathering items around the room and placing them in plastic bags. Not all wore gloves, and I feared they had trampled over traces of evidence. How many times had I argued for more stringent police forensic methods? I shrugged; too late now.

When I studied the bodies of Ellery and Anna Maria more closely, I felt bile rise in my throat. I had seen many dead, mangled bodies, but never one I had slept with only days before. I touched Anna Maria's hand, and although she had been dead only a few hours she was cold to the touch. That warm, passionate woman had never been cold. Not in all those years I had known and loved her.

Definitely a professional job, execution, mafia-style, I thought again. Anna Maria had warned me about her father's phone call, and I had the Peroni family checked; word had come back there was nothing to indicate they were up to anything more than marijuana growing ('for home use') and still flogging tomato sauce without a licence. No, this was a bigger operation. Even if Stopelli was home in bed fast asleep, he was definitely behind it. At Homicide we had a fair idea of our own home-grown hired killers, but this one had the hallmarks of an international job and whether he – or she – would lie low until the excitement died down, or make a rapid exit for home, wherever in the world that was, remained to be seen. Instinct told me the latter.

I roared at the police officers who had been in charge of surveillance of the gates and entrances to the Kendall house. How the hell did this happen? Had they been asleep? Or helping themselves to the Kendall bar? Tell me again who came in and out of these premises tonight?

Did you check their identity? How often did you check indoors? Or the gardens? On and on I raged. They shrank before me and muttered some explanations, but none of it made much sense to me. Right, the kid's nanny came home late but left soon after. Why was that? And how? The Kendalls had arrived home later, and were presumed to have gone straight to bed after having a drink in the downstairs sitting room. Did you not check that? Stupid bastards.

Too much beer and shock were now kicking in, and I hurriedly left the room to find a bathroom. Once inside, I locked the door and was violently ill. For minutes afterwards, I stood with my hands pressed on the cold sink, my head bowed. The mirror reflected back to me a clay-grey face and hard, watery eyes. All around me were neat shelves stacked with Anna Maria's perfumes, make-up, soaps, lace-edged towels, pretty ornaments and crystal containers. Her lacy peignoir. Her scent was everywhere, tricking me into believing she wasn't dead. I splashed my face with cold water.

'Boss, are you OK?'

I picked up a crystal perfume bottle and held it so tightly in the palm of my hand that its sharp corners pierced my skin, drawing blood. I didn't feel a thing. Bob banged on the door, and I dropped the bottle into my jacket pocket. I threw open the door and stared angrily at him.

'Can't a bloke take a piss in private without someone breaking down the bloody door?' I snapped when I brushed past him. He said nothing, but he was too good a cop to miss anything, especially interference with evidence. 'Where's the kid?'

'Upstairs asleep. But the nanny's still missing. Her day off. Apparently she liked a drink, and blokes, and met up with a new boyfriend in the city. She's devoted to the kid, and left a note about where she was meeting her friend. We're having the pub checked now. She came home about midnight, but left about twenty minutes later. The house-keeper who found the bodies is hysterical, but swears she saw and heard nothing all night, apart from the Kendalls arriving home just after midnight. She had the television up loud, on account of her poor hearing. The gate-keeper took the night off so left it to the police on duty at the gates, and retired to his private quarters. He didn't hear anything either, but confirms the arrival of the nanny, and then the Kendalls. He's about seventy, bit frail, been with the Kendalls for decades. I think we can rule out both him and the housekeeper.' Rule nothing out, I wanted to say, but Bob was probably right.

'The press are onto this big-time, boss,' he said. And stood back for the inevitable reaction. Damned press. Vultures. To hell with them and the whole, damned rotten world. That's the way, I told myself. Be angry. Curse. Swear. Do anything, but don't cry in public.

Bob got a radio message that the Premier was breathing hell and brimstone and demanding answers, while all I wanted to do was roar at every politician and journalist to leave me alone to do my job. I needed to let go of the rage inside me. The Premier would do as a target, and I didn't care who heard me. 'Tell the fat poncy bastard sod he can wait,' I yelled to no-one in particular. 'Wants answers, does he? Here I am up to my knees and blood and brains and he wants to chat.' Sure, he could wait. Besides, forensics hadn't finished dusting the telephone for fingerprints, and I couldn't use it. In time I would contact the idiot, but I wasn't yet ready for the world of politics, red tape, bureaucracy and blame-shifting. Heads would roll over this, and I didn't doubt it would be mine.

Also bellowing for answers was the Police Commissioner, another man I detested. He was a giant of man we called The Smarmy Midget because he had worked his way through the ranks through his skill at form-filling and grovelling to anyone who could fast-track his career. Rarely in his years of service had there been the street fight, the black eye, or confrontations with hoodlums carrying lead pipes. But why was I thinking about that now? None of it was relevant; perhaps my mind was looking for diversions and refusing to accept the reality of the Kendalls lying dead in their own home.

I forced myself to concentrate. When the forensics guys gave me the nod after finishing their work on the phone, I dusted off the fingerprint powder and dialled the private number of the Police Commissioner. I begrudged the precious minutes I needed for my job, but closed my eyes and forced myself to remain silent while listening to the screaming bullshit from this bloke I mockingly called my superior.

'How the hell could this happen?' He sounded more interested in how this affected his reputation, but he had a point. How *had* this happened? I stumbled over words, stopped, took a deep breath and began again. Words came out in measured phrases, but my mind was on the woman slumped on a silk sofa, bruised, bloodied, covered in her husband's brains and feathers from an cushion with 'Home Sweet Home' embroidered on it. Eventually, robot-like, I recited what I knew so far: 'The house-keeper found the bodies when she went in to turn off the radio and lights, thinking the Kendalls had gone to bed and left them on by mistake. I am informed the live-in nanny is missing. She went into the city and met a new boyfriend at a pub in the Rocks. We've had it checked out and the publican says they were pretty pally, drinking wine all afternoon. The bloke had a foreign accent, they had a meal and more wine, rented a room upstairs. That surprised the publican, because he took the guy for a poof. The nanny came down alone after an hour or so and left the pub carrying a small hold-all. She arrived back at the house about midnight, very drunk, not making much sense, identified herself to the duty officers, then used the security codes to enter the gate and the main door to the house.' In clipped, impersonal tones, I spoke for a minute or so more, but there was little else I could tell him. Except that she left the house about twelve-thirty, and drove off in her car.

'Well, for God's sake, get on with it, Duffy,' he said eventually. 'The whole State will be in an uproar over this. This is all we need for the reputation of the Force, a bloody political assassination. And the missus to boot. Jesus.' He banged down the phone.

My fury couldn't be contained. For some minutes I let fly, drawing on every curse and expletive in my extensive vocabulary to cover my feelings about the Commissioner and the state of the world. It felt good; well, it was better than howling. The forensics people were now taking away the champagne glasses in plastic bags. Anna Maria's glass was stained with red lipstick, the wine hardly touched and flat, the bubbles gone. Just like her.

On the marble-topped coffee table was a book opened to what I recognised as an old war-time poem. I had read it years ago. *Alone in a blaze of lights* .... It looked like Ellery had read it to Anna Maria before they died. The poem must mean something to him. Why? I picked up the book in gloved hands and noted the inscription: To Robbie, love from Dad. The dead druggie son. I imagined the scene between Ellery and Anna Maria: she would be tired, stifling yawns, glad to be home, happy with the success of the evening, black satin and diamanté high-heeled five hundred dollar shoes kicked off and lying sideways on the carpet as she curled up on the sofa and indulged a husband who was exhausted and still nostalgic for a lost son.

Despite the fog of shock and grief, it was beginning to make sense. I wasn't surprised when Bob told me a young woman – the nanny – had been found dead in a room in the Rocks pub, naked, badly cut and bruised, her clothes gone. I expected them to be found in her abandoned car. Nor was I surprised when Terry O'Brien from the Feds rang to say they had apprehended a suspicious Italian bloke at the overseas air terminal. Terry didn't much like wogs, as he called them, knowing how much I hated it. 'Acting strangely, and had no explanation for arriving in Sydney three days before with an overnight bag, and now about to leave on a 0600 Alitalia flight to Rome with a lot of cash. I have to say, Duffy, if this is your man, he's not the brightest hit-man in the world.'

'Thanks, mate.' I hung up. The phone rang again; for a crime scene and the need to preserve evidence, this damned phone was getting one helluva workout, I thought. I irritably took the handset from Bob who mouthed it was the Premier. I steeled myself.

'In view of the, eh, sensitivity of the matter, Superintendent, my office will handle the press on this,' he informed me in his cat's bum, prissy voice.

Do what you like with the fucking vultures, I thought. They would howl about crime and violence, the lack of security for high-profile public figures and scream about police ineptitude. I could see it now: A.G. gunned down in millionaire's fortress. The tabloids would excel themselves by splashing photographs of Ellery and Anna Maria in happier, glamorous days, and print themselves into a frenzy over the tragedy of an orphaned infant heiress. There was one question I had to ask the Premier, even though I predicted his response.

'Will Kendall's legislation go ahead tomorrow?'

'Well, as a mark of respect, parliament will be recessed. It's too soon to make any decision ... things will be difficult ... sensitive ... we'll play it by ear. First find whoever's behind this dreadful crime, this atrocity ...'

And he was away. He was on safe ground now, drawing on clichés that came quickly to hand to cover tricky situations: Kendall's work would be put on the backburner, set aside for a more appropriate time, looked at again when the dust settled, discussed with colleagues, and, in the fullness of time, having addressed the problem and taken readings from polls and the public, who knows what might happen? Terrified for his own safety, he stated that the Commissioner would personally oversee security arrangements for himself and parliamentary colleagues. 'At such a time, after such a lapse, Superintendent, we must be assured that every precaution is taken to protect the State's lawmakers.' Yeah, sure. Priority One.

My fury and sarcasm were palpable. I knew before I spoke that I was about to cross the line between public servant and politician, but I didn't care if it cost me my job. I started quietly enough. 'Can I suggest, Premier, as a mark of respect for a brave man you get those laws shoved through your fucking parliament before the Kendall family withdraws every donation they've ever made to your miserable Party, and before this city and its press lose interest in yet another gangland murder.' Bob hovered near me, shushing and pulling at my sleeve, but I shrugged him aside. I slammed down the handset.

Bob and I silently rechecked the perimeter of the property and studied the VHS security footage. The grainy images showed what looked like a short, slim woman wearing loose clothes and carrying a large handbag, enter the property at midnight, gait very unsteady, fiddle with the security box at both the entry gate and front door – first time unsuccessfully in both cases – and disappear into the house on the second attempt. The police on duty were seen to acknowledge her, check a list of photographs they had, and waved her through. She had left her car on the road outside. Why was that? Why didn't she drive into the garage allotted to her? Pissed? Or intended to use it later? The Kendalls came home at twenty minutes past midnight with their police escort and were ushered inside, the bodyguards ostentatiously locking the door behind them. Then the nanny left the premises twenty minutes later, clutching her handbag, mouthing words to the duty patrol that looked like an explanation that she had to go out again. She sounded very drunk, her speech slurred and deep. Was it accented? I replayed the reel.

Information came through that a car with the nanny's registration number had been found at the international airport terminal. Women's clothes and a wig in the style of the nanny's had been stuffed in a small bag and left in the back seat. Amazing. No effort made at concealment. With Terry's suspect already in custody, could we be so lucky? Surely it was too good to expect? Normally our work was like sifting through grains of sand, routine plodding copper work. Was this indeed a rank amateur, or was our killer just damned unlucky simply because a thrifty housekeeper was worried about the electricity bill instead of going straight to bed? Bob reminded me that a car was waiting to take us to Sydney airport, and I was irritated by his barely-concealed concern. It was irrelevant, but I noticed how old he looked, and how much he relied on his glasses. Did I look as old, as weary, as battle-scarred? Probably worse. I felt a hundred years old, heavy and overweight, dull, thick-witted and desperate for another drink.

'Bob, I'm guessing this is how it happened. We've seen a photograph of the nanny, but compare it with the image on the security system. I'd say a professional killer – likely from Italy, I'm thinking Stopelli in this somehow – stalked her, enticed her to a hotel, got her drunk, forced the security codes from her, killed and stripped her, then dressed in her clothes. Someone the same shape and colouring, and made up to look like her. Used her car to drive here, pretends to be dead drunk, enters with the security codes and no questions asked by our blokes when someone the spit of the nanny comes home and knows how to enter the house. Hides. Waits for the Kendalls to come home. Our killer does the job then leaves in the nanny's car that's been left on the street, drives to the airport'

'Pretty bizarre. New one on me.'

'And careless. He obviously wasn't expecting the murders to be discovered so soon. Thank God the housekeeper was watching a late-night movie. Let's look at the VHS footage again.' This time we studied it more carefully and noted how the subject clearly didn't want to be seen up close. 'That's a bloke, Bob, have a look at the angle of the arms, and the size of the feet. The main question is: who is he, and who paid him? I'll wager this bloke didn't give a damn who he killed, but pretty skilled at dressing-up. OK, let's get to the airport, and have Stopelli brought in for questioning. I've got a fair idea he's behind this.'

A young woman police officer approached us, and I knew there was one thing I could not avoid before I left that house. Bob followed me as I went up the stairs to the nursery on the first floor. It was a huge room overlooking the harbour and filled with toys and teddy-bears, bright paintings and posters, everything to amuse one of the richest kids in Sydney. It spoke of sweetness, innocence and extravagance. Love. The officer stood aside as I pulled back the pink cashmere blanket in the crib and picked up the child. She stirred, yawned, opened her eyes for a moment, and then relaxed against my chest, warm and slightly damp. She was small and dark, a miniature version of her mother.

And she was my daughter. I heard the door open behind me, and Coralyn Kendall stood there, her eyes dark with grief and rage.

'I'll take my granddaughter, Mr Duffield".

\* \* \*

We arrested Stopelli within two hours, and Bob had to restrain me from killing him with my bare hands. Between Bob, Terry and me, and some fairly muscular inducement out of earshot and sight of security cameras, the man held for questioning at Sydney airport admitted to killing the Kendalls, and eventually told us who had hired him. Maurizio Stopelli, of course. Our killer was pathetic; crying that he was a poor man, a hotel porter from Naples whose only sin was that he owed favours to an important and dangerous man in Sydney. The truth was, as the Italian police later told us, he was a vicious little cross-dresser who worked in a Naples homosexual nightclub, a heavy user of cocaine or any other drugs he could afford, and was prepared to take any job on offer for a good fee. His nickname, they told us was Sparafucile, after some hired killer in an Italian opera. It didn't mean a thing to me. Whatever he was called, this piece of shit had been promised drugs and a huge amount of money from a rich and influential Italian visiting from Australia. All he had to do was arrive, do the deed, and be out of the country, free, rich and safe. He complained he received only half the money promised, but after the job, he had no time to argue and had to leave the country quickly, or be killed himself. Bastardo, he said of his paymaster, Stopelli. 'Ow you say? Cheapskate ...' How he met and then lured the nanny to the hotel he never told us, but given the nanny's predilection for front bars, men and fizzy white wine on her days off, it wasn't hard to work out. Nor did it matter. Naturally, Stopelli swore he had nothing to do with any hired killer or murder, but a first-hand account and positive identification from 'Sparafucile' in return for promises of leniency, meant we had all the evidence we needed. Conspiracy to murder would see Stopelli put away for a long time.

After weeks of rounding up suspects involved with Stopelli's gangs and cohorts, we managed to tear apart the bulk of his drug business. And the evil bastard got what he deserved – twenty years in a high-security prison. I would have liked a longer sentence, even the noose, but that would have to do. Despite our 'promises' of leniency in exchange for information, our Italian traveller was sent down for life, but with bail he would probably get out after a few decades. After which, the Italian police were keen to extradite him for various criminal activities. In truth, he was a small fly in the whole scheme of things. A sordid, vindictive killer with a talent for cross-dressing, and who thought nothing of smashing a life or a skull for cash and drugs. It was Stopelli who I loathed with a fierce, dangerous passion.

Ellery's mother, Coralyn, worked behind the scenes to have her son's legislation raised in parliament, but even she hit a blank wall as politicians refused to touch it. They had all run scared. It fell into a hole in Macquarie Street. Me? The Premier was screaming for my dismissal for gross misconduct, foul language and disrespect towards a constitutionally-elected member of parliament. He was supported by the Commissioner and some senior levels in the police department who seemed not so much annoyed by a lapse of security ('mistakes happen, mate') but by my return to Homicide and my renewed agitation for more sophisticated police training techniques. I wouldn't let it rest. Why hadn't that 'woman' on the night of the murders been more closely interrogated before entering the house? Why were no questions raised about her leaving the house so soon after arriving home? And why was she allowed to drive away, given she was supposedly as drunk as a skunk? I had stressed to every officer on duty that night about the need to study every detail, to check everything and to take nothing for granted. They had failed me, but no matter how it was sliced, the failure was mine. The press was relentless, but I refused to engage with them. I left that for those who enjoyed the limelight.

When the dust settled, the thought of routine paper work and anonymous dead or dying bodies held no appeal. I had run out of energy and expletives, but at least I could now enjoy the whiskies I had dared not touch during those weeks of miserable, sleepless, investigative slog. I felt no sense of relief or achievement at putting behind bars the men responsible for the murders. Instead I was wracked with guilt for failing to protect Ellery and Anna Maria. And I missed her. I was a raw, jagged piece of despair and grief.

* * *

Coralyn Kendall summoned me a few days after Stopelli was arrested. She was one of the most powerful women in Sydney, the rich duchess of the Sydney social set who presided over her charities and favoured political factions with a cool eye and unbendable precision. I wasn't within a bull's roar of acceptance by her crowd, but I admired her. For some reason, she liked me, and I hoped our friendship would continue. But how could it? How could she forgive me? And how much did she know of Anna Maria and me?

I faced her in the cool, darkened library of her country home in Bowral. She had that morning completed arrangements for the State memorial service for her son, and although her face was gaunt, she hid her grief well. The white skin was carefully shaded with powder and rouge, the eyes darkened, the well-shaped mouth carefully painted, the clothes dark and severely tailored, grey hair tucked into a neat bun. Yet the ram-rod straight back and the slight tremble of her long, thin fingers with the red fingernails indicated a struggle for composure. I hoped it would remain; I could cope with anger, but I wasn't so sure about tears.

She invited me to sit opposite her. I heard Annabelle's childish giggle as she played in the garden with her dog, and we automatically glanced in that direction. Then, with a quick, brisk movement, Coralyn turned to the silver coffee-pot and delicate fine bone china cups and saucers on a tray beside her and began to pour. Her hands ceased to tremble.

'We will waste no time in recriminations, Superintendent Duffield. Or, if I may call you Duffy ...' She handed me a small cup of strong coffee. 'But there are things we must discuss.'

'I agree.'

'I know you are Annabelle's father.' I took a deep breath. So she knew. I had come here to explain the circumstances of Anna Maria and me, and to claim my child. One look at the old lady's face told me I faced an uphill, possibly impossible, task.

'Yes, I am. And here to claim custody.'

'Impossible. You can't have her, Duffy'. She didn't sound cold or hard, or particularly determined. She was weary, shocked and grief-stricken, but life would go on as she demanded. Annabelle was part of that life. It made no difference to her that she was my flesh and blood, and the only thing of value I had. 'You look dreadful,' she remarked as she sipped her coffee. She contemplated the plate of tiny sandwiches for a moment, and then absent-mindedly offered them to me. I shook my head, and she replaced the tray on the table, then stared outside at the immaculate lawn with the rose bushes and gum trees lining the white gravel path that stretched beyond her vast property. We heard the birds in the trees and the automated sprinklers that kept the gardens green and lush. She sighed.

'We've been through a great deal, you and I,' she went on slowly. 'And we have more to endure. The memorial service, court cases, and decisions about your career ...' She glanced out the window again, and a heavy silence fell in that elegant, rose-scented and carefully-shaded room. I interrupted before she said any more.

'Annabelle is my child, Coralyn, and I will prove it."

'I'm not sure how you will do that, Duffy. Legally she is a Kendall and now my ward. Nothing will interfere with that.' Something like tears glittered in her eyes. 'So I demand your discretion in this matter.'

'For fu ... for God's sake, Coralyn, she's three years old. You're what? Seventy-odd?'

'My age is immaterial. What we are talking about is the child of my son's marriage. She will inherit his estate, and in time perhaps take over the family business with her cousins. It is Ellery's legacy, and her legal right. I certainly hope she stays out of politics.' Her voice was bitter now, hard. 'We are a large family, and I am well-endowed with grand-children, but Annabelle is different. Special. Ellery had such plans ... this terrible tragedy does not alter her standing in my family. I defy you, Duffy, to challenge that position. Ellery adored the child, as he loved Anna Maria ...'

'I loved her too.'

'We all learnt to love her. But she is gone, and she would want her child given every protection and opportunity in life.'

'Then let her know her real father.'

'You're exhausted, Duffy, and as heart-sick as I am. But face facts:

what can you offer her? You're a policeman.' Coralyn was hitting her stride now, and I steadied myself for the onslaught. 'And not a very good one. You failed the most important job in your career. I have lost a brilliant son and a beautiful daughter-in-law. An infant is orphaned. I will never recover from my loss but I will minimise Annabelle's.'

'And what about my loss?'

'Learn to live with it.' she snapped. 'Yes, you loved Anna Maria, but she married my son. He turned that common migrant creature into an exquisite and talented woman. Could you have done that? On a policeman's wage? Counting dollars every payday to make ends meet? Leaving her alone while you worked night-shifts, involved in your petty public service politics, hitting the bottle on a Friday night with your mates?' She took a deep breath, and I knew there was more to come. 'And all the time knowing you could be injured or killed?' The words tumbled out like machine-gun fire. 'Come on, Duffy, you're deluding yourself. She had everything she wanted with my son ... '

'Like hell!' My anger was explosive. 'Your son couldn't give her a child.'

'Lower your voice, please. Anna Maria was an extraordinary woman. Pragmatic, a realist, and yes, I know she loved you in ways she couldn't love my son. She grabbed life with both hands. I admired that. She wanted wealth *and* a child. Ellery could offer her one, but not the other. I knew that, and so did she. I urged her to go to you.'

'You *told* her?'

'Of course. Before their marriage, I made her promise two things. First, that she had nothing more to do with her family. Second, that she would stay with my son, no matter what happened. She agreed to both conditions. In return, she would be well-catered for in terms of money, possessions and a secure place in Sydney society. I understood her, and I knew my son; he was besotted with Anna Maria, and would have accepted anything – even a lover and a bastard child – so long as she remained with him. In the event, she was a good wife and he accepted Annabelle as his own. You, my dear, were simply the means to an end.'

It was too much. We hurled bitter, acrimonious, hurtful angry words at each other, and after an hour my head ached and my throat was dry. In my determination to stay sober for this confrontation, I had drunk too many cups of coffee but now longed for a whisky. Nonetheless, I refused when Coralyn, showing no signs of fatigue or giving up the fight, gestured towards the liquor cabinet.

'Have a drink, Duffy. You could use one. I know of your weakness. So did Anna Maria, but she loved you regardless. You live a tough life, one I won't expose my grandchild to. Do you understand?' I said nothing. 'I like you. I am fond of you, in fact, but you cannot provide adequately for Annabelle's future. Not in the way a Kendall should be brought up. And in this matter, I insist on your silence. If you want money ...'

'Stuff your money, Coralyn.' I felt as if I were choking, and pulled at my tie. I turned away from those hard, accusing eyes and stared beyond her to the gardens. Annabelle was on a swing, laughing, her small legs urging it to go higher, the small dog yipping and leaping about. A slowly-darkening shadow closed over my eyes.

'I'm her father. Dear God, Coralyn, she's all I have.'

'True.'

'Then let me have her.'

'No.'

I stared at her, my fists clenched. Unexpectedly, she leant across and put her hand on my arm. Her eyes were milky-blue and tender, but her words were clear and left me in no doubt about my position. Or her intransigence.

'Annabelle is the child of Anna Maria and Ellery Kendall; she is now my legal ward. Under no circumstances will there be any public dispute about that, especially not in court. Don't even try. Can I have your word?'

'You're worried about the scandal ...'

'As you might say, Duffy, I don't give a fuck about scandal. If you make an issue of this, you will find yourself on your own. A laughing stock. I am making my position, and yours, beyond dispute.' I wanted to fight her again, even to slap her, but I sat limply in that cool, dark room until I found the strength to nod agreement.

'Thank you, Duffy. We will need each other in the days ahead ...' She went on for a few minutes, but I heard nothing. The urge to battle for what was mine momentarily returned, but was crushed against the futility of further argument. The Kendall family was too strong, too established, too wealthy, and I was what she said: failed, broken-down, probably a barely-functioning alcoholic. I could kid myself that I had seen too much, heard too much, lost too much, that life was a brutal place where you stumbled from one fight to another, with respite only from a whisky bottle, but they were thin, tired excuses.

What was left? No career, very little money, no-one to care about, and an empty, run-down flat. Few friends. All I valued was a bundle of photographs and a tiny perfume bottle that retained the merest hint of the smell of the woman I loved.

'Here,' Coralyn held out a large glass of whisky. I drank it quickly and stood up. She held out her arms and embraced me. 'You are a good man, James Duffield, and one day I pray you'll work that out for yourself.' Her back was straight when she left the room and there were no tears, an achievement that was beyond me. I helped myself to another whisky and left the premises. Ringing in my ears were the sounds of a dark-haired child calling for her dog.

\* \* \*

Anna Maria was buried alongside her husband, but I wasn't invited to attend the funeral or Ellery's State memorial service. From press photographs and television coverage, I saw Coralyn surrounded by her stony-faced family, rigidly composed and coldly courteous to the Premier. No-one from Anna Maria's family was present, and they sent no flowers, not even the violets she loved. They were placed there by me, days later. Of Annabelle, no-one heard a word.

I was sick of the entire business, and it was time to leave the whole, sordid, bloody mess behind. One way to do that was to reach for the oblivion that whisky offered.

* * *

I was very drunk, I knew that. But my thoughts were lucid. If I could have put them into words, it would have taken all night, and I would have rambled, made no sense, and I was too pissed to try. What I knew was this: my life was pointless. With Anna Maria alive, and Ellery aging, there was that fragile thread of hope we would one day be together, but now she was gone, burnt to ashes, with only a rose bush, dried-up violets, and a marble plaque to show she had existed. Not true, I corrected myself, there is Annabelle.

'Nothing, mate.' I muttered to Bob. Off-duty, we had been in the front bar of an inner-city pub all afternoon, but unlike me, he was sober. How many times had we been like this? How many years, how many drinks, how many hangovers? How often had we worked together, schemed and plotted, set up traps, played pranks, solved crimes? Always successful. Well, nearly always. I failed the one important time.

'You OK, Duffy?'

Bob's concern irritated me. No, that wasn't true. I loved him; not that I would ever tell him. I wished he worked harder for promotion instead of being stuck at my side, loyal, hard-working, decent, married. *He* had something to live for, lucky bugger.

'There's nothing left, Bob. Not a bloody thing.'

49

'You've gotta give this up, mate, or you'll kill yourself. Let's get you home.'

'Where and what is home?' I had thought about this for days between and during my drinking marathons. 'Nowhere and nothing, is the answer.' How blissfully drunk I was. What had Coralyn said? Oh, yes. How could I forget? You drink too much. Sure, Coralyn, I drink too much. Goes with the job. You wouldn't want to see or hear what I've been through, watching the man who arranged to kill Ellery and Anna Maria sneer from the witness stand. 'Bastard ...' I muttered to no-one in particular. I stopped. I didn't want Bob to think I meant him. 'Not you, Bob, but all those swines we arrested ... I hate how they've destroyed lives and don't give a ...'

'You did good work, Duffy.'

I envied Bob his wife and children, his contentment with so little. I was becoming maudlin. 'Sorry, mate. Home, you say?' Home to me wasn't Sydney any more, not without the little house screened by trees that faced the harbour where Anna Maria and I had met. There I could slough off crudity and toughness, not think about a drink, and show this beautiful woman how much I loved her. How I wanted to always be that tender, kind, soft. Sober.

I was tempted to tell Bob about Annabelle, but I suspected he knew. He pushed me into his car, and we drove through the gaudy streets of Kings Cross, down William Street and onto the Parramatta Road and towards the western suburbs. All so familiar, with or without the flashing police lights and sirens. I sipped from my whisky flask, and remained silent. We pulled up outside my flat, a red-brick three-storied, badly-built, carelessly maintained block that had never seen a harbour view in its life. This was home.

'I wasn't born in this country, Bob, did you know that? No, I was born in Scotland. Do you think my life would be different if I'd stayed there?'

It was fruitless to speculate. I hadn't been back to Scotland since

I left Glasgow as a kid of ten, and hadn't given it much thought since, apart from the times that Anna Maria and I had shared experiences as migrant kids. But I had mulled over this for days. Thoughts had tumbled through my brain like a high-speed newsreel: how I gripped my mother's hand when we left the ship at Sydney Harbour, me dressed in short trousers and a Fair Isle jumper; how I hated the heat and humidity, how my mother pined for my dead father and how she worked hard to buy a house and make a new life.

We rarely spoke about Scotland except when letters arrived from her mother in Glasgow, and then she would talk about soft rain, green fields and tenement buildings; a life she loved but chose to leave to find a better life, not for herself, but for me. I remember once saying to her I wished she hadn't. School bored me and there was nothing to interest me in the parks and beaches, so I became a gang-leader, rebellious, the one other kids approached when they wanted their enemies sorted out. Later, I became a policeman because I liked the idea of motorbikes and guns. But when my mother was killed in a drunken hit and run accident, all I wanted to do was catch bad guys and punish them. A tough guy, yes, but terrified of girls until I saw Anna Maria Peroni.

So why did Scotland beckon now as a new start, a retreat from hell? God, I felt sorry for myself. My head hurt. Even Bob's patience ran out as he heaved me out of the car. He helped me upstairs and shoved me on the bed while I held my head in my hands. He was right; this had to stop. I was killing myself. Clear thoughts fought their way through the drunken, sick waves. I didn't want to die, even if there was nothing much to live for. But I had a daughter, and one day she might need me. What if she found me in this useless state?

* * *

Bob was not surprised when I told him a week later that I was resigning from the police force and leaving the country. We drank coffee. I had to be sober for the meetings ahead.

'I have to do this, mate.'

'Yeah, I think you do,' he said quietly.

The Commissioner barely suppressed his pleasure when I handed in my badge. We had had too many fights in the past for me to be civil, and I suspected he was disappointed that my insubordination and the enquiry into the lapse of security in the Kendall case had been dropped. He muttered something along the lines that I 'could have had a brilliant career, but ...' paused, then wished me well and asked about my plans.

'None of your fucking business.' Over the years when he had blocked my ideas to update reform and efficiency, I had longed to tell him to go to hell, but today it just sounded crude and childish. I left without shaking his hand, and slammed the door behind me.

I knew my meeting with Coralyn Kendall would be difficult. Our meeting this time took place in her harbourside home in Elizabeth Bay, and I was aware of my badly-ironed shirt and a suit that needed a dry-clean. She would have noted my shaking hands.

'I'm leaving Australia,' I said bluntly, and drank the strong black coffee she offered. The cup clattered in my hands, and I prayed I wouldn't drop it on the Persian rugs.

'I know, and I am pleased.'

In a rush of fury, I put down the cup and stood up. 'Listen, I made a promise to you. You have Annabelle. Why gloat now I'm leaving the country?'

'Duffy, Duffy, sit down. You are exhausted, in mind and body. You must leave. Questions in parliament and the police force were raised about this ... tragedy, but they have passed over – with my help. You've done your work. I'm glad you're leaving, but not because I fear you will cause trouble. You made a promise, and I trust you. The truth is, if you value your health, you cannot continue as you are. You know that. I share your anger and grief, but I am an old woman, and you are a young man. You have lost Anna Maria ...' she sighed. 'but, as I always say, life goes on.'

'Life without her is empty.'

'Your life together went no further than secret meetings and public pretence. How could that compare with the life my son offered her? You didn't stand a chance ...' It was too fast, too ruthless, too unrelenting, to combat. I let her go on. 'I share your grief, and your disappointment that my son's work won't see the light of day until some brave political soul sees its worth. Until then I won't rest. I owe you and Ellery that.' She took my hand and leant in towards me. 'Dear boy, your birthplace, Scotland, is very beautiful, and the Scots are a strong, stoic race. They understand that life is about purpose, but it's not without its pleasures. Pray God you find the peace you need.'

The turn of conversation caught me off-guard, and I quickly reminded myself I wasn't here to indulge the absurdity of my dreams, or any mythical Brigadoon in Scotland.

'I ask one thing of you, Coralyn,'

'Go ahead.'

'If I always let you know where I am, will you keep me informed about Annabelle? Will you do that?'

'Gladly.'

I had another request, but I doubted she would grant this one. 'When she's old enough, will you tell her who her father is?' Coralyn's expression was thoughtful but shrewd as she considered my question. The silence was unbearable as I waited for her to answer.

'I can't promise that. In time, perhaps. As you reminded me, I am an old woman, and she is a baby. Possibly one day, when I can no longer protect her, she may need to know her real father is alive.' She hesitated and picked up a small, leather-bound book on the table beside her and handed it to me. 'Have this, Duffy. It was the last thing Anna Maria read before ... she died. It may give you some comfort, somehow, at some time ... ' She began to sob, in an elegant and controlled manner. I held her, shocked at the fragility of her thin, frail frame. She spoke against my chest. 'You will never lose your daughter while I am alive. You have more courage than you know, and I hope you find happiness or at least peace of mind by going back to your roots and starting a new life.' I rose to go, but she held on to me with remarkable strength. 'A moment more, my dear,' she whispered, 'I have forgotten how comforting it is to be in the arms of a good man.'

She stood at the doorway until I drove through the gates and they closed behind me and locked with a final electronic snap. I glanced at the book I had thrown on the seat beside me, its pages flipped open at a well-marked poem. 'Make your daughter proud of you,' were Coralyn's last words to me. 'As I know you will do.'

\* \* \*

*No man is an Island, entire of itself; every man*
*is a piece of the Continent, a part of the main ...*
John Donne (1572-1631)

# PART TWO:
## THE ISLE OF CRIACH, SCOTLAND

FIFTEEN YEARS LATER

# CHAPTER ONE

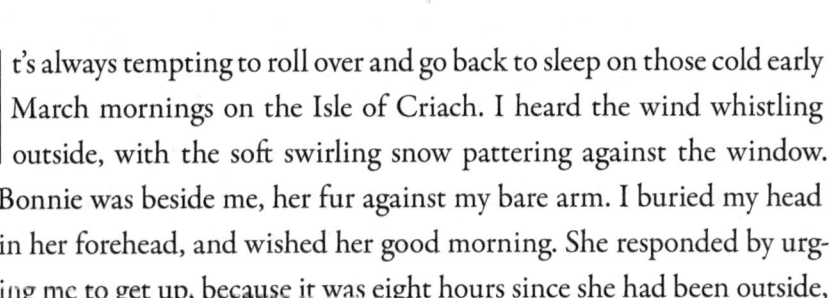

I't's always tempting to roll over and go back to sleep on those cold early March mornings on the Isle of Criach. I heard the wind whistling outside, with the soft swirling snow pattering against the window. Bonnie was beside me, her fur against my bare arm. I buried my head in her forehead, and wished her good morning. She responded by urging me to get up, because it was eight hours since she had been outside, and she had to inspect her property to see what had happened in those hours. Good girl, I whispered to her, and got up to let her outside.

Silence. It was a perfect day for being at home, reading in front of the fire – those 'kindly books that hold me late', as the old war-time poet Sassoon once wrote – or even plotting the next chapter of my own book. But Bonnie and I had a busy day ahead, and an important meeting with our friend Andy Cameron, in the village pub. Andy and I had a lot to discuss. I peered outside at the garden, not expecting to see any sunshine or blue sky, and not at all surprised at the depth of snow on the ground. It would be a busy morning shovelling it away from the paths and around the shed. Not a good day for 'spring' tourists or climbers, I thought, and caught Bonnie as she rushed inside, shaking the snow from her fur, tail wagging happily in welcome as though we had been separated for weeks.

From the kitchen downstairs came breakfast preparation sounds and delicious smells. Bonnie watched as I shaved, showered and dressed, undoubtedly thinking this habit of scraping the face with a sharp object, standing in running hot water, slapping on lotions and covering the body with layers of material, was a curious human activity but one she accepted with good grace. What are we doing today, she was probably thinking, and then judged by the selection of the clothes I chose to wear. Jeans or corduroys and woolly jumpers for desk work, sheepskin overcoat for long walks or trips to the village. Heavy safety gear and boots for mountain treks. Bonnie loved everything about our life except the occasional appearance of a suitcase which meant I left her for a few days, but trusted I would always return. We see Andy today, I told her, and she wagged her tail. I immodestly tell myself I am Bonnie's favourite person, but Andy is assuredly second.

She was not quite so fond of the woman in the kitchen, humming and singing tunelessly some songs from a London West End musical. I waited for the call when the eggs were boiled exactly right, the bacon crisped to perfection, the home-made croissants warm and buttery, and the special New Guinea coffee perked the required number of times. Then the summons: 'Duffy, breakfast's ready.'

Fedora Forbes-Brown was a thirty-five year old very, very attractive woman and a fabulous cook; fun company if you overlooked her phobic need for order and neatness. She was a generous soul, and I cared for her, perhaps even loved her in my own limited way, but I wasn't *in* love with her. Those days were well and truly over. Whenever she rang from London to say she was coming to visit, to 'put me to rights', as she said, I rarely deflected her unless a publishing deadline loomed, or, frankly, when I wasn't in the mood for company. But when my agent was happy, and time hung heavily, I didn't mind her company and the delicious food she cooked. Or her warm body.

On and off for two years now, Feddy had either flown up north and I had picked her up at the airport, or she had driven the long distance from London to see me. My island was accessible only by local ferry, and when she arrived in her latest-model BMW car it was stacked with food and wine from Harrods, sometimes a new jumper for me, the latest videos and taped television crime series, and an impressive Louis Vuitton suitcase crammed with her cashmere and tweed winter gear, including a mini-kilt. Even in summer she packed a raincoat and wellington boots, because she learnt early on that there was rarely respite from rain, wind or snow on Criach.

Old Hughie Ferguson, the ferryman and master of *The Criach*, had a face that displayed the characteristic polite but passive curiosity of the Criach Isle inhabitants, but he never lost his fascination with the tall woman whose squeals of delight could be heard from the deck even when the ferry was ten minutes from the jetty. I knew that within hours, news would whip through the village that my girlfriend was back, and there would be questions raised about my intentions. Did I intend to marry this English woman? That was something that Feddy herself often raised during her visits. After wine and an excellent meal, tipsy and pink-cheeked from the old kitchen wood oven, she would tentatively raise the question of us spending more time together. Perhaps living together? Either in her London flat, or even (with a snort of amusement or incredulity) here in frozen, backward Criach? Each time I sharply closed down the conversation. No, it would never work, I repeatedly said. She was a wealthy socialite, used to life in London with her marketing business, opera, art galleries, museums, long lunches and trips to Paris to buy clothes.

What she saw in me was a mystery. I was pretty much as she described me: a hermit, a recluse, only venturing out amongst people when I went to the Criach village or nearby mainland towns for supplies, or sometimes to Glasgow to see my agent, banker or dentist. I never visited

Feddy in London. My island highlights were sharing a meal with Andy in the pub, climbing mountains, fishing, bird-watching, and rambling amongst the lochs and heather. I enjoyed being at home in my old stone cottage with its low ceilings, the lamps turned on in the early afternoon against the approaching gloaming. Outdoors, I loved the squeak of snow underfoot. 'You have the slippers and the faithful dog, Mr Thistle Man,' Feddy remarked once, 'but you need a wife.'

I most definitely did not; I was content with my solitary life. I had no intention of changing it, even if I knew I was being hurtful when I evaded Feddy's questions about the future. I made it clear enough that while she was a beautiful woman whose company I enjoyed (I didn't add, for short periods), I was not the man for a stable, committed relationship and future partnership. I don't know why she doesn't accept the situation, and insists on coming to visit every few months, but she does. How can I tell her there is no room in my heart for anyone after Anna Maria?

Bonnie nudged my hand to remind me that breakfast was ready, and for her there was always the prospect of bacon and bits of fried egg. I loved her happy canine acceptance of another day of curious smells and walks, preferably up the mountains and along the streams. She was four years old, and the locals and I had given up trying to establish her lineage, knowing only that her Border Collie mother was the best sheepdog on the island, but whose instincts had led to an anonymous liaison and six unwanted pups. Ronnie McNair, my neighbouring sheep farmer, had arrived at my doorstep one winter morning with a small bundle of black and white fur tucked snugly inside his jacket.

'She'll never be a sheepdog, Duffy, but she'll make a nice wee pet.' I hesitated, but didn't want to offend Ronnie, or look into those round, black, shiny eyes and say I didn't have a place in my heart for a small creature that fitted into the palm of my hand. Within twenty-four hours I was irretrievably in love again, this time with a pup. We suited each other, she lying under my desk at my feet as I worked, exploring the fields and mountains together, sharing meals, talking to each other as humans and dogs do, and sure, she may not have made a good sheep dog, but she was brilliant on mountain slopes where she was fearless, sure-footed, and with the keenest nose in locating lost mountaineers. We liked and disliked the same people. She could converse with me without saying a word, make me laugh, and showed me things in the fields and mountains I had never noticed before.

I half-listened to Feddy at the breakfast table as she chattered about life in London, how busy she was with 'clients', dinner parties and shopping, spring sales and the thrill of finding a fabulous new Turkish restaurant in Soho.

'You're not listening, are you?'

'Mmmm.'

As far as I was concerned, she could have been describing a recent trip to the Gobi Desert. To her credit, she had long ago given up trying to find out about my life in Australia, or why I chose to live alone in a remote north-west Scottish island. On those issues, I remained silent. Tight shut.

Feddy wouldn't know that I had arrived in Scotland exactly fifteen years ago. Nor would she have recognised the man who stood outside the Glasgow tenement building of his only relative, Grannie McPhedron, on that bleak, cold and blustery day. My arrival was a cheek, because I had never replied to the letters and birthday cards she sent me in Australia. But I was broke, exhausted, and needed a bed for a few nights.

'Come in, laddie.' She didn't seem surprised to see a big, miserable, shivering, jet-lagged, hung-over bloke on her doorstep, lugging a battered suitcase. There was warmth and humour in her face, and it bore such a close resemblance to my late mother that I was momentarily startled. Beyond her, I saw a softly-lit room and a glowing electric fire. 'Och, come on in, son, yer lettin' the cold air in. Ye'll be wantin' a cup of tea, maybe even a wee dram to warm you up. My, my, there's no doubtin' yer my daughter's son.'

Over the two years I lived with her, Grannie McPhedron brought me back from the living dead. I initially told her I was on holiday and planned to hire a car and tour the Highlands, and to all my fabrications and fantasies, she nodded and agreed it was good to get away to the clean, clear air of the Scottish countryside. I wasn't exactly lying. I wanted to drive into oblivion, where nothing reminded me of Australia, or Anna Maria. Grannie fussed over me, insisted I stayed with her and made my bedroom warm and 'cosy-like'; she cooked hearty meals of Scotch broth, tatties, stews and dumplings. At the end of the day she enjoyed a sherry to my whisky, but never asked why I was in Glasgow without a job or money, or why I never made plans to return to Australia.

Of course her keen Scottish instinct told her I was troubled. I learnt early on that Grannie was a spiritual soul, 'fey' as she called it. She could predict things, deaths and calamities in particular. I didn't believe her then, but eventually came to realise she really could look into souls and broken hearts.

'There's a wee island you should visit,' she told me once when I came home drunk after a day in a Glasgow pub which ended in a fight and red-raw knuckles. She talked about a place where she and my Grandfather had spent their honeymoon; I could tell it held happy memories. 'A bonnie wee place, son. Quiet. With big high mountains, heather and wee streams ...' She put down her knitting and was lost to memories for a moment. 'There's an old legend about how the biggest mountain, The Old Lady of Criach, shelters those with a troubled heart, but she can be a harsh mistress if you don't respect her powers to save or slay. Och, the views! Ye'd like it, son.'

How did Grannie know that a tiny north-west Scottish island, accessible only by a ferry with limited room for cars and passengers – when the weather permitted – was what I needed to tame my anger and bitterness? I went there in the autumn, planning only to please Grannie, but I was instantly drawn to the place. It was shadowy and damp, the mountains covered in snow and crowned with clouds, the fields misty green and dotted with white sheep. The Old Lady of Criach did look threatening, but – call it imagination or too much to drink – I sensed a kinship with the old girl. It was the silence that I liked. It was deep and intense and surrounded me in a way I found impossible to describe. I simply *felt* the hug of its power.

It was sparsely populated with farmers and fishermen, population 160 souls. And nothing has changed in the thirteen years I've lived here. The village is small and pretty, with a grocery store serving as a chemist and post office, and a solid old stone pub called *The Heather and Eagle* offers fine fish meals and limited accommodation; there is a dusty gift shop that makes soap infused with heather for tourists, and further out, tucked away amongst the mountains and fast-running streams, a small distillery that turns out remarkably good whisky.

You'll see an old stone Presbyterian church and parish hall on the way from the ferry to the village. There is no school, and kids are ferried to the mainland in term-time, but is often cancelled in the winter when the weather is too dangerous for crossings. Newspapers and mail arrive on a haphazard basis. There had once been a handsome castle, but which was now stones and bricks amongst weeds and nettles. Criach hasn't seen an English laird for a century, not since the last one succumbed to ill-health and lack of interest in anything Scottish, especially taxes. When the lease expired, Criach people and tourists were allowed to fish and roam wherever they liked, although hunting and fire-arms are strictly forbidden. Visitors are restricted because there are few facilities for them, but the locals welcome serious hikers, campers and climbers, so long as they mind their manners, cause no problems, do not trespass, leave gates as they find them, and pick up their rubbish.

Communication has always been difficult. With modern

technology my new computer is useful for my writing, but our faxes, mobiles and telephones work intermittently, and so, as in the past, we rely on the postman, Jimmy McClure, who learns everybody's business as he scooters around the island delivering mail and parcels. Hughie the ferryman is the island's main lifeline as his ancient old ferry carries passengers, mail, cars, furniture and sometimes the odd horse, cow or goat across the twenty-minute stretch of often wild sea that separates us from the nearest mainland town of Kilsney.

When I first visited the island and walked aimlessly around the beach and fields, I stumbled across the place I instinctively knew I was meant to find. Nestled at the foot of the Old Lady of Criach, not far from the seashore, was a neglected two-storied cottage boarded up and fortified against the weather and unwelcome visitors. Perhaps I was drunk, but I felt so drawn to it that I imagined it was mine.

I met Andy Cameron on that first trip. I cringe when I think of our first encounter. I had drunk beer all the way from Glasgow, my three-hour journey taking me first by train and then by ferry. I checked in at the *Heather and Eagle,* had another drink, and then wandered around the coastline for an hour or so, picking up stones and flinging them into the sea, enjoying the sound of the sea battering against the rocks as the afternoon turned dark and the wind whipped at my jacket. After I saw the cottage, I felt more depressed, knowing I could never afford to buy it. I was hungry, frozen, melancholy, in need of further drink, so, with the skies darkening, I headed back to the pub.

A tall, well-built but stocky man was in the bar reading an old Glasgow newspaper, a lager at his elbow. He glanced up as I approached him, nodded briefly to acknowledge me, and then returned to his reading. It was ridiculous, but there was something about his round, pleasant face, blue eyes, curly sandy hair and Fair Isle jumper that annoyed me. Even his accent irritated me when I heard him joking with Kenny, the publican. The warm room, the easy banter between the patrons, the sheepdogs lying at their masters' feet, the smell of soup and bread, coupled with the island's pervading moody atmosphere, exacerbated my melancholy and sense of aloneness. I wanted to lash out at something. Anybody.

'Does it ever stop raining in this bloody place?' I demanded of Andy when I went up to the bar beside him and ordered a beer with a whisky chaser.

My voice was loud, my Australian accent harsh, my aggressive friendliness at odds with the warmth and geniality of the room. He briefly looked up from his newspaper and answered quietly.

'Och, mercy, aye, but not often right enough.'

'You live here?'

'No, I'm from Inverness.' He returned to his newspaper, but I gave him no peace. For the next twenty minutes I jabbed at him like a punch-drunk boxer, flinging questions at him, rough and intrusive. He didn't lose his temper, even when I followed him to the dining room where he clearly wanted to enjoy his haddock and chips in peace. Without invitation, I joined him.

'What does a bloke do here for fun?

'Fish, walk or ...'

'That's fun?'

Andy put down his cutlery, dabbed his mouth with the tartan napkin and looked at me closely for the first time. Had I known him then as I now do, I would have recognised the challenge behind the friendly invitation. And been warned.

'... well, there's always a wee bit of mountain climbing. Our Old Lady of Criach isn't the highest mountain in Scotland, but she's the toughest and most interesting. Would you care to join me tomorrow for a wee bit of a climb?'

I thought about the black granite mountains hiding behind the mist and snow and slapped Andy on the shoulder. 'Sure. Sounds great.'

Hell, I had once been fit, athletic, up for any competitive adventure. I still had it in me.

Andy was about to teach me a lesson I would never forget. Between the time he hammered on my door at seven the next morning and dumped me back at six that night, I was tormented by the cold and sleet that seeped into my clothes and bones, despite the heavy raincoat, as we trudged up that Old Lady of Criach. My head ached, my feet and hands were frozen, my breath came in short stabs as I put one boot in front of the other to climb that huge, damn, mocking piece of rock. Andy watched as I slid and fell, ignored my pleas for a break, a drink, and kept pushing upwards. I was a sorry sight, but some remnant of pride made me determined to continue. We didn't make it anywhere near the top, of course, but I was too hung-over and miserable to feel any sense of achievement at making any headway at all.

If I made a fool of myself in Andy's eyes on the way up, I consolidated it on the downward journey. At one point, I yelled I'd had enough of his prodding encouragement, and would make it down on my own. I trudged through the gathering mist and darkness, gripping the slippery slush and stones under my feet, and becoming so lost I nearly wept with fear and frustration. Unknown to me, Andy was always close. Only when he couldn't bear my distress any longer did he appear from the mist to rescue me. Never will I forget my relief when I saw that round face in the balaclava, and heard a Scottish voice that meant safety and a return to warmth.

The next day I learnt from Kenny the barman that Andy Cameron was a local legend; the leader of the regional mountain rescue team, trained and experienced to tackle any kind of emergency. He had won countless medals for bravery and saving lives, here and overseas. And well-used to the antics of inexperienced and arrogant idiots who refused to acknowledge the dangerous combination of alcohol, altitude, ignorance, wind, cold and snow. Some paid with their lives, Kenny said; she can be an auld bitch, that mountain. 'But there's a helluva lot of folk who owe their lives to oor Andy.'

I was subdued and sober when Andy later that day came into the hotel carrying a fishing rod and basket. I felt foolish, embarrassed about my clownish behaviour, yet wanting to share those moments of wonder when I had looked down from the mountains through a break in the clouds and saw from a great height the expanse of sea beyond. I felt infinitesimally small, a mere speck within a wider, wonderfully spectacular world. But words were difficult. I wanted Andy to like me, but it was unlikely he would have time for a crazy drunken lout he had carried down a mountain like a child.

'Thanks for your help yesterday, mate,' I said eventually.

'Nae bother at all,' he said, and handed Kenny some freshly-caught fish, 'If the cook would be so kind.' When he grinned, his unexpected generosity struck me like a pleasant punch. 'Would you care to join me, Mr Duffield, in a nice wee bit of trout?'

That night I shut my mouth and listened. I learnt Andy came to Criach a lot, sometimes to fish and climb or to lead rescues when climbers were in trouble. Often to train the young lads. In spring and summer he brought tourists to the island, 'Small groups, mind,' he said, 'this is no place for tramping about and spoiling things.' Of his private life, he gave nothing away, and beyond asking which part of Australia I came from, he asked no questions about my past. It was late when I went to bed, sober.

Grannie noticed I was different when I returned to Glasgow. I had a plan for us. I lost the urge to drink heavily and inveigled myself into the lives of the neighbours, playing football, sorting out gangs and delinquents, finding more shift work as a security guard in one of the few remaining working docks along the River Clyde, and putting away a few quid each week in a savings account. I started to write. Grannie was pleased ('ever since you were a wee boy, James, you've been good at composition') and liked it when after dinner we sat in the front room, she knitting, the electric fire blazing, and me battering away at an old typewriter I bought for four quid in a Gorbals pub. I wrote stories based on the everyday funny, sad, poignant events I witnessed in Glasgow streets on a daily basis.

I invented a fictional crafty but irascible Glasgow police detective called Inspector Galvanney, who began to live in my head as though he were real. Having finished my stories, I didn't know what to do with them. I protested, but Grannie persuaded me to send my stuff to various publishers and magazines. I wasn't surprised when they were rejected. I sank into despondency while Grannie was cheerfully persistent.

'Och, we'll no let a wee thing like that bother us,' she said, and sent them off to different publishers. 'I've got a good feeling aboot aw' this,' she would say. She was a regular at the post office, with her big envelopes, stamps, and confident predictions to the post mistress that her grandson would one day be a famous writer.

I couldn't pretend to be an overnight success. I just slogged away. Galvanney was eventually accepted by a small London publishing house. I was pleased that Grannie was alive to share my first royalty cheque, small as it was. We celebrated with dinner at the Grand Central Hotel in Glasgow because she had always wanted to go where the film star, Roy Rogers and his horse, Trigger, had once stayed. I wanted to thank her for her support and confidence, but she would have none of it. 'Och, son, yer mammy and I always kent you were clever. It's a damn shame she's no here tonight wi' us.' True. But I only wanted Anna Maria with us, sharing my modest success. I ordered another Drambuie, aware that, despite my earlier euphoria, I was becoming maudlin. It was time to stop, order a taxi and go home. Grannie insisted that a bus would do just fine, thank you very much, but we laughed as, worse the wear for the last Drambuie, she tripped and tumbled into the black cab. 'Och, ye didne see ma knickers, did you son?' We laughed all the way home.

Grannie died a year after that. When she became sick, I looked after her with the neighbours and her many friends, bringing cups of tea and new editions of *The People's Friend*. I spent hours sitting at her bedside, listening to her talk about her life, how much she loved roaming the Highlands with Grandpa when my mother was small. 'Mind that wee island I told you about? Criach. When I'm gone, son, go there. Try and be happy.' I wept when she died, and again when the lawyer told me she had left her freehold house and entire savings to me in her will. I knew she was frugal, but was surprised at how much she had saved.

By then I existed modestly on the earnings from the fictional Galvanney, and articles and short stories I contributed to magazines and newspapers. With my meagre savings, and Grannie's inheritance, I wondered if I could now buy my house on Criach. Would it still be available? There was only one way to find out, and as soon as the legalities were settled, I was on the first train to the Highlands.

It was eighteen months since I was last on the island, but there was my house, still boarded up and waiting for me. Considering its condition, it was a bargain. I was warned it was in need of extensive renovation, but I didn't mind. It would do me fine. I threw myself into the job like a crazy labourer. I cleared paths, scythed weeds, painted, plugged up holes and scraped decades of mould from surfaces. Slowly, I saw a handsome home coming back to life to reveal its character: tough, protective and practical. Built to last against the freezing winds and snow.

I still loved Glasgow, and mourned for Grannie – how I missed her, and wished she had been alive to come to Criach with me, as we had planned – but this wee cottage, this wee island, were now my home. In the spring when I arrived, the weather was surprisingly mild, the fields green, the days long, and some months after I arrived, tired and frustrated after a day of trying to build dry stone walls, I walked to the village pub for a quiet drink and a meal. The locals were still reserved but becoming friendlier now that they saw I intended to live on the island, but minded my own business.

It was good to see Andy in the bar, this time wearing his coach driver's uniform with the blue and white Scottish Saltire flag embroidered on the padded waterproof jacket, over his name tag, 'Andy'. Just as before, he was reading a newspaper and drinking a beer. When I entered the bar, he looked pleased to see me. We shook hands.

'Well now, welcome, Mr Duffield. You've become a Criach landowner, I hear,' he said in his soft Inverness accent. It hadn't taken long for news to rip around the island, but I still looked surprised. 'Och, mercy, you'll get used to the local communications systems.' When he accepted my offer of a drink, I was vain enough to feel proud that he now saw a leaner, fitter, sober bloke from the earlier one who tormented him. 'And you've lost your Australian accent.'

'I've lost a lot more than that, Andy,' I said sheepishly. Over a drink that led to dinner, the conversation slid into topics like the weather, sheep, the scourge of summer midges, safeguarding mountain climbers, hikers and ramblers attracted by the island's isolation and spectacular scenery; the superb quality of the island's lamb and sea-food, the difficulty of hauling furniture from the mainland. The conversation was easy, companionable, but I had to get something off my chest. 'Andy, I never apologised for my behaviour the last time I was here. I'm sorry I was such a fool.'

'Och.' He waved his hand, 'you were a brave man to attempt that climb. And one day, if you like ... ' He stopped suddenly, fearing he had encroached on my privacy, and remained silent until we resumed our conversation about the best way to clear the snow from footpaths and plug up draughts in old cottages.

After that, we arranged to meet regularly. Our routine rarely changed: once he had his tourists settled and 'at leisure', we met at the pub to share news over drinks and a meal, either sitting at the bar or in front of the fire. We never spoke about politics, or the state of the world ('I'm no of a mind to journey into the dark arts of the politician's mind,' was his comment), although I noted how well-informed he was about government legislation that involved his Highlands.

In autumn and winter when there were few tourists, he came privately to fish or to climb the Old Lady of Criach and her sister mountains, living in a small cabin near the sea which had been built by his father decades ago for family holidays. In time, Andy invited me to join him on his mountain climbs, and with his patience and my determination, I became good enough to reach the summit of the mountain that once mocked me. My body became hardened by the exercise and the rough, often brutal, weather conditions. My police training kicked in when instant decisions had to be made on the slopes, and I was as proud as a kid at Andy's slight nod of approval.

Gradually Andy and I talked more freely, more frankly. His father had taught him everything he knew about climbing. 'It was a grand time, Duffy,' he said. 'It's a magic island. So much to see and learn.' Much, much later he told me about his wife, Isabel, who had shared his love of the outdoors, but who had died giving birth to their son. The child had lived only a few days ('a wee thing, Duffy, so helpless'). In time, he talked about his travels around the world where the thrill of high peaks attracted him, but, as he said, he was always happy when the wheels of the plane touched down on Scottish soil and he was back in his house in Inverness or his wee cabin on Criach. 'I'm a Scotsman, Duffy, and my mountains always welcome me home.'

Over the years and in tiny segments, I confided parts of my Australian life that were still painful, but faintly scabbed over. He listened carefully, whisky glass held to his chest while he stared into the fire, never interrupting or commenting. No words from him were necessary; it was too personal a thing, this glimpsing into another man's soul, to complicate it by words.

I settled into my new life. Sure, there were times when dark moods struck and no matter how hard I ran, how much wood I chopped, dug into the hard, icy ground, or how I struggled with a new plot for Inspector Galvanney, the past would not let me go: Anna Maria's bruised face, Annabelle as an toddler, giggling on a swing with her dog, Stopelli's bitter sneer from the dock, Coralyn's hard face telling me I couldn't claim what was mine. And yes, the whisky beckoned. But I learnt. When the damned black dog of depression, guilt and regret came to haunt me, I learnt that whisky wasn't the solution. Often, late at night, alone with Bonnie, I stared into the fire and remembered Anna Maria as she had been in our tiny bolt-hole in Sydney; warm, and so very welcoming ...

I was shaken into the present by Feddy's voice, asking me if I wanted more coffee. I was momentarily disorientated. I had been sitting at the kitchen table, my coffee cold, staring out the window at the mountain, absent-mindedly smoothing Bonnie's ears as she patiently sat beside me waiting for her breakfast treats. As Feddy refilled my coffee, she reminded me in slightly peevish tones that I had chosen to spend the day with Andy, rather than with her. Today is different, Feddy, I explained, but didn't say why.

I surreptitiously patted the letter in my shirt pocket to make sure it was still there, and once again felt the stabs of anxiety mixed with hope and anticipation. If it had been impossible to ever forget the nightmares of the past, I had at least quietened them. Yet it took only one visit from Jimmy the postman and a letter from Australia to remind me that the past still walked every step with me.

After breakfast I spent an hour or so clearing the snow from the pathways until it was time to drive into the village. I assured Feddy I would be home before it got dark; she in turn promised on my return to have the cottage spring-cleaned, and roast duck with a spicy orange sauce simmering in the oven and ready for dinner. Not for the first time I thought what an exceptional woman she was; kind, accommodating and very forgiving. I wished I could give her what she wanted, but I was incapable of doing that, and it was dishonest to even try.

Keen to start the day's activities, Bonnie urged me on. She looked slightly impatient as I kissed Feddy goodbye on the cheek, and then collected my overcoat and scarf. From the back seat, Bonnie's tail was wagging and when I flung myself into the Land Rover, she put her paws on my shoulder as if to urge me on: come on, come on, Andy's waiting. Feddy waved me off, her eyes twinkling a promise that suggested more than a culinary feast that night.

As I switched on the ignition and slid on to the rough road that led to the village, I patted my shirt pocket yet again. Bonnie followed my every action, her ears pricked. What's ahead, my furry friend, I whispered to her, good or bad? Who knows? Get on with it, she silently responded.

Andy sensed I was troubled but it was not his way to rush at a problem. Besides, there were too many people in the pub to speak privately. We sat down on the bar stools and ordered beers. He looked as he always did – shiny-faced, clean-shaven, well-pressed, good-natured, and fit beyond his forty years. We joked with Kenny briefly, and then our conversation turned to conditions on the mountains, my book newly published, my vegetable garden and what I laughingly called my 'hot house' where I coaxed Australian plants to grow. Normally we could spend hours discussing finches and eagles, but today we cut it short, and only when our meals and drinks arrived did we move to the fire where, as Andy said, it was more 'cosy-like'.

He had barely taken a mouthful of his poached salmon when I handed him the letter. From under the table, Bonnie's ears pricked up as she saw the object which had given me such a shock when Jimmy delivered it yesterday. I had recognised the Australian stamps and postmark on the blue air mail envelope, and knew it was not Coralyn's routine Christmas card with the promised, but brief, reference to her granddaughter, Annabelle. The letter had taken over four weeks to reach Criach, which didn't surprise me. Bonnie had padded after me when I sought solitude at the foot of the mountain to open and read, then re-read, the contents of the two thick sheets of paper. After that, I sat in stunned silence for an hour, my mind spinning, until the cold drove me home to hide the envelope in a locked drawer, alongside old photographs, Anna Maria's perfume bottle and the book of war-time poems from Coralyn. For the remainder of the day I sat at my desk pretending to work on a new plot, but few words on the computer screen made any sense to me. I gave up, and told Feddy I was taking Bonnie for a walk. I wanted to check who had arrived on the afternoon ferry, but I was too late. Old Hughie had gone home, his last delivery of tourists and the noisy schoolkids off-loaded, his ferry tied up securely against the impatient surge of sea against the jetty. I returned home and sat for a long time looking into the fire, pretending to listen to Feddy, but in truth was deep in my own thoughts and keen to see Andy the next day to talk about this piece of news. To ask his advice.

Andy squinted to read the letter. When he finished, he slowly read it again, just as I had done, while I waited for his reaction. He was silent as he considered its contents; his quick, intelligent mind knew what the expensive notepaper with the spidery handwriting meant to me. After some moments, he handed me back the letter and picked up his knife and fork.

'Och, lad, have you not been waiting a long time for this? Whatever happens from here, you know it has to be dealt with. To my mind, it's a good thing, long overdue ... ' Bonnie nuzzled his hand as he leant across to feed her a scrap of salmon. His eyes were serious and contemplative when they met mine for the briefest of moments, then he added quietly, 'It's a wearisome thing to have emptiness in your heart when you know it should be filled with your own kin.' I knew he was thinking of his wife and son, and he sighed deeply. 'You've been given a chance to fill that gap. Will you not grab it? You're a smart man, a lucky one, with a good mind and heart. Trust me, it will all work out.'

I wanted to believe him, but to tell the truth, it was difficult to know how to deal with what I knew was about to rock my life and my island.

* * *

# CHAPTER TWO

vents moved fast after that, but I was unprepared for the speed. I arrived home after seeing Andy to find that Feddy had indeed thoroughly doused the cottage with disinfectant, scrubbed every available surface, including Bonnie's basket, and stacked my books and music tapes in alphabetical order. My meagre wardrobe was colour-coordinated, although by tacit agreement my working rescue gear and office paperwork were off-limits. As promised, a duck was roasting with oranges and vegetables in the old wood-burning oven, and I sensed from Feddy's fierce welcome that it would be difficult to persuade her to return to London a few days after she arrived. How could I explain I wasn't in the mood for romantic company, and that she was a complication I couldn't tackle at the moment?

Bonnie lay on the bed while I changed out of my damp clothes. After seeing Andy, I had stopped the car half-way home and walked for an hour or so in the drizzling rain with Bonnie, who was always happy to be amongst her favourite smells and with me in deep thought. I had much to think about, but none of it made much sense. Nor had any plans come to mind to deal with whatever was about to happen. Cold and wet, Bonnie now crossly rearranged her basket to her own liking, dragging the blankets across the floor and rubbing her own scent on them to combat the evil disinfectant. I was sympathetic to her annoyance over her bed being interfered with, and called her to my side so I could rub her dry and offer words of reassurance, but it may well have been that I was the troubled one in need of comfort. What's up, she seemed to say. That piece of paper again? I rubbed her face.

'I'm still a copper, old love,' I muttered into her fur, 'and I want to believe Andy because he's always right, but my instinct tells me we've got a helluva long road to travel before this comes right.' Feddy stirred in the kitchen.

'What did you say, darling?'

'Nothing,' I shouted back, 'just talking to Bonnie.' She appeared at the doorway, all short tartan skirt, shiny knee-high boots and pink cashmere sweater. Her face was flushed from the kitchen heat, and she looked as delicious as the duck smelt in the oven.

'Duffy, you treat that dog like a child.'

'And why not?' I glanced up at Feddy appreciatively to deflect any further criticism. 'You look lovely.' It was true; it was easy to charm Feddy, and hard to hurt her. I kissed her warm cheek and patted her backside, self-conscious about my struggle to make flippant conversation while my head was spinning around events I had no wish to share with her. 'When's dinner?'

'It can wait.' Her blue eyes were suggestively wicked. She was two people, this London lady with the classy accent: pink rubber gloves and Draino one moment, black suspenders and French lacy knickers the next. When I made an elaborate show of finding and opening a bottle of her favourite red wine, she predictably pouted at her advances being rejected. I handed her a glass of wine and gave myself a good measure. We sat at the elaborately-set dining-room table with the glowing candles and flowers she had brought from London, watching the steam rising from the platters of food. I saw her take a deep breath.

Here we go again, I thought, and mentally steadied myself for a conversation I would have given anything to avoid.

'Duffy, we have to talk ...'

'Feddy, we've been through this before, many times. There's nothing more I can say or add. Please, let's just enjoy the ...'

'Fine, but there's something I *must* tell you. I love you dearly, but you're a difficult man to reach. You're clever and fun, but you lock me out. You shut everybody out, except Andy. The only thing you truly love is your dog. I have no idea about your past, your life in Australia, why you're here on Criach. Honestly, sometimes I think you arrived on this god-forsaken island, fully formed, without any past history.'

'Maybe that's how it is, Feddy,' I said quietly. The platter of duck meat and vegetables lay between us uneaten. I noted that Feddy seemed unusually emotional tonight. She took another deep breath, and then began to serve the food onto the warm plates. Bonnie's nose twitched at the prospect of some duck, but her instincts were alive to the tension in the room and looked at me with curiosity and concern. Treats another time, she wisely thought. Feddy took a sip of her wine and reached out to touch my hand. I knew I wasn't going to come out of this conversation with any credit.

'You're like a thistle. Prickly. Apart from Andy, you keep everyone at a distance. Especially me. It's very difficult, because I know there's more to you ...' She looked soft and rather beautiful in the candlelight and not for the first time I was thankful she was so different from Anna Maria. I marshalled my thoughts, protests and explanations, knowing I was unfair, hurtful, but, as always, and as I had explained to her interminably, I was unable to offer her anything more than visits, a warm, receptive bed, appreciation for delicious meals, and goodbye after a few days. How could I make her understand that I adored her, but simply could not give her the commitment, love or security she craved? It wasn't personal; I couldn't give that to any woman.

'I cannot offer you what you want, Feddy, or what you deserve.'

Feddy drained her wine, and I reached out to refill her glass. She took another deep breath before she spoke again. 'I know, I know. You've told me so often. Well, if there's no place in your life, I've decided to make some new plans. I'm going to open a new branch in Paris. I'll move there permanently. I won't see you, Duffy ... well, not very often.'

'Great idea, Feddy,' I said, and too late realised there was far too much enthusiasm in my response. 'You love Paris, your French is perfect, and you're a natural marketer. Look how you discovered the soap the girls make in the village, and promoted it all over the country. You were brilliant, and you'll do well with your new branch. Good on you. Let's open some champagne to celebrate ...' I rattled about in the fridge for a cold bottle of her favourite Veuve Cliquot, ignoring the tears that were forming behind the blue, beautiful eyes.

'Why *won't* you make a commitment, get married, or live with me?'

'I can't, Feddy.'

'Even if that means it's all over between us?'

'I guess so.'

Again, I knew the speed of my reply was unnecessarily hurtful. Feddy rose to go into the kitchen, where she began to slam plates into the sink. Bonnie now lay on the rug in front of the sitting-room fire, slightly panting from the warmth, her black eyes not leaving my face for a moment. I imagined she was cheering me on. Go on, she seemed to say, good work; you'll never get another chance like this. But then she was suddenly on her feet, alert and barking, the first to hear a car approaching outside, stop, doors slamming, and then footsteps hurrying up the path. Her agitation increased as her tail wagged tentatively and then became a flurry of black fur. She clearly liked whoever was behind the door. My heart was beating fast; I knew who it was.

I flung my napkin down on the table, took a deep breath and walked towards the door. It opened to an icy wind and light swirling snow, and to Andy standing behind a tall, surly young girl with dark eyes who looked very cold despite a heavy, grubby padded jacket, shabby woollen beanie and scarf. Her hands were bare and blue with the cold. The brown leather boots were muddy and soaked through. A bulging backpack and guitar case covered in stickers were slung over her shoulder, and she seemed unsteady on her feet. I took it all in within seconds.

My heart seemed to stop beating. In her letter Coralyn had warned me of Annabelle's possible arrival, but I was unprepared for the astonishing likeness to Anna Maria. And here she was before me. Annabelle Kendall as a younger, much taller version of her mother, olive-skinned and with eyes so brown they were almost black, strands of long dark hair with snowflakes and golden highlights falling from beneath her beanie. But unlike you, Anna Maria, I thought, there are no smiles from a mouth that is wide and beautifully-shaped like yours. And if I am not mistaken, our daughter is very, very drunk, or drugged.

'Duffy, I'm sorry I couldn't ring you,' Andy muttered as he pushed Annabelle inside and towards the fire. Momentarily, they brought gusts of the cold inside with them, and I shut the door hurriedly. 'The phone lines are down again, but this wee lassie was looking for you. I found her in the pub, a wee bit financially embarrassed, no-where to stay, so thought it best to bring her here.' I stared at Annabelle, hardly hearing Andy. It was impossible that this girl, now eighteen years old and heiress to a fortune, had no money. But then again, as Coralyn's letter had revealed, Annabelle was a difficult, unpredictable, delinquent granddaughter. Defying her normal good manners, Bonnie jumped up and down excitedly on Annabelle's legs and wagged her tail. Only now did Annabelle's expression soften slightly as she scratched Bonnie's head.

'Duffy, who is it?' Feddy appeared from the kitchen and stared at the unexpected and uninvited visitors. She was pink-eyed from weeping, but hadn't lost her haughtiness. 'Do tell the girl we don't do bed and breakfasts, dear.' Annabelle raised her hand, scowled, and with one upright finger indicated what she thought of Feddy's welcome. Andy's eyebrows were slightly raised, but I also detected a small suggestion of wry amusement. Perhaps he was reminded of a previous Australian with similar manners and attitude. Come in, come in by the fire I said as I fussed over them, taking coats, and mumbling offers of food, wine, tea or coffee. In truth, I was hardly aware of what I was saying or doing. Annabelle reluctantly took my hand when I offered mine in welcome, but hers was limp and cold, and she quickly stood back to avert any further attempt at physical closeness. Her eyes were slightly unfocused, I noted. She slumped onto the sofa and dumped her backpack and guitar on the floor beside her, shivering as she held her hands to the fire to warm them. I repeated my offer to get her anything she wanted, perhaps a hot drink to warm her up.

'Yeah, I *could* do with a drink. A strong one. I guess you know who I am, right?' Her accent was Australian, but the product of a private school education.

'Of course I know who you are ... ' Before I could say anything else, Feddy appeared again but was pushed back into the kitchen by Andy with the suggestion that perhaps he could make himself useful by helping her put together some hot food and coffee for the wee lassie. I heard Feddy's protests until a word or two from Andy brought silence apart from the clatter of plates and the snapping of the oven door.

Judging from her unsteadiness and her slurred words, the last thing Annabelle needed was more alcohol, but I gave her a brandy anyway. Bonnie sniffed at the backpack and wagged her tail; her eyes moved from Annabelle to me in something like a question mark. Whoever this is, she appeared to say, I like her. I wondered what reason Annabelle had given Hughie on the ferry, or Kenny at the pub, as to why she wanted to see me. She hardly sounded like a fan of mine or my writing. Would she claim the relationship? At the moment, that mattered little;

here she was, under my roof. Hostile, frozen, angry, drunk, but my daughter.

Andy appeared with coffee and a plate piled with hot roast duck and potatoes, which Annabelle accepted with a muffled thanks as she wiped her nose on her jumper sleeve. From the speed with which she demolished the food, it was obvious she was starving. I was on the verge of replenishing her plate when, a few minutes later, she vomited into Bonnie's basket, who didn't mind one bit; no doubt it was infinitely preferred to disinfectant.

'Oh, for goodness sake, what's happening now?' Feddy refused to be silenced another moment, but retreated in disgust to the kitchen. I handed Annabelle a towel, and took Bonnie's basket outside. Andy made plans to leave, but I urged him to stay and plied him with coffee. At this moment, he was a lifeline. I wasn't yet ready to tackle Annabelle's aggression and anger alone, although I knew I must. And soon. Despite the many times I had dreamt about being reunited with my daughter, this was hardly how I imagined it. I was apprehensive and sorely out of my depth.

'I would have picked you up from the ferry, Annabelle. Or from Glasgow or Edinburgh. London. Anywhere at all. Why didn't you let me know you were coming?'

'Rack off.' It may well have been another, more explicit word she muttered into her woollen scarf. She stretched out on the sofa while I stoked the fire, and when she kicked off her boots I noticed her socks were damp and grubby. Her clothes were good quality, but well-worn. 'Just fuck off.' There was no doubt now about her vocabulary. 'Except you, Mr Cameron.' She glanced in Andy's direction with an almost apologetic nod. 'Thank you for the lift.' When she lapsed into a sleep or coma, I covered her with a blanket. From the dark circles under her eyes, the worn clothes, the rough edges of her backpack and the raggedness of her fingernails, I guessed she had lived rough for a while. The guitar I had no idea about. What had she been doing in those weeks since leaving Australia, without money or clothes, and presumably travelling alone?

While she slept, Andy told me in low whispers how he had found her in the village pub, having walked from the ferry, demanding to know where I lived. She was wet, muddy, bedraggled, and aggressive. He didn't say it then, but I later found out from Kenny that she had regaled the patrons with her views about the 'crap writer, James Duffield, who uncovers crimes and lies, and saves women from danger, but what the hell would he know about all that?' Kenny and his patrons eventually became annoyed with her, and when she admitted she had no money to pay for a hotel room or her drinks, she accepted Andy's offer of a lift to my cottage, if she was so keen to meet me. As she got into Andy's coach, she warned him if he tried 'any funny business', then, 'mate, your mating days are over.' She had been sullen and silent on the short journey, and Andy remained diplomatically silent.

When he left to return to his cabin, Annabelle was still passed out on the sofa. There was no escaping Feddy in the kitchen where she was smoking a cigarette and drinking wine at a pace I'd never seen before. I poured myself an unusually large whisky and looked enviously at her cigarette. The kitchen was cleared of debris, now as pristine as though nothing unusual had happened in the past hour. Feddy had prepared herself for our confrontation. She had re-applied her lipstick, and her long blonde hair was loose around her shoulders; her face was pale but composed. Normally she was a happy drunk, but tonight she was miserable and angry. I could hardly blame her, it was hardly the romantic end to the day she had envisaged. But more important, how could I explain Annabelle? I had no idea whether she wanted it known I was her father, and I was in no mood tonight to discuss my past to Feddy.

'An explanation, please, Duffy,' she said huffily. She drew on her cigarette, its filter stained with red lipstick. 'I have worked and cooked all day to make this day perfect; I have been patient, understanding, accommodating. I have offered you an alternative to this lonely wretched life, one that most men would at least think about.' Her eyes flooded with tears. 'And what do I get? My dinner ruined, Andy ordering me around like a hired maid, and a foul-mouthed hippy vomiting all over the place. And you say ... ' her voice faltered, 'you say it's over between us. What is happening, Duffy?'

'I'm sorry I've hurt you, Feddy. In my defence, I can only say I've never lied to you.'

'Who is she?'

'She's a girl from Sydney.'

'So she stays, and I go? Is she a newer, younger girlfriend?'

'Don't be daft.'

As Feddy left the kitchen, her heels clicking on the old stone tiles, Bonnie whined. She too found it unbearable to see the pain in Feddy's eyes. I wanted to tell her what a wonderful woman she was, a magnificent cook, a generous, passionate lover, that I loved her company but couldn't, wouldn't, trust myself to love another woman the way I loved Anna Maria. How for eighteen years I had missed my daughter, ostensibly lost to me, but who was now in my house, angry and antagonistic. But I said nothing.

The quiet closing of the bedroom door was more wounding than if Feddy had screamed obscenities and slammed it shut in my face. With her in my bedroom and Annabelle on the sofa, I was relegated to the rarely-used spare room. Bonnie was with me in a split second. She too was homeless, with her basket outside in the rain. I stroked her, and she licked my hand. You did the right thing, she seemed to say. Did I, Bonnie? Why do I hurt people? But that was a question the wise little creature couldn't answer. The house was quiet, the embers in the fire shifted, and eventually Feddy stopped sobbing. Annabelle snored.

The house was ready to sleep, but I couldn't close my eyes. I unfolded Coralyn's letter and read it again. Once I had an affectionate, lovable, beautiful granddaughter, she wrote, but since leaving school Annabelle is uncontrollable, spiteful and rebellious. 'I have done my best, but she is beyond all of us. I don't have much time left on this earth, days only, and so – as you once requested – I have told her about you, and where you live. She is very angry with me, and you, and determined to find you, and I warn you, she is difficult and aggressive, drinks too much and I suspect takes drugs. Because of this, the rest of the family have challenged her inheritance, which she can now claim as she's turned eighteen, but money means nothing to her. She intends to leave without saying goodbye to me, and without means or financial support. If she finds you, and she will because she is wilful and resourceful, I hope you can make her understand our motives all those years ago. She reminds me of your troubled days, and just as I was confident you would ulti-mately be successful and find contentment, I pray you can help your daughter do the same.'

But could I? Feddy was right: I had lived so long within my own private world, with my selfish pursuits of books and isolation, moun-tains, birds and fish. Feddy was a slim link to another world, but there was always the nearby ferry to take her home.

I didn't hear Feddy come into the room, and even Bonnie didn't stir. She looked sad and tired, her cheeks smudged with mascara. I rarely saw her without her glasses or contact lenses, but tonight she didn't care. Her woolly dressing gown was drawn tightly around her waist as she sat on the edge of the bed.

'Is it really over?'

'Feddy, you delivered the ultimatum, not me. And you had every right to do it. Go to Paris, be successful, be happy without me, because, believe me, I don't bring much joy to anyone who comes into my life.' She began to protest, but I put a finger to her mouth and shook my head. 'You deserve much, much more than this ...'

She shrugged me off, sighed deeply and then began to speak very slowly, her eyes locked onto mine. 'You are a selfish, lonely man,' she began, 'And yes, it may take some time, but I'll try to forget you. I will be successful. We don't all hide away from life like you; some of us live it, get touched and hurt by it. I think something happened to you once, and you're too damned scared to let it happen again. You don't fight back, Duffy, you retreat. I saw your face tonight when you saw that girl. I realised then that the tight-shut James Duffield lives with demons and memories that torment him. I wish to God you'd let me help you, with whatever it is that troubles you.' I had never known Feddy to be so intense, honest, or wounding. And she was right.

I held her close as she slid into bed beside me. I wasn't proud of myself.

*   *   *

I sat beside Feddy as she drove to the ferry early next morning. This time there were no playful farewells, simply a stilted embrace as we stood on the jetty. She looked white and strained, but still lovely. To me, the seagulls seemed louder, more fractious, the wind chillier, in that grey bleak morning air. The old mountain brooding and judgemental. I didn't like myself much.

"Who is she, Duffy? I deserve to know that.'

'In fairness to her, Feddy, I can't say just yet.'

She raised her eyebrows and sighed as I helped her onto the gangplank. 'So many secrets and lies,' she said quietly. 'I said last night I would forget you and get on with my life, but the truth is, despite everything, I only want to be with you ... and I hope, Mr Thistle Man, one day you'll tell me this isn't really goodbye.'

I was spared a reply. 'Did that big lassie catch up with you last night,

Duffy?' Old Hughie shouted over to me, a soggy cigarette between his lips as he pulled in ropes and made ready to leap aboard. I nodded 'aye'. Feddy's car was safely on board, and now she turned to me and kissed me on the cheek. *'Au revoir,'* she whispered hoarsely, and then strode up the gangplank. I watched from the jetty as the old boat cast off and made its way across the choppy, grey water until Feddy became a lonely speck in the distance; I was barely aware of the drizzle until Bonnie's jumping up and down with tiny yips brought me back to earth. Things to do, she chided. People at home to look after.

I jogged home to find Annabelle still fast asleep on the sofa. I cleared out the spare room and prepared it for her, then cooked breakfast, found I couldn't eat it, gave it to Bonnie, then tried to read yesterday's newspaper, but didn't understand the words. I wanted Annabelle awake, rested and reasonable. To like me sufficiently to listen, to let me explain. But why should she like me? She hardly knew me, beyond being the man who fathered her when her mother was married to another man, and who later fled from Australia. Not a pretty story. How much did she know about the murders?

'I'd shag a snowman for a coffee ... ' I turned to see an unwashed, hung-over young woman who seared my heart because of the astonishing resemblance to her mother. But that was where the resemblance ended.

'Good morning.'

'That,' she muttered, 'remains to be seen.'

Indeed it did.

\* \* \*

# CHAPTER THREE

A ction, food and hospitality were the best strategies in situations like this, I decided. Just the way Grannie McPhedron had taught me.

'How do you like your coffee, Annabelle?'

'It's Annie.'

'OK. Everyone calls me Duffy, Annie.'

'I'm hardly going to call you Daddy.'

The tensions between us reflected the coldness of the house in the morning light, with none of the soft shadings from the late after-noon when the lamps shed a friendly light, and the fires warmed the low-ceilinged rooms. I handed Annie a strong coffee and asked what she wanted for breakfast. In several colourful phrases she told me she ate anything except porridge, black pudding, haggis and turnips, then looked down at Bonnie's bowl and remarked with a hint of mischief, 'What the dog's having looks good.' She looked pale, with dark circles under her eyes, and from the thickness in her voice, and the sleeve she intermittently drew across her nose, she had a cold, or even 'flu. There was nothing wrong with her appetite, though, and she began to eat the sausages and bacon, tomato and fried bread before they were out of the frying pan. I made more toast. No sooner had she eaten, and drunk two cups of coffee, than she was in the bathroom retching. I remembered my own hung-over days and left her alone. When she reappeared an hour later, she was showered and perfumed – courtesy of Feddy's French toiletries – wearing blue jeans torn at the knees, a thick, loose lambswool sweater and the well-worn boots still muddy from the day before. Her long hair was shampooed and tied back in a long glossy pony-tail.

The fires were lit, but the house was still cold and Annie hunched her shoulders and wrapped her arms around her chest. Outside it began to rain, and the wind was picking up. It was going to be a miserable day, perhaps in more ways than one.

'It'll warm up inside soon, I promise,' I said. 'Everyone complains about the cold in Criach, but we know how to get a good fire going.' Even to my own ears, I sounded stiff and stilted. If there was a sensible and sensitive way to connect with a daughter after an absence of eighteen years, I hadn't cracked it. But then again, she wasn't making it any easier.

'Wouldn't be the only thing to complain about,' she muttered. 'I see the very friendly English lady with a cork up her bum has left the premises. She your missus? Mr Cameron is nice, though, I like him.'

'I'm not married, Annie. Feddy is a friend, and she's gone back to London ...'

'Feddy? What a name! Feddy and Duffy, you sound like a couple of poodles in a circus act.'

'Annie, I wish you'd told me you were coming. I would've been more prepared ...'

'Or run away? No, I wanted to surprise you, see how you would react, but I kinda knew Granny Coralyn would spoil my surprise. After she dropped the death-bed confession about my absent father, I was so angry I had to get out of that place. No point in hanging around to weep at her grave, watching that horrible Kendall family scramble over her money. They're all vultures. I didn't say goodbye to Granny ...' Her voice faltered for a second, and she bent her head. The nape of her neck looked defenceless and very young, and when she spoke again it was barely a whisper. 'I thought she'd live to be a hundred, just to drive me mad ... but she ... died so quickly.'

Again, I detected a quaver as she spoke, and she hurriedly left the room. I watched her go, surprised not so much that Coralyn was dead, because she was old and had been ill, but that Annie pretended indifference when she was obviously upset. I poured myself a coffee, and Bonnie jumped on my lap. What do you say to a sad, grieving, hostile kid, I asked her, when she belongs to you, needs help but there's no way on God's green earth she'll accept it. She licked my hand. Sure, Bonnie, I said, your way is affection and loyalty, fun and forgiveness, but this is a pretty complex and hard nut to crack. For her, as well as me.

'Well, I'm off.' Annie reappeared, zipping up her jacket and carrying her guitar case and backpack. 'Don't worry, I'm not heading to your precious village pub to tell the world you're the world's dud dad. Quite frankly, you're not worth the trouble. I've met you, seen how you're doing, which, as it turns out, is pretty nicely, thank you. You, in turn, have seen your bastard spawn. That's it. No more to be done or said.'

'Hang on,' I was on my feet in an instant. 'Why did you bother coming here in the first place if you didn't want to talk about your mother and me? Didn't you want to get to know me, learn the truth?'

'Truth? Seems pretty clear to me. You shagged my mum, a married woman. Made her pregnant. She and the bloke she married for his money subsequently died as a result of a police fuck-up – *your* failure – then you left the country ... '

'Stop it, Annie. I loved your mother and her death nearly destroyed me. Be angry, but know the facts. You weren't abandoned. I wanted you desperately, but your mother chose another life and I was forced to accept that. Your grandmother refused any access ... you must listen to me.' She hoisted the bag on her back.

'Nup. No point. I accept I'm the progeny of a gold-digging whore and a shagger. An orphan. Orphan Annie, that's what they called me at school. I just wanted to see you, to see what kind of a bloke could live with what he did. And I find you've got a good life. Living the fantasy to match your friggin' awful books. Your problems all behind you. So I'm off. Thanks for the free bed and breakfast your girlfriend, Feddy ...' she snorted, 'didn't want to offer. You're quite a pair.'

'You are so wrong, Annie! About your mother ...' I was shouting at her now, but she ignored me, shrugged, and headed for the door. Agitated, Bonnie ran in front of her, as though she was trying to block her exit. 'Where are you going?'

'I dunno. After this freezing hell-hole, anywhere where I can find some sun. I like your dog, though.' She bent down and rubbed Bonnie's head. "Your dad's an arsehole,' she whispered, and then looked up at me. 'I like her better than you.'

She slammed the door behind her and was almost at the end of the pathway when my nerves snapped and I raced after her. 'Come back here,' I yelled as I flung the bag from her shoulders and snatched the guitar. Alarmed, Bonnie jumped on my legs and began to bark. Was this a game, or was protection needed? And if so, for whom? Me or the girl? Poor Bonnie; she was as mixed up as I was. 'This is ridiculous, you're here now, so let's sort this out. Get back inside and sit down where it's warm!' The icy wind blew in our faces until I forcibly pushed her towards the front door and into the hallway, then slammed the heavy door shut behind us.

'Stay there!' As she sank down on the sofa and stared into a fire that obstinately refused to catch, I doubted if my heart would ever regain an even beat. 'You can't just arrive like this, sleep off a hang-over, and then leave without telling me where you're headed and what you want from me. I will give you anything you want. There's a storm brewing, you're broke and tired. Besides, we owe each other some explanations, surely?' She pulled a face and crossed her arms as she stared into the fire. Bonnie waited for some familiar words that would explain the situation to her, her eyes anxiously darting from me to Annie.

Damn. The telephone rang in the hall and I hoped it would be Andy, but feared it would be Feddy. It was neither. I hadn't heard from Bob Connelly since he had visited Criach some years ago, and despite my present agitation it was a relief to hear his familiar booming Australian accent. 'Duffy!' The line was clear, but he bellowed as though to cover the miles that separated us. 'Howzit going in that great ruddy cold part of the world?' I suspected this was no cheery social call. Too many things were happening, too quickly, and none of them was coincidental.

'Just as cold, Bob. How's hot and humid Sydney?' The weather established in our respective parts of the world, he moved on to the real point of an expensive international telephone call.

'You remember Maurizio Stopelli?' Of course I did. Barely a day went by that I didn't, at some time, think of that evil swine. 'Well, just a heads up. He's been released from prison.' I closed my eyes and leant my forehead against the cool brick wall. So what? We always knew he wouldn't do the full twenty years. Bonnie was beside me now, watching anxiously. 'Word is, he's out to get you.'

'Of course. They all say that.'

'He's returned to Italy. I thought you might like to know he's on your side of the world.' All I could say was, 'okay', and then we hurried on to other matters: his promotion to Assistant Commissioner and near retirement, his family, how much he had enjoyed his recent stay in Criach; we discussed who was still in the police force, who had retired, and new procedures brought in to safeguard forensic evidence. 'Just like you always argued for, mate.' A hesitation alerted me to more news. 'Ah, one more thing. We have a new Premier, a protégé of the old

95

Kendall woman, Roland Perritt, who we'd remember as Ellery Kendall's old chief of staff. Became a politician some years ago, done well for himself, and worked his way up to leader and is now Premier.'

'Yeah, I remember him. A good guy, liked a drink but couldn't take the harsh stuff.'

'Well, he's dredged up Ellery's old anti-drug stuff. Stopelli's release has opened up interest in the Kendall case and the press's raking up old records.'

'They'll soon lose interest. Thank God I'm out of it.'

'Well, that's just it, Duffy. The *Sydney Mirror* plans on doing a big splash on drugs and crime, and since you were the policeman involved in the Kendall murders and now a bit of a celebrity crime-writer, they're sending a journalist to Scotland to interview you. Probably there by now. Thought you should know.' I heard his cigarette lighter flick open. 'I'll fax you some press clippings ... ' Right now, the last thing in the world I wanted to see were old images of Anna Maria and Ellery, or talk to any journalist. 'And you'll never believe this, mate. Talk about rich kids.' He took a long drag of his cigarette. 'There's a summons out for the arrest of one of the young Kendalls, Annabelle. The family dobbed her in for stealing some money and shoplifting after the old girl died, but she's disappeared. Last known to have boarded a Qantas jet for London. Nothing after that. Just disappeared.'

'She's here, in Scotland.'

'Yeah? What's she doing there?'

'Bob, she's my daughter.'

'Jeez. That's a turn-up for the books. Then again, that Kendall case hit you real hard, and I always wondered why. I kinda figured ... well, good luck. Sounds like your island's getting pretty crowded, mate, so take care of yourself. Big hello to Bonnie, and let me know what you want me to do about this theft and shop-lifting charge.' I told him to have it dropped; he still knew how to work the system.

I returned to the sitting room to find Annie dozing on the sofa. The fire was now blazing, and she looked warm and relaxed. I put a soft lambswool blanket over her. Bob had brought up more old memories, and I sat and stared at her as my mind sifted through images of the past. Like the time when Stopelli was taken down from the courtroom, and how he spat a vow at me that he would make me pay one day. It was possible he would be stupid enough to attempt some kind of revenge now that he was released from prison, but more likely it was empty pride and bravado. A journalist might turn up, but what more could I say about something that happened fifteen years ago? The arrival of both, or either, could disrupt my peaceful life, but the only person I cared about, and who had to be protected whatever the cost, was Annie.

The girl I last remembered as a three-year-old child playing on a swing with her dog was caught right in the middle of all this, and still struggling with the truth of her birth and whatever Coralyn had told her of Anna Maria and me. Surely it wouldn't have been in the cruel terms Annie had flung at me? Perhaps Annabelle just wanted to hurt me? In truth, I couldn't blame her.

Annie stirred from her sleep, pushed away the blanket, frowned and then rubbed her eyes with her knuckles. 'Sorry, I fell asleep ...' Drowsy, caught off-guard, she sounded like a very young child. She was so much a mirror image of her mother that more unbidden memories came to mind; this time of Anna Maria sleeping in my bed and waking up slowly, arms outstretched and inviting me to join her. God, how I still loved that woman; how clear the memories remained.

Annabelle was now fully awake, and the gentle sleepiness was gone. She glanced outside the window. It was barely three o'clock in the afternoon, yet it was darkening outside, the grey clouds low in the sky. The wind howled straight from the Atlantic Ocean and carried snow from the mountains. She shivered.

'When does the ferry leave?'

'It won't go today. The weather's too rough.'

'Does anything ever happen in this shit-pit of a place?'

Oh, Annie, if only you knew. There's a lot about to happen. You've brought the world to my safely-barricaded sanctuary, and somehow, together, we're going to have to see it through. Maybe we'll be friends at the end of it. I glanced up at her angry face as she strode past me towards the spare bedroom, slamming the door behind her. Maybe not.

\* \* \*

# CHAPTER FOUR

The good thing about living on a small remote island in Scotland is that you get to know its inhabitants pretty well. The bad thing is that they get to know you equally as well. Within hours of Feddy leaving, teary and tense, and Annie arriving, drunk and abusive, I knew that all of Criach would be well-briefed on current events. I had lived with these people for many years now and had slowly gained their trust, but I was still sufficiently a curiosity, a newcomer, to make me interesting.

I was accepted. I minded my own business. I drank in their pub, pulled people off icy cliffs with Andy and the mountain rescue team; I fished and bought their raffle tickets; I danced at their weddings and drank at their wakes. I donated books to their library and helped them find lost sheep on cold winter nights. I helped the regional police on the mainland when asked about suspicious people or activities in the region. I attended their Burns' suppers and once agreed to be a guest speaker. Despite all this, I had two strikes against me: I never went to church, and had an English girlfriend. Maybe three, as I didn't join their bid for Scottish independence.

I now provided them with enough gossip to keep the tongues

chattering up and down the high street for days. There hadn't been so much excitement since the day poor, plain Fiona McCallum was left standing at the altar in a borrowed wedding dress while her erstwhile groom disappeared across the sea in a stolen rowing boat. Given the ammunition I had given them, I could picture the Criach housewives now, chins tucked into their headscarves, heads bobbing, arms crossed, clutching shopping bags to stout bodies against buttoned-up overcoats.

'Did you hear thon nice Mr Duffield threw that English lassie oot of his hoose? Will he no make up his mind?'

'And whit aboot thon big lassie who turned up on the ferry, shoutin' and bawlin' about wantin' to see him ... I hear she might be some kind of folk singer from Australia, had a guitar, or maybe she's a wee niece ... except she's no that wee.'

Oh yes, I could imagine the gossip. Not that the Criach folks would ever confront me directly with their curiosity.

The next morning I decided to see Andy in the village before he left for the mainland. I had heard nothing from Annie's room since we shared a stony, silent dinner last night, and after which she fled upstairs with the best part of a bottle of red wine. Before I left the cottage, I left a note to say I would be home soon, but to help herself to anything she wanted. Even as I wrote, I knew I sounded like a staid and boring old aunt. Bonnie was excited to see the car keys, but hesitated and looked towards Annie's bedroom, as though to enquire whether we shouldn't include our guest.

I found Andy checking his coach and putting snow chains on the tyres, while his tourists finished their lunch before the last outing of the day, a visit to the nearby distillery. I gave him a hand, then we went inside to the pub's warmth for a welcome coffee. We had barely begun a conversation and taken a sip when there was a commotion at the hotel entrance. Bonnie leapt from beneath the table with a small, sharp, delighted bark. Annie had arrived on the back of the only motor-cycle on the island, the one that belonged to the closest thing we

had in Criach to a hoodlum, young Lachlan McClarty. As Andy and
I watched, we saw Annie dismounting with her backpack and guitar,
appearing to thank Lachlan then telling him to get lost.

When I approached her, she suggested I do the same. Andy was now
outside, gathering up his rowdy group and ushering them towards the
coach. He walked over to Annie with a smile and shook her hand. She
looked pleased to see him, and for a second I saw the glimpse of Anna
Maria's smile.

'Nice to see you, young Annie,' he said heartily. 'Unless you've got
anything else planned, would you like to see a bit more of Criach? Why
don't you come along and join us for a wee tour? You'll enjoy it. We stop
at a nice wee distillery that might interest you.'

'Sounds good, Mr Cameron.'

'Andy, please.'

She turned to give me a deliberate look of disdain as she heaved her
backpack and guitar inside the coach, then took Andy's offered hand
and climbed inside. His tourists followed, chatting and arranging and
re-arranging themselves in the best seats. I left them to it. I had only just
walked back into the bar as the coach left when Kenny shouted over to
me that I was wanted on the lobby telephone. I hoped it wouldn't be
Feddy, for I was in no shape for fights, accusations or pleas for further
discussions. But luck wasn't on my side that day.

'Thought I'd find you there,' Feddy began, sounding peevish. I
frowned and pressed the phone to my ear to hear above the background
babble of Glasgow voices and taped music behind her. 'Your mobile
phone doesn't work, never does ... anyway, never mind that ... I think
you should know I had a call on *my* mobile from an Australian journalist, a woman who's in Scotland and wants to get in touch with you.'

'How did she get your mobile number?'

'She rang your agent's office. They refused to give your number, but
suggested I might be able to contact you.'

'And what did you tell her?' Too late now, but how I wished I had used a *nom de plume* for my books, but vanity had over-ridden common sense. Although the fly-leaves merely said I lived on a small island in Scotland, I didn't trust Feddy to get even with me by freely giving the journalist any information she wanted. She hesitated before she replied, and I knew she was lying, or at least was flirting with the truth.

'Nothing much,' Feddy was shouting over the noise in the background. 'She did most of the talking. She's visited people in your old Glasgow neighbourhood, for what she called background material. Said she wanted to talk to you now about some murder in Sydney you were involved in. I thought you might have been the murderer she was after ... ' she laughed nervously, 'until she told me you were a top cop. I did not know that.'

'Did she say anything about ... the girl who came to the cottage?'

'What?'

'The girl, Feddy, the girl who came to the cottage.'

'No. Why should she?'

'Be honest, you *did* tell her where to find me, didn't you?'

'I may have, in a roundabout kind of way. Why the fuss? Look, if she found out where you lived in Glasgow, your little hideaway island will be a doddle. You sound a bit rattled, sweetie.' She adopted a mocking tone, 'Big bad world invading your hidey-hole? Well, welcome to the real world.' There was a silence, and she continued in a smaller, contrite voice. 'Sorry. That wasn't very nice.'

'Feddy, don't get involved with strangers who ask about me, or want to know where I am. Please take care, and let me know if she, or anyone else contacts you again. Promise?'

'Of course, but I'm off to Paris soon. So, once again, goodbye Mr Thistle Man. Unless, of course ... ' There was now a forced gaiety to her voice, and I heard the clink of glasses and chatter behind her. She sounded tipsy, if not dead drunk. What was she doing in a Glasgow pub? She normally headed for London at the speed of light, not stopping until she reached the English border and 'home'.

'Please take care, Feddy. I'm sorry about everything.'

'Me too.'

I hung up and found a table by the window, where I could look out onto the expanse of fields and mountains beyond. Anything to calm down. Kenny brought me coffee and a meat pie, and when I finished eating I spent the next hour pretending to read the day-old newspaper, but it was impossible to concentrate. I could take care of ex-cons and journalists, no bother, but how to cope with a sad, possibly vengeful, ex-girlfriend and a stubborn, anti-social daughter?

Come off it, Duffy, I told myself sharply, stop feeling sorry for yourself. How about a thought for Feddy who's shown you nothing but kindness and generosity; or a kid who's been left an orphan by a murderer? And who finds out on the deathbed of a grandmother she adored that her life was a lie? No wonder she wants to strike out and hurt. I understood her dislike of the Kendall cousins who sounded like a mendacious and nasty bunch. And if she stole and shoplifted, she obviously needed the money for her airfare to get away from them, or just wanted to annoy them; she would be good at that. I deserve her anger. But was it pure anger that motivated her to travel across the world to meet me? There must be more to it than just to tell me what a rat bastard I am. Curiosity? Below the venom and bad language, confusion and feigned toughness, there was something else: tiny flakes of politeness, of gentleness. Vulnerability. Bonnie loved her, and she was a fine judge of character. Optimistically, I told myself that Annabelle had travelled thousands of miles to confront me, and that surely was a starting point for reconciliation?

I left the pub and took Bonnie for a long, brisk walk. It was getting dark when I returned to the village, just in time to see Andy's coach approaching the pub, lights blazing through the light mist. I heard music and singing. I thought how good it must be to sing away your problems in the protective company of someone like Andy. As the coach got nearer I saw the bright indoor lights, with the passengers turned to Annie as she sat on the arm of a seat near Andy, strumming her guitar and singing. Everyone joined in what seemed like a chorus. It was like watching a stage show finalé, and when the coach came to a standstill, there was loud applause and cheering when Annie stood and bowed to her audience, laughing and tossing her hair from her face. Andy was first off to help the happy, chattering tourists as they tumbled off the coach and raced to the warmth of the bar. Last off was Annie, her cheeks pink, her hand firmly in Andy's as they laughed and stepped down from the coach. Yes, she did indeed have her mother's beautiful smile.

'I've invited Andy home for a meal,' she said as she brushed past me and gathered Bonnie up in her arms. 'Hello, Bon Bon, you should have come with us, it was fun.' The remark was definitely for my dog, not me. She stroked Bonnie's ears, whose tail indicated sublime pleasure at having Annie and Andy together. 'But first, as you Criach people say, a wee drink.' She giggled. Andy – and possibly the trip to the distillery – had worked some magic. Home. She said 'home'. Maybe I was in with a chance that we would become friends. Maybe in time, when she knew the whole story, she could learn to trust me. Maybe even love me.

We all piled into the bar. 'You owe Kenny twenty-six quid,' she snapped at me after ordering drinks for everyone, as well as a bottle of whisky to take home. 'You can afford it.' Within an hour, having won the hearts of everyone in the bar, now definitely tipsy and cheery, Annie struggled from the hotel with her guitar and a bottle under her arm.

As I reached for my wallet, I wondered how to make my daughter stop drinking so much.

\* \* \*

# CHAPTER FIVE

A nnie and I drove home in silence. It was too dark and pointless
anyway to interest her in Criach's spectacular scenery, while she
sat hugging her backpack and her bottle of whisky. Bonnie sat between us, delighted to be so close. Once home, Annie fled upstairs to
the spare room and shut the door behind her, yelling to let her know
when Andy arrived and dinner was ready. While I was no chef, Grannie McPhedron had taught me how to cook basic meals and Feddy had
stocked the freezer with recently-caught fish. Immodestly, I told myself
my chips were popular; some people say they're the best they've ever
tasted and seem to mean it. So a meal was no problem, and maybe the
combination of a warm house, good food, Andy's company and Bonnie's love of fun, would soften Annie's antagonism towards me.

Andy arrived soon after. It mattered little to him if he was on the
freeway or lumbering over the icy, rocky roads of Criach, he drove his
coach as though it were a scooter. He was clad in his Fair Isle jumper
and sheepskin jacket, and helped himself to a drink as he warmed
himself in front of the fire. Annie skipped down the stairs, her hair
brushed loose, curling around her shoulders, and took the glass of
wine he offered her. From the kitchen, I couldn't make out much of

what they were saying, aside from registering that their conversation was friendly, free of expletives and Annie laughed. Bonnie appeared to be enjoying the company, and certainly the potato crisps that Annie offered her.

When I called them to table, I poured generous glasses of white wine and then glanced over at Annabelle with concern. As soon as I spoke, I knew how stupid I was. 'With your cold, Annie, you really shouldn't be drinking so much.' Within a second, she picked up her wine glass and slowly drank the entire contents, all the time staring at me in defiance. God, what was making me like this? A shrew, a nag? The look of rebelliousness and contempt in my daughter's eyes said it all. Andy pulled out her chair and refilled her glass. I put the plates of fish and chips in front of them.

'Just wait till you taste these chips, lassie, *and* the fish from our local streams.' Andy rubbed his hands with satisfaction and anticipation as he sat down and shook out his napkin. Annie ignored me, but picked up a chip and inspected it. 'But first, I want to hear where you learnt to sing like that.'

Annie's eyes brightened and she began to eat. Under Andy's clever questioning she told him (not me) that she had always loved music. Granny Coralyn had insisted she study the piano, which she liked, but preferred the guitar. Unknown to her disapproving grandmother, she had busked in Sydney streets from the age of fourteen to earn her own money. Not that it was much, but it was *hers,* she emphasised. And when she left Australia, she busked in London and Glasgow to pay for food and a bed. 'I just love singing,' she ended, 'particularly folk songs. I mean, if you're gonna make music, it's gotta mean something to somebody.'

'Your mother loved singing,' I ventured to say in a very quiet voice. 'She had a beautiful voice.' Annie's head swung in my direction, her eyes wide, the hostility momentarily gone. She was silent, her face soft for a few moments as she digested this information.

'Until it was snuffed out, you mean,' she snapped, the softness gone. In its place was bitterness, and tears very close. 'Thanks to you.'

'What are your plans now, Annie?' Andy was quick to intervene.

While I retreated to the kitchen to make coffee and put together some cheese and oatmeal biscuits, I heard him suggest that she might like to spend some time on the island. 'Take a wee rest,' he said. 'You've had a long journey and you're a bit weary.' Maybe, she said, but she had no money and relied on busking. That's impossible, I wanted to shout out; she was a rich Kendall, for God's sake. But I forced myself to be silent and remain in the kitchen to eavesdrop. Andy continued in his quiet, persuasive way. 'There's always the pub, lass. I can arrange for you to sing there Fridays and Saturdays, or when the tourists come in.' She didn't snap at him, so I presumed she didn't entirely discard the idea. When I reappeared, feeling like the unwelcome guest in my own home, Andy sent me a warning signal across the table to be silent as he pressed home his advantage. 'The pub's far too expensive, and accommodation elsewhere is pretty tight and not very grand. But what about here? Duffy's got a spare room, and he's close enough to the village and the ferry.'

The response was instant. 'And hell will freeze over first. I don't want to be here, any more than he ... wants me. I'm off as soon as that death trap of a ferry gets going. You're a good friend, Andy, but he ...' She stood up, dragging the chair behind her as she flung down her napkin and stared hard at me, 'he doesn't deserve you. You don't know the half of what he's done. Goodnight.' She ran up the stairs, and then we heard the bedroom door slam shut. We both raised our eyebrows. Nice try, Andy, I thought.

'Och, it'll all work out, son. She's a fine wee lassie. Bruised, confused, weary, grieving for her granny and the mother she never knew. She reminds me of you, all those years ago. Have faith in her, and in yourself. I'll have one more wee whisky with you, and then I must be off.'

We chatted for another hour about inconsequential subjects I couldn't recall the next day, until he picked up his jacket and car keys. 'Thanks for a most interesting evening, Duffy.'

I watched him drive off into the dark, and wondered if he was right. Or was it just hope? Would it ever work out? I admired his confidence, but I felt bereft of certainty. I cleaned up the kitchen, and when Bonnie leapt into bed with me, she sighed and laid her head on my shoulder. I love that wee lassie, she seemed to say, and so do you. That isn't the problem, I told her, of course I love her, but how do I get her to even like me? Bonnie had no answer, for it had been a busy day, she'd eaten far too many potato crisps and was fast asleep.

* * *

The cottage was strangely quiet the next morning. The wild weather of the previous day and night had gone, the sky clear and wintry grey. I had slept late and uncharacteristically very soundly, either from mental exhaustion and maybe drinking more whisky than normal. I discovered the reason for silence when I entered the kitchen and found frying pans congealed with fat, breadcrumbs, bacon rinds and bread slices scattered across the table, coffee beans strewn from bench to floor. Annie had made herself the full Scottish breakfast. I found her room empty, and she was gone. A glance outside the window and the open shed door told me that so had my car.

She probably had gone to the ferry. If I jogged fast, I could catch her. Bonnie loved the run as we raced the mile to the jetty. My mind worked through what I had to do: first find Annie and make her stay long enough to explain about her mother and me; watch the ferry passengers for either a journalist or a criminal, or both, and alert the mainland police that Stopelli might appear on their patch. The priority, of course, was to find Annie.

The ferry was securely tied up, with no sign of passengers or Old Hughie. That wasn't so unusual for his ferry timekeeping was perennially eccentric and random. In reality, he ran his own version of a timetable. Bonnie and I ran on to the village and the pub, and I wasn't surprised to see Andy's coach parked outside. Alongside my car. Inside enjoying an early lunch were Andy, Old Hughie and Annie, and from the muffled chatter and laughter coming from their table, they gave every impression of being old mates enjoying good food and each other's company. Andy beckoned me to join them and pulled out a chair, Old Hughie continued to chew his cottage pie as though it were a tough steak, and Annie ignored me by staring out the window and ruffling Bonnie's fur. I didn't sit down.

'Can I see you for a minute, Andy?'

Outside, we pretended to inspect the coach's snow chains as I asked him what the hell was happening. He outlined the morning's events, and I listened apprehensively as he spoke: he had found Annie at the jetty, intending to leave on the morning ferry but had no money for the fare. Nonetheless, she was determined to get herself and my car across to the mainland, although, as Old Hughie told Andy, she was a wee bit vague about where she was going after that. Besides, she had enormous trouble getting my car onto the confined ferry space.

'You know Old Hughie, Duffy, he wouldn't have bothered about a fare, but he suspected you didn't know your car was leaving the island. Annie tried to convince him she was running an errand for you, then I came along and persuaded her to delay her trip for a wee while. So the three of us decided to have a wee bite together.'

'How come you were passing by the ferry this morning?'

'I had an idea she might try to leave.'

'Thanks, Andy.' Aware I should have been alert to that possibility myself, I briefly told him about the prospect of Stopelli and the journalist travelling to Criach. As I spoke, I knew I sounded distracted and barely making sense. My main worry was Annie. How was I to keep her here and care for her until she settled down and saw sense? But what made sense to me might not make sense to her. I sighed in despair.

'Be patient, man. She's tired and angry, and hasn't a penny to bless herself with, although.' From his jacket pocket he fished out my watch – an old one, not worth much, but to me priceless because Anna Maria had given it to me from her first pay packet. It was engraved 'James and A.M.' inside a silly little heart. He handed it to me, and chuckled with amusement. I was astonished. This was an Andy I didn't know and one who was totally out of character; he who couldn't steal an apple from a public park was now chuckling over larceny. 'She's a homeless wee soul, Duffy, so take her home and look after her. She needs that, son.'

'Andy, you've seen what she's like with me.'

'But she's your flesh and blood, and you'll do what's right. Be patient. Be firm. She needs a rest, a place where she feels safe. She's a courageous wee soul, but she's near the end of her strength. Oh, and by the way, you might like to know that she *has* now agreed – just a wee while ago – to sing at the pub. Which means she'll stay for a while. Kenny's told her there's no accommodation available at the pub, so she'll have to take the offer of a room with you. See? It's going to work out fine.' I suspected some jiggery-pokery had gone on between Andy and Kenny – I knew the pub wasn't full – but if it worked out the way Andy felt it would, I was grateful.

We walked back to the dining room. 'And by the way, Old Hughie tells me that an Australian woman arrived on the early ferry this morning. Mid-thirties, smartly turned out, although he says she has no idea about the conditions here on Criach and she'll freeze to death in a wee thin coat. I think it might be your journalist. She's booked into the pub for four days, paid a small fortune for the hire of Kenny's old Cortina and already asking the locals about you, and how to find you.'

'What's her name?'

'Mariella Ridge. Have some lunch with us, Duffy, then get Annie home. The weather the now is fine, but there's another storm brewing. Oh, and here, you'll need your car keys. I'd hide them, if I were you. Your daughter is a fine wee singer, but she's not so good at the driving.' He handed over the keys with a faint smile.

Annie ignored me when I returned to the dining room, and was sullen while I ordered sandwiches and a beer for myself. She refused my offer to buy a round of drinks, and looked pale and weary, avoiding eye contact with me. Conversation was stilted, the group laughter gone, and when I suggested it was time to leave, she shrugged and remained seated and silent. Old Hughie's curiosity was palpable, despite his natural Scottish tact. He played with his pipe and when he eventually got it going, I asked him to look out for a passenger who might travel alone, Italian-looking, about sixty. He nodded, 'aye', and then mentioned the Australian woman who had arrived that morning with a suitcase large enough to indicate that she planned to stay more than a few days.

The entire village would now know about Mariella Ridge, and, if she were as nosy as she was in Glasgow, she would dispense my past to anyone who showed the slightest interest. I consoled myself by knowing that while the Criach folk were curious, they don't open up easily to strangers. I would get word around that she was no friend of mine. But that was a problem for later; in the meantime, it was important to get Annie home and safe, and once that was done, to check the locks on doors and shutters.

Annie half-heartedly listened to the conversation between Andy and Old Hughie, mainly about the weather and fishermen, silent and white-faced, sweaty. She picked at her fingernails and stared out the window as the wind gathered speed and the day became greyer. I saw Criach as she saw it from her eyes: cold, miserable, lonely. Friendless. I longed to shelter her, keep her warm, convince her she was safe with me, have her come to love the island and its people, as I did. It was a lot to expect of her, but I had to try. As I picked up my jacket and paid the bill, I asked her if she was ready to leave. Seeing the look of disdain on her face, I swiftly, wisely, changed tack.

'Bonnie and I would love it if you came home with us, Annie, until you sort yourself out. You'll need somewhere to live when you're working at the pub. You'll be free to do whatever you want.' Bonnie was far more persuasive: she put her front paws on Annie's knees and the two pairs of dark brown eyes met in mutual admiration. The tail wagged slowly at first, then more enthusiastically as Annie put her arms around the furry body.

'The hotel's full and charges too much,' she muttered, 'so I'm stuck on this bloody Arctic island, otherwise I wouldn't be going anywhere near your cruddy cottage.' Old Hughie puffed at his pipe and looked into the far distance as he feigned deafness and disinterest. 'So OK, let's go.' She sounded exhausted and resigned as she said her goodbyes, letting Andy carry her guitar and backpack as we walked outside into the misty, chilly air. When I saw what I had missed before, my nerves snapped, and I lost my temper.

'Oh, for God's sake ...' My almost brand-new Range Rover was stoved in on the side. Smashed and dented. I turned on Annie, who looked unrepentant while Bonnie quickly jumped into the front seat and anxiously peered out at us. Rarely had she heard me raise my voice. 'Did you do this? Trying to get on the ferry?' Annie shrugged and rolled her eyes. Andy ran his hand over the deep dents and scratches, and tried to sound casual and unconcerned.

'Och, it can be fixed. Could've been worse ...'

'Not much worse. Have you even got a licence?' I turned on the culprit.

'Shut up.' She hardly raised her voice, but the tone was deadly. She snatched her guitar and backpack from Andy and strode off down the road, slipping in the mud and slush as she tried to keep her balance and hold on to her possessions. It was a sad sight. Bonnie whined and scratched her paws on the car window.

'Go after her, Duffy.' Andy's voice was barely above a whisper, but it was a command nonetheless, so like the one I sometimes heard when we were in the mountains on a rescue mission. You did not ignore it. I ran to catch up with Annie, and when I drew up alongside her, she increased her stride and angrily turned away from me. The temperature was now almost sub-zero and her hands without gloves were blue, although her face was flushed and her eyes too bright. Tears streaked her cheeks. I caught her by the shoulders and turned her around to face me.

'A truce, Annie. Please. I'm sorry. I don't give a ... I don't care about the car. I was stupid to go on about it. Come home with me. Stay as long as you like, until you're rested. We have an awful lot to say to each other.'

'You had eighteen years for that.'

'No, I didn't. Give me a chance. What did Coralyn tell you?'

'That you were a loser, an alcoholic cop.' She was shouting at me now. I doubted that Coralyn would have used that harsh language to her granddaughter, but that was immaterial if Annie believed it was the truth. I wrested her backpack and guitar from her.

'There's another side to the story. Come on home, Annie, and let me explain. Please. It's far too cold to talk outside like this. You're freezing, and you'll make yourself ill if you stay outdoors much longer.'

'I really hate you, you know,' Annie muttered.

'I know, sweetheart. But give me a chance.'

She was either about to faint or fall to the ground, and I caught her in time before she slid into the snow. Andy raced towards us and helped to carry her back to the car. She was limp but recovered slowly and angrily, resisting my efforts to steady her and support her while she walked. From the car's cabin, Bonnie wagged her tail when she saw us coming back, and when Andy opened the door and helped Annie onto the front seat, she licked Annie's cold face. Nothing was said, because this girl was now too spent and exhausted to protest when I leant across to clip on her seat belt. Bonnie placed herself between us, so relieved to have us together again that she barely glanced at Andy as he waved us off.

Within minutes in the warm car, Annie was asleep, her head resting on her chest. Her bare hands looked vulnerable and childlike as they lay crossed on her lap. All the fight had gone out of her, and I prayed this meant some progress. I also prayed there were no visitors at the cottage. But God was either busy or paying me back for past sins.

Parked outside my gate was a battered old Cortina.

\* \* \*

# CHAPTER SIX

When Bonnie saw the car, her bark was not a welcoming one. I couldn't agree more, I said to her under my breath. I remembered once again how much I hated journalists, and no doubt this was the woman from the *Sydney Mirror* following up, as Bob Connelly had warned, the old Kendall case. Annie woke up and glanced at the car and then me.

'For someone described as a hermit crime-writer, you run a pretty busy social life,' she mumbled as she unclipped her seat belt and prepared to make a quick dash for the front door.

The woman stepped out of the battered old car as I pulled up outside the garage. Yes, middle-thirties, tanned, dark-haired, smartly-dressed in a coat that was more suitable for a Sydney winter than a Criach spring. There was something Mediterranean about her. 'It's a journalist, Annie, and I have to get rid of her. We haven't settled one thing yet, and that is, do you want people to know I'm your father?' She shrugged unhelpfully.

'Please yourself. Who'd believe a liar anyway?'

The woman was now tapping on the car window, and Bonnie was going mad with frustration. Annie ran up the path, head down, ignoring the greeting from the visitor. When I walked over to her, the woman offered her frozen hand and I reluctantly held it for the briefest of moments. My attitude clearly indicated she was neither welcome nor wanted. Bonnie's fur rose on the back of her neck. I clicked my fingers and she was instantly beside me, quiet, tense and watching every move the stranger made.

'Mr Duffield, I'm Mariella Ridge. I'm here from ...'

'I know who you are, Ms Ridge, and I have absolutely nothing to say to you, not today, or at any other time. I'd be grateful if you'd leave my property, in fact, I'd prefer it if you left the island. There's nothing to learn here.'

'You have Annabelle Kendall with you.'

'So? None of your business.'

'Interesting that she should travel so far to see you. Did you know she's up for theft and shop-lifting in Sydney, and with the old lady Kendall dead, the family are trying to disinherit her? She's a handful. But I'd rather talk about the murder of the Kendalls, Ellery and Anna Maria, if you could spare some time. I'm doing a feature ...' The woman started to shiver and I was conflicted between the natural instinct to offer shelter and warmth to someone who was about to collapse if she stood in the open with flimsy clothes for much longer, against my hatred of nosy journalists scrabbling through the debris of my life. All so they could sell a few newspapers whose purpose was to lie, shock and thrill their paying readers. I compromised; I took off my jacket and handed it to her.

'Wear this, or you'll catch your death of cold. I'm sorry you've wasted your time and your newspaper's money, Ms Ridge, but I won't discuss a case that happened fifteen years ago, in another country. Case closed. Go home. Leave the jacket at the hotel, I'll pick it up later. And I strongly advise you to get back to the hotel now, otherwise you'll find the roads hard to handle in the dark and snow. You could become disorientated, and that's dangerous.'

The wind almost blew us off our feet as we stood facing each other. It was good to feel angry. The damned stupidity of people who came to Criach without proper gear, ignorant of how quickly the weather could turn dangerous. They climbed the mountains with no thought of safety or precautions and then poor sods like Andy and me had to spend hours, sometimes days, getting them down to safety. And here was a woman in a clapped-out car and in light clothes ... God, I was angry. We were sick of scraping bodies off icy roads or carrying them lifeless or injured down the mountains. Would they never learn that Criach in full storm mood was no place for the stupid or ill-equipped? Or that the Old Lady of Criach was deadly serious when she threatened those who treated her as a sports game? I glanced again at the woman shivering beside me, and doubted if Mariella Ridge had driven through anything trickier than a haze of sun-tan oil on Bondi Beach. I nodded an unfriendly goodbye.

Bonnie and I left her abruptly and sprinted for the front door. When I had shut and bolted it behind us, I peered out the kitchen window and saw Mariella staring at the cottage; my heavy padded jacket was far too big for her, but at least she was more protected from the weather. There was something beyond disappointment on her face, but I didn't reflect too long on how she might be feeling, apart from wishing she and Kenny's battered old banger were gone from my sight. I wouldn't have been surprised had she persisted and knocked on the door; I was ready for that. Instead, she looked at the cottage for a minute or two with a reflective look on her face, light flakes of snow starting to fall around her. Just go home, I said under my breath. Beat it. Knowing her profession as I did, no doubt she was planning a fresh approach. They never give up, these vultures, I thought.

Inside the cottage Annie appeared to have recovered but was still pale and shaky. She found a fresh packet of potato crisps, and was munching them while trying to get a decent picture from the television set. The rooms were cold, and I hurried to build up the fires, light the lamps and brew some coffee. She stamped her feet and flapped her arms around her chest.

'What? No highland hospitality for your friend?'

'She isn't a friend, Annie. She's trouble. And here to rake over the ... past. About Ellery and Anna Maria. So best stay away from her.'

'They would be alive today, if it weren't for your stupidity.'

'Don't you think I remind myself of that every day?'

'I doubt it. You've got a lovely life ... ' She gestured around the sitting room which now glowed in the mellow light from the lamps, with the fire beginning to blaze and crackle in the grate. It looked very cosy. Bonnie lay across the fireside rug and looked from Annie to me. She didn't like the way this conversation was going, and, besides, it was nearly her dinner-time. 'You won't get rid of the press, you know, Mr Important Crime Writer. Nor can you write your own plot this time.' Annie had a nice turn of phrase, I thought, but more to the point, she was right. What happened now was mainly beyond my control. She sat on the sofa, her legs tucked under her, and accepted the cup of scalding hot coffee I handed her, ignoring my question about how she was feeling. Was she feeling better? I sat opposite and risked holding out my hands to her, but she ignored the gesture and looked away. Undeterred, I decided it was time to talk.

'What do you want of me, Annie? Tell me, do you want people to know I am your father? That gives that journalist a great story, but it's up to you. Did your grandmother give you any advice?' I saw the tears well up in Annie's eyes, but she brushed them away angrily and blew into her hot coffee. Her cheeks were flushed pink with fever. 'What did Coralyn *really* tell you?'

There were a few moments of strained silence before she spoke, staring into the fire as she smoothed Bonnie's fur.

'Grandma talked about you just before she died. She liked you. She said you had tried to take me away after my ... after they died, but she wouldn't allow it because she wanted me to grow up as a Kendall, not the daughter of a policeman. You drank a lot, she said, a wild man. When I heard that, I wondered what my mother saw in you. But then again, I can't remember what she was like, apart from being a tricked-up, glamorous socialite from her photographs, champagne glass in one hand, microphone in the other. Grandma spoke about her son a lot, but rarely about her daughter-in-law. None of my mother's possessions was kept, except her jewellery which are probably mine now I've turned eighteen. I don't want them. I have no idea where they are; probably in some bank safe, somewhere. Who cares? I don't want anything from the Kendalls. I loved Grandma, but I hated the rest of the Kendalls. Rich, thick and selfish. I never fitted in, and maybe they kinda knew I wasn't one of them. When Grandma wasn't around they called me a half-wog, half-Itye. They were horrible snobs. But who cares? I'm rid of them.'

'I'm sorry about that, Annie. That was cruel. Your mother was Italian, and proud of it, even if her family ... well, that doesn't matter. What *does* matter is what you want me to do. I can tell the truth about us, or I can say nothing. I'll do whatever you want, but, believe me, I'd like to tell the world you're my daughter.' She gave her usual shrug, but I persisted while there was peace. 'You must understand, Annie, that I loved your mother more than I've loved anything in my life, then or since. You're right to ask what she saw in me, but she *did* care for me. I pleaded with her to marry me, and it broke my heart when she married Ellery, and I was almost insane with grief and guilt when she died. Yes, because of my mistake. And yes, Coralyn refused to let me take you, no matter how much I begged her. My life was a kind of living hell afterwards, until I came to Glasgow and then Criach to escape from it all. But I always hoped I would see you again ... I loved you as a baby ...' She stroked Bonnie's ears and listened quietly, and I took a chance. 'I still do.' The shrug again.

So far so good, I thought, but Annie looked distinctly unconvinced. That was all in the past, and we were now living with the consequences. I wanted her in my life to care for, and at the moment that involved making her realise there were people who wished me, and possibly her, harm. It was my job to safeguard her from potential and unwelcome interlopers, Stopelli and Mariella Ridge. I took a deep breath. 'Annie, we've got some problems to sort out.'

'*You* have. I'm off to bed.'

'Don't you want some dinner?'

'Later, maybe.' I watched as she climbed the stairs. Half-way up she suddenly and unexpectedly turned back and grinned, her eyebrows raised. 'Maybe some chips?' Time stood still for me. It was like seeing Anna Maria when she laughed and teased. The past came back in a rush: a wonderful, silly, loving scene with Anna Maria in our secret tiny harbour house. At that moment, I was no longer in the Scottish Highlands; I was in Sydney in the 70s, trying to cook a meal for Anna Maria I knew she loved: crayfish mornay and chocolate ice-dream. But all she wanted was chips. In bed. She was warm, soft, confident of my love for her, delaying the time when she had to return to her husband later that night. She had whispered again and again how much she loved me. 'But am I a wicked woman to marry a man who does not have my heart, and to come to you like this?' There was no answer. 'All I know is I cannot live without you, dear James.' Annabelle was conceived that night.

Now our daughter was upstairs, running a bath with the remains of Feddy's expensive bath oil. She needed a mother because she was unwell, angry, sad, bewildered, grieving, and vulnerable underneath the harsh and hostile veneer. Who could blame her? She had grown up surrounded by wealth and privilege, but lacked the things most kids took for granted: parents who unreservedly cared for her, who offered security and an uncomplicated family life. All her life she was dogged with the ugliness of death, marked because she was different and tormented by the Kendall family because of her migrant connection. If she had lived, Anna Maria would have fiercely protected her daughter against her hostile relatives, made her proud of her inheritance, taught her all those things that mothers do; maybe even told her one day who her real father was. Coralyn Kendall alone had loved this girl, but on her death-bed had admitted to the lie, and to keeping her apart from her biological father. Now, with Coralyn's death, Annie was left with that despicable Kendall clan that she hated. No wonder there was anger. There was a lot to spread about.

Over the past fifteen years I had assumed that Annabelle had a happy life – I admit I was often jealous, sometimes resentful – but I knew I could never have given her the extravagance of a Kendall upbringing. True to her word, Coralyn had sent me a card and brief note each Christmas to say that Annabelle was healthy, pretty, with a smile that would melt ice-bergs, was a fine equestrienne, played the piano beautifully, was the star of the school's theatrical and choral club, the fastest swimmer. But never enclosed a photograph. In the last three years, the letters were shorter, more cryptic. 'Annabelle is still lovely (despite the paint she wears on her face) and no doubt she could pass her exams (if she applied herself), but she is always in trouble, one way or another ... ' At the time, I thought it was normal teenage rebellious behaviour, with Coralyn an older woman unable to keep up with young kids and their wayward, modern ways. Now I wasn't so sure.

I had almost finished cutting up some steak and chopping potatoes into chips when Annie came downstairs, this time wearing Feddy's pink terry-towelling dressing-gown and matching fluffy slippers. She poured herself a glass of wine, and sat down at the kitchen table. Bonnie looked up expectantly, then at the open packet of potato crisps. Annie laughed as she dropped a crisp into Bonnie's mouth, then ruffled her fur. When she turned to me, however, there was no light-heartedness.

Just a cold look of dislike. I decided now was not the time to ask Annie to stop feeding Bonnie so many potato crisps.

'You could have come back for me,' she said.

'Your grandmother made me vow that I wouldn't. She agreed to tell you the truth only if she felt you needed to know. And I think you *do* need to know the truth, Annie. I'll say it again. It's as simple as this: your mother and I loved each other. But we wanted different things. I pleaded with her to marry me, but she had a fear of poverty and being an outsider in a country that wasn't her own. She wanted so-called respectability and security and thought a rich man like Ellery would offer that. He had everything I didn't: status, houses, maids and flunkeys, he could give her jewellery, clothes ...'

'And like a whore, she took them.'

'Your mother was never a whore!'

"OK then, a gold-digger.'

'Where are you getting these ideas? Your mother was very fond of Ellery, and he was besotted with her. We all were. I could love her, give her what he couldn't – a child – sure, but she chose another man to marry. Don't you think I hated myself for that? Don't judge, Annie. At least not until you know all the facts ... '

'The facts are fucking clear enough to me!

'You just won't listen, will you?'

I was shouting now, frustrated because I could, in all honesty, see the situation from her perspective. She was on her feet and shouting back at me, her temper matching mine, expletives tripping from that expensive private school-educated mouth. So much for the intimate father and daughter chat. This wild-eyed girl was so angry she had trouble breathing.

'She wanted a baby, she desperately wanted you. We both did ... Christ, Annie what's wrong with you?' Her chest was heaving now, every breath laboured and noisy. I'd seen asthmatics before, and knew instantly she was in trouble. 'Where .... ?' She pointed upstairs. I took the stairs three at a time, and rummaged through her backpack. I glanced quickly at her meagre possessions while searching for the inhaler, noticing but tossing aside a dog-eared paperback edition of one of my books, one corner of a page turned back. Her leather wallet was open but there was no money inside apart from a few coins and a small photograph of her mother, but not Ellery, tucked into a slot. Bonnie tried to be helpful, her wet nose snuffling amongst Annie's clothes and oddments. Thankfully, there were no syringes or white powder in small plastic bags.

Thank God the inhaler worked like magic, and Annie gradually became calm again, her eyes no longer wide and frightened. In her panic she clutched my hand while Bonnie sat beside her, licking her face and looking up at me, begging me to make things right.

'Why don't you go to bed, Annie?'

'And why don't you go and ...'

We were back where we started. Having shown her vulnerability, Annie now flew at me with an almost manic intensity. My temper rose. 'Look, Annie, I didn't force you to come here looking for me. You made that decision. All I wanted in life was your mother and you. To be a family. So don't load any more guilt on me, sweetheart, because I gave myself the lot ... '

Bonnie began to bark and leapt at the front door. I shouted at her to stop, my nerves at breaking point. 'Annie, listen to me. I was only a cop, okay, maybe a drunkard, angry, bitter, pissed off at the world and denied the only things I wanted. Then Coralyn refused to let me have you, and maybe I don't blame her. Yeah, I'm not proud of all that. I'm not proud of myself. But I wanted you then, and I want you now, Annie. I want to love you, take care of you, the way I did for Anna Maria before Ellery came along with his millions, and thugs like Stopelli came along and destroyed their lives. Just tell me what else I could have done?'

'Just *shut up*. Bloody justifications. Admit it, you cling to this cosy new life because, damn it, you didn't – couldn't – cope in the real world!'

Bonnie was barking furiously at the door and I angrily spun around to stop her. Too late, I realised someone was knocking loudly, and who probably had heard the whole furious exchange between Annie and me. When I flung open the door, I imagined the look on Mariella's face showed that she had stumbled across one of the greatest stories of her career. There was something else though, and I searched for the right word. Concern? Shock? Surely not.

'The car broke down,' Mariella said quietly. 'I had to leave it up the road, and walk back here. Can I call a taxi?'

'We don't have taxis in Criach.'

'Will you drive me to the village?'

'No, I can't leave Annie. She's unwell. Besides, there's a storm brewing and the roads are pretty treacherous.' There was nothing else to do but to invite this foolish woman inside, despite my suspicion that the broken-down car explanation was a ruse to come back and torment me. 'OK, come in. We were just about to have some supper. Help yourself to a drink.' Impatiently, without any display of hospitality or welcome, I gestured towards the fire and drinks table, and went back to the kitchen.

A shivering, frozen, Mariella gratefully warmed herself by the fire. Bonnie watched her suspiciously and then joined Annie who had fled to the kitchen, and who was now sitting at the table, scoring the old wooden top with a sharp knife. I took it away from her and threw it in the sink. She looked moody but had calmed down. In a whisper, I asked her how much she reckoned the woman had heard of our fight.

'I'd say the lot. You know you're going to have to offer her a bed for the night, right? Highland hospitality and all that ...' She glanced over at the snow that was building up outside on the window sills. 'So I'll just say goodnight.' She got up to leave, then lingered at the kitchen door. I was chopping potatoes and glancing now and then with concern at the gathering storm outside, but turned to face her and wish her goodnight. She was staring at me.

'You tell a fine story,' she said.

'It's the truth ...'

Mentally, I searched for a clue from the tone of her voice. Was there scorn, or sarcasm? Some semblance of belief? I put down the knife and stared hard at the snow outside. Was it possible to believe that Annie was entertaining doubts, raising questions in her mind about the harsh story she had built up in her mind about Anna Maria and me? For the first time I felt a whisper of relief creep through my soul.

'But I don't believe a word of it.'

Her scorn was lacerating as she fled upstairs. I heard the bedroom door snap shut. Bonnie pawed me to remind me about her own dinner. You're making headway, she seemed to say. But no more risks; just leave her alone.

Outside the storm raged, and there was no question of attempting to drive Mariella to the village, or leaving an unfed and unwell Annie alone. I put some chips and steak on a plate, with a puddle of tomato sauce, and took the tray upstairs to her. I knew she had a secret stash of wine in her bedroom, and added a tumbler. There was no reply when I knocked on the door, so I left the meal outside. As I reached the last downstairs step, I heard the door open, the plate scooped up, and the door quickly shut again. I shook my head; it was hard not to smile.

Downstairs, Mariella and I ate our meal in strained silence, but after a few glasses of wine, she began to talk about Sydney, how crowded it had become, how the real estate prices along the harbour had escalated and homes were now accessible only to millionaires or the Asian market, the personnel changes in the State police force ('and about time, too'), her job as a senior *Sydney Mirror* crime reporter, how my books were becoming popular since they had been converted into a television series, and how the Kendall case ... and that was where I stopped her. I gathered up the dishes and showed her the sofa, the bathroom, and a pile of blankets.

'Surely we could drive to the village?'

'No. I can't leave Annie, and you don't understand Criach storms. Goodnight.'

'Goodnight, Duffy. You know, I mean you no harm?'

'I'm sure you don't. But then again, perhaps you have no idea what harm you could cause at the expense of a ... what, is it still called a "scoop"? Take it from me, Mariella, there's nothing much happening on Criach, unless you want to hang about and see the next poor sod being carried off a merciless mountain.'

'I only want to help, Duffy. Get your side of the story on record.'

'Sure. It's what journalists do best. I discovered that many years ago.' My sarcasm and disgust were obvious and unpleasant, and I didn't like myself. I felt that my safe and welcoming cottage – my home and haven – had been infested because of the intrusion and hostility that people like Mariella and Stopelli brought with them. Not to mention the unwelcome memories of failure that were now shoved in my face. How I begrudged being drawn back to that world.

In the silence of the cottage when the lights were out and Bonnie and I took to our beds, I thought about the day, and in particular this woman, this journalist. Despite my antagonism towards her vocation, I couldn't help but think how different she was from the many hard-bitten journalists I had known in Sydney. She was persistent, but took the hint. Tonight, she accepted that I would not speak about the Kendalls, and didn't pry further or harass me for any information about my young house guest. Perhaps she was not quite the threat I imagined her to be. That was when I pulled myself up short, wide awake. For God's sake, she is a top journalist sent here by her newspaper at great cost, and who's just stumbled across a story that will light up Sydney. Her life's work is to bleed you dry of information for her tabloid shit-sheet. That's the only reason she's here. No threat? Pull yourself together, man.

But there was something about this woman that was strangely familiar. I wracked my brains to think back to those days in Sydney, in parliament house. I would ring Bob tomorrow and ask him what he knew about this woman's background. There was some connection there, somehow, somewhere, with the Kendalls. I had no idea why I thought this, but instinct told me there was more to Maria Ridge than she was willing to divulge. My suspicion of her grew.

What a day. Surely fate had played enough tricks, good and bad. I should have known better. After a fitful night of rest, the doorbell rang early next morning, and I knew from the droop in Bonnie's tail it wasn't a visitor she welcomed. Or wanted. I opened the door in my dressing gown to find Feddy on the doorstep looking pale, as though she were hungover, wary, and unsure of her welcome. Her arms were full of bags of delicatessen food and groceries, but not from Harrods. I recognised the Glasgow labels.

'Hello, Mr Thistle Man. Do you mind if I come in?'

Bonnie slunk away and left me to it.

* * *

# CHAPTER SEVEN

eddy's composure wavered when she glanced behind me to see Mariella eating breakfast at the kitchen table. Even to me, it looked intimate. Worse, Mariella was drinking coffee from a Wedgewood mug that Feddy had given me on a previous visit.

'I see you have a guest, Duffy,' she said with a chilly smile that didn't reach her eyes. 'Where's your other little friend?' I ushered her inside and helped her with her parcels, introduced her to Mariella and explained about the car breaking down, the storm, the enforced stay-over and how Mariella would soon be going back to Sydney and her newspaper job. 'Oh, yes,' Feddy said, and I had to admire her coolness, 'Ms Ridge and I have spoken on the phone. How do you do?' With the brisk gestures that were so familiar to me, Feddy pulled off her leather gloves and offered her hand. Mariella looked curiously at this fashionably-dressed woman who was incongruously out of place in Criach, and, after a moment's hesitation, took the offered hand. 'I see the Criach weather isn't bothering you,' Feddy's eyebrows were raised as she spoke. The kitchen radiator was burning on high heat, the fire in the front room was blazing, and in the warmth Mariella had taken off her jacket to expose a tight jumper. After a quick glance which took in the high-street label, the cost, and the poor-taste fit, Feddy turned to me. 'So where's the other visitor?'

A good question. I was worried about Annie. When I took her a coffee earlier in the morning, she had been huddled under a mountain of blankets with no intention of emerging. Her voice was croaky, and she looked hot and feverish. Then again, I was relieved that she wasn't present to witness this confrontation, and spared her acidic interpretation. I had to admit, it wasn't a good look. Feddy's eyes were glacial as she glanced at the pile of greasy dishes in the sink, last night's chip pan still on the stove, the clutter of wine and whisky glasses on the bench-top.

'Annie's upstairs in bed.'

'Another hangover?'

'No. Some coffee, Fedora?'

She hated being called Fedora. And standing there in my dressing gown, with two women facing each other with hostile curiosity, I thought how the charade of formal politeness always came to the rescue. How the courteous, glib, practised words and lies roll off the tongue when needed. You'll be okay, mate, I said as a rookie cop to reassure a man trapped inside his smashed car, knowing he would be dead within the hour; you'll be fine, mum, I promised my dying mother; if marrying this old man makes you happy, then go ahead, that's how much I love you, I told Anna Maria on her wedding day; your decisions, sir, not mine, I told the Police Commissioner when he blocked my ideas for improving police forensic efficiency; I'm fine, I told Grannie when I first arrived in Glasgow. Of course I'm lonely when you're not here, I tell Feddy without blinking an eyelid. All a travesty. The time for honesty had arrived, but not with a journalist within a bull's roar. I had to clear the air with Feddy.

'Nothing happened between me and that woman.'

'I know that, Duffy.'

'What are you doing here ... no, don't say a word. Let me get dressed, Mariella sorted out and back to the village, and I'll be back. We can talk then.'

'Yes, we need to talk.'

I drove Mariella to her car, got it started, said goodbye and told her to go home to Sydney and forget the Kendall story, because there was nothing new to tell. We shook hands and she said she would be nearby if I wanted to talk. Hardly, I snapped. There was nothing I wanted to say to this woman, and she would learn that my patience and hospitality had a very precise end-point.

Back at the cottage, Feddy was sitting in front of the fire, nursing a cup of very strong coffee. She had tidied the kitchen and put away her gifts and provisions. Order had been restored. I flung off my jacket and sat next to her, closer than I actually intended. I was more puzzled than annoyed by her return; in truth, I was pleased to see her because I needed her. I was also curious about her strange overnight stay in Glasgow.

'Well, I got as far as Glasgow, and I couldn't drive any more. My eyes were sore and I was exhausted. I found a hotel to stay the night, some dreadful place, but the people were nice even if I didn't understand a word they said ...' When she told me which pub, I suppressed a wry smile. I knew it well; rough, but safe enough for women. 'I slept the night there and next morning when I went down for a late breakfast, I got caught up in some kind of party ...' I could imagine it; swept up and entertained by some of the finest unemployed drinkers and singers in the city. 'I woke up this morning with a dreadful headache, all packed and ready to drive home. But something stopped me; I don't know, Duffy, I sat in my car and thought about a lot of things. You and me. About the unkind things I had said. How pushy I had been. I had no right.' She sighed deeply. 'I'm not going to Paris. The truth is, I'm still prepared to accept any part of your life you're willing to share.'

'That isn't worthy of you, Feddy.'

'I know, but there you are. Besides, you're worried about something, and you know me – plucky old Fedora who likes to rescue ...' She laughed, but it was a sad appeal and my heart went out to her. 'Seriously, Duffy, I know you won't open up easily, but will you give me a chance?'

'There's a lot happening, Feddy. And to tell the truth, I'm glad you're here, because I *do* need your help.' She brightened instantly, her eyebrows raised, eyes wide. True, this was what Feddy liked best: being useful, practical, solving problems, putting 'things to rights'. 'This is the situation. I have a girl upstairs who is exhausted, without money or warm clothes, ill, and won't accept help from me. She'll flee as soon as she can, and I worry about her safety. It won't be easy, but will you help me look after her? I'm out of my depth.'

'Who is she, Duffy?'

'She is my daughter.'

'Ah, I see. And is there a mother, a wife?'

'No, her mother is dead. I have no wife. It's a very complicated story ...'

At that moment Annie appeared, wrapped in a blanket. She was pale, cold and miserable, and looked at both of us with unfeigned animosity. Feddy was on her feet in an instant, and with the efficiency I always admired, had told Annie she must return to bed. Now. This minute. But first, she said in her no-nonsense manner, let me see what state the bedroom is in. Maybe clean sheets and a radiator for that cold room, and a lemon drink to be going on with?

I was astonished at the meekness with which Annie accepted the bossy directions. Fifteen minutes later Feddy came downstairs and reported she had warmed and tidied the room, made the bed fresh and comfortable, and installed Annie in it with a promise to return with a breakfast of her choice.

'You're right, Duffy. She can't go anywhere in this weather, she's not at all well. Here, help me with the bacon and sausages. And we'll get some fresh coffee going.' We worked together amiably until breakfast was cooked, placed on a tray, and Feddy raised her eyebrows to ask if I wanted to deliver it upstairs to my daughter. No, I wasn't ready for another rebuff. Feddy returned within a few minutes to report that the breakfast had been eaten almost before she left the room. I thanked her, and she hugged me. 'It's nice to be needed, sweetie. She's a lovely girl and when you're ready, tell me more.'

For the next two days, the three of us lived together quietly, with Annie avoiding us wherever possible. She remained in bed for most of the time, reading, eating and watching the television we moved into her room. Feddy cooked and I chopped wood to keep the hot water supply and the oven going. She left one afternoon to catch the ferry without her suitcase so I knew she intended coming back, but I didn't ask any questions. She returned in the afternoon with bags of clothes for Annie: warm jumpers, a sheepskin jacket, heavy jeans, scarves, gloves and under-wear. 'She's got a gorgeous figure, Duffy, but my goodness, she's had a rough time of it. Her clothes are rags. And she tells me she's managed by busking, eating pies and baked beans in hostels. Then tramping through rain and storms to get here. She really wanted to see you.'

Up until then, Feddy had wisely and thankfully waited for me to explain the curious situation she found me in, but the time had come to be completely honest. After dinner, with the room warm and softly shaded by lamps, Annie fed with hot, nourishing food and in bed watching television upstairs with Bonnie, I sat Feddy down in front of the fire with a large glass of red wine. I sipped my whisky in between deep breaths to prepare myself for a hard conversation.

'Feddy, Annabelle Kendall is one of the richest girls in Sydney. I have no idea why she's travelling without money or credit cards. What I know is that, just before her grandmother died, she was told I was her biological father. She feels she's been lied to, and she's angry, hostile, hates me, and won't listen my side of the story ...'

'Which is?'

'It's complicated. I loved her mother. She loved me, but I wasn't enough for her. She was a migrant girl, beautiful, vivacious, but insecure. She chose to marry into an established, wealthy Australian family to get what she thought would be acceptance, security. All those things I couldn't offer her. It broke my heart, but she was determined. It wasn't long into her marriage when we began to see each other again; in truth, we couldn't live without each other. And while she had every luxury she ever wanted, her husband couldn't give her a child. It wasn't planned, but at least I gave her the child she wanted. Annabelle was born, but she was a Kendall ... ' Feddy's face became visibly pale, her expression one of ineffable sadness. She said nothing, and I forced myself to continue. 'For political reasons, Annabelle's parents were murdered, and I was the policeman in charge of their security ...' Feddy's blue eyes filmed with tears, but still she remained silent. 'I tried to claim custody of Annie, but it was hopeless. I was dealing with a rich, influential family. And what was I? A man without money or means, and I drank too much. A failure. When the grandmother refused to let me have Annie, I left the country. There was nothing else I could do.'

Feddy held my hand. Dear God, I wanted to cry. Bonnie had tripped downstairs and I now felt her paws scraping against my legs; her furry black face a picture of quizzical concern. I heard a noise on the stairs, and looked up to see Annie staring down at us.

'Liar!'

She turned quickly and raced back upstairs, but Feddy was quick to follow her. I heard the bedroom door slam, and then a lot of shouting, the substance of which I couldn't hear, but it seemed fairly evenly divided between Feddy and Annabelle. Bonnie was agitated and fretting, and I felt the overwhelming urge to flee the cottage, walk, run, do something physical to stop the hard pain in my chest. Come on, girl, I said, let's check the ferry. We still have to deal with a journalist and a murderer, I told her. And that has to be easier than coping with combat between a daughter and a girlfriend. Bonnie was as relieved as I was when I gathered up my keys and headed for the car, as though she too had decided, yes, let's get away. We are of no help here.

It was good to get out in the cold air. Old Hughie told me that there had been no single, Italian-looking men on the ferry that day, but two young foreign boys had been on the late-afternoon service. They spoke a strange language like German, but their English was good, and they looked like keen backpackers. 'But I did hear a word something like "Annie" a couple of times amongst their blether.'

That was interesting. I drove on to the pub and found Andy preparing to leave the island. We had a quick coffee while I hurriedly brought him up to date with what had happened since we'd last met, in particular the arrival back of Feddy.

'I've told her about Annie. But I'm not sure if that's what Annie wants. To tell you the truth, Andy, I'm not sure what she wants. Certainly not me.'

Andy nodded, but said it was always a good thing for the truth to come out to face daylight. He promised to return within a few days, this time without his tourists, on account of, as he said, you might need a wee bit company and the fish are biting. Before he left, I asked him what he knew about the two foreign boys from the ferry.

'Aye, Israeli kids. Fit, strong, nice-looking. Keen to do a bit of climbing, and I promised to take them up The Old Lady if they waited a few days until I returned. In the meantime, I've suggested a few wee mountain tracks they could tackle, but if you've the notion you might like to give them a hand. There's something you should know, Duffy, and that is that they're looking for Annie. Nothing sinister, don't worry, don't react like that. I gather they met her in London when she was there, and one of them, the bigger lad, seems a bit sweet on her ... '

I was instantly alert. Anyone connected to Annie, looking for her, at this particular time, sent off alarm bells.

'How can we trust them, Andy? Israelis, for God's sake ... how ruthless are they?'

'Instinct, Duffy. Instinct. Trust me. These lads aren't your enemy.' He told me their names which he had learnt from the pub register. David Levine and Ari Rosenthal. In his inimitable way, Andy had discovered they were both aged twenty-two and final year students from a medical school in Tel Aviv. Nice lads, he assured me. 'And I didn't mention you, Duffy. I'll let you sort that out.'

I trusted Andy with my life and followed his instructions on the mountains without question or hesitation, but I was still a copper and refused to rule out suspects. Sure, we get some British or European gap-year students on Criach, young kids who want to climb or hike, but Israeli lads? We rarely saw them. Despite Andy's confidence, I was wary.

I decided it would be wise to say nothing to Annie until I knew more about these boys. As soon as I was home I intended to make some phone calls. That is, if the phone lines cooperated. I wanted to talk to Bob Connolly about Mariella Ridge, and then to my useful police mate on the mainland, Sergeant Duncan 'Corky' McCorquodale, to ask him to check any police records on two foreign students.

I was forced to drive home slowly and cautiously because of the increasing force of the wind and snow, and I swore under my breath when half-way home I came across Kenny's old Cortina parked at the side of the road. Mariella Ridge was sitting in the driver's seat, looking cold, miserable and glum. She had an extra jumper on, but still wasn't dressed for the weather. I shouted over to her to get into my car and warm up, which she did with a grateful mutter of thanks. When she had scrambled inside and slammed the door behind her, I snapped at her, demanding to know what the hell she was doing in this weather, in a parked car without heating and one, at that, that was fit only for the wrecker's yard. Bonnie listened, fully approving of my anger.

'Bloody thing broke down again.'

'You should have known that old death-trap wouldn't get you far. I'll drive you back to the pub, but that's it. I'm not your taxi service.' Indeed not, Bonnie seemed to agree, perhaps put out at the delay in getting home to Annie, if not Feddy, and her dinner. I turned up the heating and faced Mariella. 'I wish you'd get this straight. There's no point in hanging around. I have no interest in talking to you about anything that happened fifteen years ago. For me, it's over. I don't want to talk about, think about, or have you write it up as a salacious feature article. Is that clear?'

'Very. But you don't have much say in this. Whether you like it or not, the world is about to arrive on your doorstep. Your old adversary, Stopelli, is serious about coming after you. To harm you.'

'Yeah, yeah. How do you know that?'

'I'm an investigative crime journalist, Duffy, and I'm good at my job. The Kendall case has a special interest to me. I begged my editor to let me cover the story when I heard Stopelli was out. I interviewed him a few times in gaol, and he became quite talkative. Boastful. I discovered he managed to make as much money inside gaol as out of it. He hasn't mellowed one bit, and has a special place in his heart for revenge, and is determined to see you pay for what you did to him.' I closed my eyes. I didn't want that grim, sordid world to come any closer. 'He said when he was free, he would find you.'

'I know all that, Mariella. Most crims I've known swear innocence, even when they're caught with a smoking gun in their hand, or their fist is wrapped around a knife in the back of some poor sod, declaring on their grandmother's grave that they'll pay back those who spoiled their innocent lives. Heard it a million times. So what?'

'Stopelli's different. Dangerous. He's obsessed, and he'll track you down. You're not hard to find. Dear God, I did, easily enough, despite the mangled instructions your girlfriend gave me.'

'And that's it? You're here to cover the confrontation between him and me? Good copy for your newspaper, eh?'

I started up the car and headed for the village. I wanted this woman, and all the sordidness she brought with her, out of my car and far from my life. But as we drove through the snow, she insisted on talking. The windscreen wipers worked overtime to clear the sludgy snow, but it was impossible to drown out her voice.

'You're wrong to ignore this, Duffy. It's serious. The whole Kendall thing is about to blow wide open again, because of Stopelli. I knew the Kendalls. And what happened to them was ... dreadful. I wasn't in their social world, of course, but I was happy to provide publicity for their charities. Their deaths were ...' She hesitated, seemingly reluctant to finish the sentence. When she spoke again, she took an entirely different tack, one for me that was unwelcome and painful. 'You didn't notice a young reporter like me, but I saw you around parliament house a few times when you worked with Ellery Kendall. All the girls had a crush on you, but you never noticed. You were very guarded about your private life, but naturally there were rumours ...'

'Just shut up, Mariella.' Bonnie put her paws on my shoulders and nuzzled my cheek. Home, she seemed to say again. No more of this. We pulled up outside the pub and I leant over to open the door for Mariella. 'Take my advice as an old copper who's not quite lost the heart for battle: leave it alone. Whatever happens with Stopelli, I can look after myself.'

'And ... Annie? What about her?'

'She's in my care. Another piece of advice, Mariella: catch the next ferry out of here.'

'And my advice to you is this, James Duffield: Stopelli is evil, and for fun he'll torment you by destroying anything, or anyone, you love and value. He wants to see you suffer. And he's prepared to travel anywhere, do anything, to do it. He's an old man now, and sick. He hasn't much longer to live, so he doesn't have a thing to lose.'

'OK, sure. That's great copy. Your editor will love it. But I don't care what you write for your paper about that old shit. It'll obviously be dramatic, an exclusive scoop from Sydney's top crime reporter, Mariella Ridge, but it'll last two days, because it's old history. Who cares any more? As the cliché goes, nothing to see here, the caravan's moved on ... '

'I disagree,' she glanced at Bonnie. 'Stopelli hasn't finished with you. Or anyone – anything – you care about.'

'I warn you, if you report any part of that private conversation between me and Annabelle Kendall the other night, I swear to God I'll not only discredit you, but your press credentials won't be worth a bumper ever again. And that's before I sue the arse off you.' Angrily, she stepped out of the car and moved towards the pub entrance, then turned around to face me.

'Just be careful, Duffy. Especially with Annie.'

'Why should you care? Another twist for your story?

'No, but ... ' The wind whipped away her words. 'Oh, forget it.'

I watched her disappear into the warmth and conviviality of the pub, and wondered again what this woman was really after. Again the old copper antennae warned me she wasn't being honest with me. The sooner she was off the island the better, with or without a story about a Kendall paternity scandal that, at this stage, I refused to verify and so far, she couldn't prove. My gut tightened. Today there were DNA tests, and she could have collected samples easily enough from her stay in the cottage. If Stopelli turned up on the island, she had an extra twist to her story. If he tried to harm me, as she claimed he would, she'd have a damn good story. And if he hurt Annie – a Kendall – she'd have the makings of a sensational story. Because it would, in all likelihood, by followed by manslaughter. I'd kill the bastard.

I knew she was right about one thing: Stopelli was cruel enough to destroy anything or anybody I cared about. I put my hand on Bonnie's head as she lay sleeping across my lap. She was as deep in thought as I was.

\* \* \*

# CHAPTER EIGHT

When I got home I was relieved to find my cottage warm and smelling of good food and women's perfume. Music played in the background, and everything looked comfortably in its place. Feddy wore a tartan apron as she checked her chicken and tasted the sauce, offering a sample to Annie who perched on the kitchen stool in her new clothes, her cheeks pink and shiny. The pair of them were drinking gins and tonic and chatting in that way that people do when they are comfortable with each other. Bonnie excitedly greeted Annie with a wagging tail and licks to the hands and face, and although I expected my daughter to leave the room as soon as I appeared, she stayed to hug Bonnie. 'Hiya, Bon Bon', she crooned, and ruffled her fur, 'I missed you, babe.' It was, I had to admit, a rather reassuring scene. But how long would the peace last?

The whole evening, as it turned out. Annie was quiet, but civil, and I noticed how she occasionally glanced at me under lowered eyes. The meal was, as always, delicious, and Feddy kept up breezy chatter about her two nights in Glasgow, and how she couldn't work out why everyone in the bar called her 'hen' until told it was a term of endearment. Or why next day her wallet was empty and crammed with credit card slips until she remembered buying drinks and food for everyone. She didn't mind one bit, she said, because they were fun. And kind. And it was good to laugh, even if she was very, very drunk and couldn't remember anything the next morning.

'I needed it,' she sighed.

Annie looked rested and warm in her blue jeans and a soft pale pastel wool jumper that highlighted her olive-skin and dark hair. Feddy had chosen well; there was no doubt her stylish flair matched her generous, practical heart. It was hard not to sneak a look at Annie in sideways glances, to see how beautiful she was, and how, apart from her height, so like her mother she was. She loved Feddy's food and helped herself to second helpings, drank a lot of wine, and offered an occasional wry comment about her stay in London and Glasgow, but little else. She ventured no questions of me, or Feddy.

Later that night in bed I asked Feddy how she had worked the miracle with Annie, and how she had pacified her to at least the level of civility. Despite my wishing her far from Criach only a day ago, it was good to have her close. But I didn't want her hurt again, even if it was hard to resist her. She looked gorgeous in her silk nightgown, and smelt of expensive perfume. As she wriggled closer to me, she chuckled softly. Her hair was soft under my chin.

'For a start I put her right about you being a liar. I told her I've never known anyone so brutally honest as you. As for me, well, you had your secrets, Mr Thistle Man, and I had mine. You never asked, or showed any interest, so I never mentioned them. But the truth is, when I was Annie's age I was as angry and rebellious as she is now; no, probably worse. We have a lot in common. We're both rich kids who've never had a mother to love, or to love us. My mother died when I was five and I was left with an old-fashioned establishment father who was committed to the Conservative Party. "Brought up" probably isn't right; he hired nannies and instructed them to produce a well-mannered "lady". And then he married an appalling woman, some sort of poverty-stricken aristocrat who drank a lot of sherry and couldn't stand the sight of me. All I remember is being told to be quiet, not make a fuss, be polite, and to remember my manners. Not embarrass the family. Find some gormless rich sod to marry. But when I was sixteen or seventeen, I wanted fun, to get out into the streets and swing with the wild ones. London was crazy then. My father locked me up after he caught me at discotheques and nightclubs, then banished me to a Swiss finishing school. I was worse when I came home, and he threatened to disinherit me. That made me more defiant. Rows. Fights. Locked rooms. Getting belted. So I packed up and left home, penniless, painted-up, wearing the shortest skirts, and shacked up with the first decent-looking boy I could find. Got pregnant, of course ... '

'You have a child?'

'No, I lost it. Just as well, because I couldn't look after myself, let alone a baby. The father, naturally, fled when he found out. But I was sad and guilty and drank a lot and took drugs to obliterate the whole horror show. I followed a new hippy boyfriend to Paris where we lived like poor, homeless bohemians. Such idiots. I took no responsibility for my life, for anything, really. Hated myself, and tried everything to excess to make myself feel better. Then I met Jean Paul, a dress designer ... well, he convinced me I had a bit of talent, scrubbed me up, let me work in his studio and taught me all about fashion and marketing. For the first time, I loved doing something.'

'What happened then?' Why did I know nothing about this? The answer was, of course, that I hadn't bothered to find out. I was too busy safeguarding my own secrets by shoving up the barricades lest anyone get too close, especially persistent ones like Feddy. But I had to admit it was an extraordinary feat of selfishness to *never* ask Feddy about her past, or why she bothered with a cranky old hermit like me who offered her nothing.

Feddy nestled closer against me, her voice steady but wistful, not so much for good times past, but for mistakes she had made that could never be corrected. I knew the feeling. 'Go on, Feddy. I'm listening now.'

'Jean Paul's clothes became quite famous for their wackiness, and he was spectacularly good at promoting himself, but once he hit the big time, he dumped me for another so-called "muse". By then, though, I'd become a bit smarter and more confident, so I took what I'd learnt from him and knocked on every Parisian door looking for any job in fashion, sales, marketing, anything where flair and flattery were needed. I worked in restaurants, boutiques, hotels. I was good at my work, made a bit of money, rented a nice flat in the Latin Quarter, swore off drugs and too much alcohol, unsuitable men, and scrapes with the law. I became known in the restaurant and marketing world because I got results and made money for the owners. I didn't want to return to London ever, but was forced to when my father was dying, and we staged a kind of reconciliation. My stepmother had drunk herself to death years ago, so, as an only child, I inherited his entire estate. God, can you believe it, but I was so angry! Then I decided to use the money to set up my business in London, and you know the rest.'

'I wish I'd known.'

'You were never interested, sweetie, but I longed for the day when you would ask, show some interest. You are always so self-contained. I knew if I strayed too far into your life, made too many demands, you'd shut me out. And the time I did overstep the mark, you did exactly that. And I'm sorry.'

'Did you talk to Annie about this ... your past?'

'Of course. I understand her. I told her how I was once like her, angry, aimless, hostile, hating authority figures. We miss our mothers, Duffy. From what I gather, the grandmother was a good soul, but it isn't the same as knowing your mother's always there, close, looking after you. I can barely remember my mother, but I loved her. Everyone did. She was fun. All her friends told me that, and when she knew she was dying, how she was heartbroken knowing she would never help me grow up. Can you imagine, Duffy, missing someone you've never really known? Like Annie is right now. So sad.'

'Feddy, I am sorry ...'

'Let's talk about ourselves another time. What's important now is that Annie recovers from everything she's been through. Maybe I helped; I hope so. We come from the same place, the same battlefield. Instead of listening to preaches about manners and gratitude, and curbing defiance and anger, I said, go for it, girl. Rebel, don't follow rules. Run your own race. Value your talent. Be original.'

'And she listened?'

'Eventually. Once she knew I was on her side, and she was free to do whatever she wanted, without traps or expectations, it was pointless to fight with me. She feels she's on her own, lied to by people she trusted, and is trying hard to work things out as honestly as she can. She's been through a lot, coming to terms with a new life now her old one has shifted under her feet. She's curious about you, Duffy, but she doesn't know you, or whether she can trust you. Maybe you'll disappear, as you did before. She's come a long way to meet the man she's been told is her father, and you've much to learn about each other. Most of all, she needs a refuge until she works it all out. There's a lot of you in her, Duffy, my dear; she's tender but tough, and she won't be pushed. She's quite a gal.'

I felt a rush of affection – even love – towards Feddy and held her tight. 'You're a wonderful woman, Feddy. And I ...' She put a finger to my mouth.

'No. Not yet ...'

\* \* \*

Feddy left the next morning. We were silent as she manoeuvred her car into the tight space on board the ferry. She had a long journey ahead of her, and as we stood on the jetty, I made her promise to go straight home to London with no stops in any Glasgow pub. Laughing, she agreed. I looked at her lovely face and bright blue eyes and thought about every act of kindness and patience she had shown towards me, despite my lack of appreciation. Yes, she had pestered me about the future and I had been cautious, like an animal avoiding capture, but I always convinced myself with the fiction of always being honest. In truth, I had shut off my past, and shown no interest in hers. Why she loved me, or even tolerated me, I had no idea. I certainly didn't deserve it.

'Thank you, Feddy. For everything.'

'I'd love to stay with you, Duffy,' she said, 'but this is something you and Annie must work out for yourselves. And you will. I cannot help you anymore. Until you come to terms with your daughter, and sort out this man you tell me who's threatened to harm you, and deal with the journalist woman, you won't rest. I know you. I am a complication you don't need at the moment. I know what you wanted to say last night, but the time's not right. I hope that time *will* come. When you're ready, you know where to find me. And I meant what I said: I'll take any part of your life you're prepared to offer. That's how much I love you, Thistle Man.'

There was nothing left to say so I held her tightly and buried my head in her sweet-smelling hair until the ferry's whistle blew. Nearby, Old Hughie hadn't missed a thing.

\* \* \*

I stood for some minutes on the jetty and watched her go. Andy had returned to the mainland with his tourists, so there was no point in jogging into the village. Besides, I had that phone call to make to Corky in Glasgow about the Israeli boys before I tracked them down, and then a quick drive around the island to talk to the locals to ask if they had noticed any unusual activity at sea, or had seen anyone who might have bypassed the ferry and arrived by private boat. With the inducement of cash, it was possible that a small boat and an expert sailor could slip inside a sheltered cove, hide, and just as quickly be gone.

Mariella had said the ageing Stopelli was ill – but not so sick that he couldn't get himself from Australia to Europe. The question was, if he was determined to come to Criach to confront me, how would he do it? By regular means, making no bones about it? It was unlikely he could smuggle himself unseen on the island, and even more improbable that he would remain hidden. Would he come at all? How reliable was Mariella? I suspected she would be pretty reliable. But then again, why would an old, sick man make a long, tedious journey to do the dirty work himself? He had the money and could easily hire some desperate druggie who didn't fuss too much about the job so long as the next hit was paid for. He had done it before.

Something told me that there was something *personal* about Stopelli's oath of revenge. He hated me so intensely that I sensed he would want to face me, enjoy inflicting whatever cruelty he had in mind. I shook my head to clear it of those kind of thoughts. Was I being paranoid? Or just realistic? What was it I had always drummed into Bob Connelly as a junior sergeant: consider every contingency.

I turned and headed for home, glad of the cold, clear air which always made me feel better. Bonnie was delighted to run alongside me. We found Annie in the kitchen eating toast and marmalade, playing her music cassettes at top volume. She had lit the fire, however clumsily, but the rooms were warming up. She made no attempt to leave when I poured myself a strong coffee and joined her, leaving it up to her whether she chose to talk or not. She didn't.

For the rest of the morning and afternoon, while Annie lay

spreadeagled on the sofa, listening to her music on earphones, I made phone calls then worked around the cottage, examining the door locks and shutters, chopping piles of wood to keep us warm and with hot water, and then cleared the build-up of snow around the paths and windows. I tested the snow chains for the car, then, cold and shivering, I stamped my boots at the back door and came inside to check my climbing gear. I heard the phone ring, and hurried to answer it. It was Corky.

'Nothing on those Israeli kids, Duffy. Final year students, about to graduate. Clean. No suspicious record of any kind.' I thanked him, but still felt uneasy. Given the timing, and my belief that there's rarely a thing called coincidence, I felt they had some role to play in the events of the past few days. But I remained silent. Corky went on. 'And thanks for the heads up about Stopelli. We're checking airlines from Rome into London, Glasgow, or Edinburgh. We'll let you know should anything turn up.' I thanked him again, and reminded him about private flights; Stopelli had a lot of cash to splash about. Corky hesitated before adding, 'Aye, of course. And possibly using a different name, a different passport. You know how crooked these bastards work.' Yes, I assured him; I certainly did.

I asked Annie her if she wanted to go into the village for a meal, but she shook her head. She looked warm and comfortable, and was enjoying her music. I was keen to meet these Israeli boys, so I told her I would return in a couple of hours with food. She shrugged and turned her music up. Bonnie looked uncertain about whether to join me, or stay, but in the end leapt into the car with something like reproach that we were leaving Annie behind. You're a wee turncoat, I told her, but she wagged her tail and looked unapologetic.

Kenny owned the only pub in Criach, and it was a safe bet that any visitors to the island, especially student campers, would head there at some stage for a beer if not accommodation. I passed the ferry and saw Old Hughie locking up for the day, looking pleased to be heading for his first beer and whisky chaser of the day. He waved to me, while his passengers dispersed into the gloaming, huddled into overcoats and thick scarves, rushing for the warmth of waiting cars. Some locals, after a day on the mainland for appointments or supplies, strode off on foot in the direction of their homes or farms. I offered lifts to a few stragglers, but was waved away. They were happy to be back on Criach and well-used to the brisk walk home.

Instead of driving straight to the pub, I decided to take a rough path that led to one of the popular walking tracks leading to the mountains, mainly from curiosity to see who was around the area and rambling through the glens and lochs. It would be wise for anyone to now head for cover and safety; the weather was likely to turn very soon. The car bumped and churned its way through the mud and slush, and I was forced to drop to a low speed. The place was empty of walkers as far as I could see, which was good. Then I saw two hazy figures in the distance. I drove up closer to them, curious, but more concerned about warning them about the weather, and saw two tall, good-looking, tanned lads, striding at a good pace through the mist. They were warmly dressed, their sturdy boots mud-caked, and they carried good, sensible backpacks. It began to drizzle, and night was drawing in. These lads should head for their accommodation, and smartly.

'Can I give you a lift, boys?'

'Thank you.' They piled into the car and each shook my hand as they cheerfully introduced themselves as David and Ari, tourists and students on vacation. I had found the Israeli boys. Their English was perfect. Bonnie shifted to make room for them, and sniffed their backpacks with interest. 'We have been hiking today,' the boy called David said. 'We have met the famous Andy Cameron and he promises to take us up the mountains when he returns in a day or so. We are not experienced, but we are keen. Until then, we walk on this beautiful island, looking ... '

'How did you hear about Criach?'

'We met an Australian girl in London.' I clutched the steering wheel so hard my knuckles were white. 'She told us about it. She planned on travelling here.'

'Oh yeah. What was she doing in London?'

'Trying to earn money to travel on to Scotland. She wouldn't talk about it much, but we gather she was looking for someone in her family.'

'What was her name?' Of course I knew the answer before the question was out of my mouth. My heart was pounding.

'Annie Kendall.' When Bonnie heard the name, her ears pricked up. 'Such a great girl. She didn't much like people, but we got on well. She was very sick when we first met her, and she had nowhere to stay. She had been busking and was a pretty good singer and musician. We helped her, and when she was better, she was fun. We met up for meals and drinks ... ' They glanced at each other and began to laugh at a shared joke. And what was funny, I wondered grimly. 'We got kicked out of one hostel because of the noise we made.' I couldn't share their amusement, as the thought of Annie singing for money, cold, hungry, sick, lonely, and evicted into unfriendly London streets made me feel nauseaus. 'But when she moved on, London wasn't the same so we came to find this island about which she spoke. Do you know of her? Or where shall we find her? We have made enquiries, but people are very tight-lipped here, you know.'

'With strangers, yes.' The lights from the pub were now visible, but I wanted the conversation to continue so I could learn what Annie had told these boys about the 'family' she was looking for in Scotland.

Ari turned to his friend and spoke quietly, although I picked up what he said. 'We agreed, David, we give it two more days, and if we don't find her, we go home.' I knew then there was more than friendship between David and Annie. Andy was probably right; these lads were not our enemies. I drew up outside the pub, pulled on the handbrake, and turned to David and Ari.

'I'll tell Annie you're here.'

'That is cool. Thank you. But what is your name?'

'James. I'm Annie's father.' There, it was out.

\*   \*   \*

# CHAPTER NINE

was almost home when I remembered my promise to bring food home for Annie. I wasn't worried, because there was plenty to eat in the cupboards and freezer, and stacks of her favourite potato crisps. While she had given the bar a bit of a hit, it was still well-stocked. Once home, I intended to tell Annie about her Israeli friends, but she was locked in her room, watching a noisy television programme and didn't answer me, so I left her alone. It had to wait. Outside it had turned dark and the wind blew the snow so hard against the windows that I pulled the heavy curtains across, and stoked the fire. The sitting room was warm, and I poured a small whisky to sit with Bonnie, she to anticipate her dinner, and me to think about this new turn of events. To make sense of what was becoming a jigsaw puzzle.

Annie came down the stairs and without a word helped herself to a glass of wine and a packet of potato crisps. When she sat down in the big easy chair, Bonnie leapt from my lap and curled up beside her. I was about to tell her about the Israeli boys when the phone rang.

It was Andy, shouting down a very dodgy telephone line. 'I'll be back tomorrow, Duffy, for a few days fishing. I'll be there on the morning ferry.' We rang off. He may well have planned to fish, but his real reason for returning was to stay close in case of trouble. I was about to sit down when the phone rang again.

'It's like the country telephone exchange in here,' Annie muttered. I ignored her.

This time it was Corky, and the line was just as bad. 'Hello there, Duffy, just so's you know, we've tracked down your Mr Stopelli. Arrived in Glasgow last night, travelling from Rome and London, booked into a city hotel, Grand Central, for two nights. Our old mate, Roddy – ex Glasgow copper – concierge at the Central says Stopelli made enquiries about getting to your island. Naturally, our man has helpfully offered to make all the arrangements, so we'll know his movements. Bold as brass, not trying to hide a thing. Big tipper. Flinging cash about like a man without arms.'

'Thanks, mate.'

'Nae bother. I've alerted the local boys, so they'll probably be around your area in the next few days if Stopelli does travel north. Might drop by myself. Give my best to Andy when you see him, and let's hope we keep the idiots off the mountains in this weather. It's a strange spring.'

I topped up my whisky and stared into the fire, my only thought now on how to handle what looked like the reality of Stopelli arriving on the island. Annie watched me with interest, her hand delving in and out of the crisp packet then to her mouth with quick, precise movements. She sounded vaguely interested in my phone calls. Had I received bad news?

'Good and bad, Annie. Andy's coming back tomorrow and ... '

'That's good. But ... what's the bad?'

'It looks like the bloke I put to gaol fifteen years ago is planning on travelling north to Criach. It won't be a friendly visit.' I hesitated, softening my voice. 'He's the one who paid to have your mother and Ellery ... '

'I know about Maurizio Stopelli! I hate him! How dare he come anywhere near us!' Her voice was shrill, and there were sudden alarm and tears in her eyes. Bonnie licked her face and tried to pacify her. It did not pass me that she had uttered the word 'us'. I sat down beside her and held her hands; thankfully, she did not pull away.

'I hate him too, sweetheart. I'm ready for him, and the local police are on to him, but we have to be careful. I don't want you out of my sight until it's been sorted, and he – and that damned journalist – are off the island.'

'At least Grannie didn't lie to me about *him*,' she said bitterly, 'but why did she have to lie about *you* all those years?'

'She did what she thought was best for you, for her family. I didn't fit her plans, but you really need to know ... ' The words tumbled out. For the next fifteen minutes I talked about the fun, wonderful years her mother and I spent together before she married Ellery, both of us young, naïve. How we knew it was wrong, but we couldn't give each other up. How she desperately wanted a baby; how much she loved the little Annabelle who arrived, and whose father couldn't share her. How beautiful Anna Maria was, clever, sang like an angel, and wanted only to do good work for kids who were troubled, addicted, or home-less. I described the sheer horror of investigating their deaths while forced to hide my relationship with her. The guilt that was like glass shards cutting into my skin. How I had nearly killed Stopelli when I arrested him, and how I had pleaded with Coralyn for custody of my child. How, in the end, if I couldn't have her, the only way to escape the nightmare was to leave Australia and live in Scotland. 'Of course I didn't want to leave you, and I bitterly regret every day since that I didn't fight Coralyn harder for you. Or that I didn't protect Anna Maria and Ellery. He was a fine, important man, Annie.'

'But why did they kill my mother?'

'Your mother wasn't the target. She was just there, in the way. It was Ellery they were after. Killing him was a warning to stop the laws he was about to take to parliament. Sadly, it worked.'

'Okay then, answer me this. Why did my mother marry a man for his money when you say she loved you?' I detected scorn in Annie's voice, and I had to tread very, very carefully. Bonnie's black eyes followed me, as if to offer encouragement.

'The Peroni family were hard-working Italian migrants with not much money, but had a good business in their market gardens. Anna Maria was ambitious, different from her brothers and sisters, and didn't want a life growing tomatoes. She was scarred as a kid by the taunts of rotten red-necks about being an Italian, a wog. It was the times, Annie. Some guys were once unwise enough to share their bigoted views in front of me, and risked spending the next few days in hospital regretting it. I know your mother loved me, Annie, but she was driven by something I couldn't change. She needed security, and I couldn't provide the kind she wanted, no matter how hard I tried. She knew that police sometimes got injured, even killed, and the thought of being alone terrified her. As happy as we were together, Ellery offered her what she craved – at least materially. I knew I had lost her. Not entirely, but ... '

'You lost her because you were both cowards.' Her words cut like a razor.

'Cowards?'

'Yeah. Neither of you had the guts to be honest with your lives. You hid behind lies and pretence, kidding yourselves you had no choice.'

'Maybe we deserved that, Annie,' I said softly. 'And maybe you're right. But what matters now is that you know the truth, and we have to work out what we do from here. I love you and want to look after you, have you stay here as long as you want. Keep you safe.'

'I don't want anything from you,' she said. 'I like having nothing.'

'Why?'

'Because if you have nothing, you can't lose it, or have it taken away. I wish my mother had known that.'

'So do I, Annie.' I doubt if she heard my words. At that moment, she looked exactly like the three-year baby I had held in my arms in a Sydney nursery many years ago. 'So do I.'

I left her holding Bonnie, tears streaming down her face.

\* \* \*

Feddy's frozen food came in handy as I defrosted one of her curries and called Annie to come to dinner. She had spent the past few hours in her room with Bonnie, and there hadn't been a sound. Had she believed me? My mind was in turmoil with the intensity of our conversation and the prospect of Annie suddenly fleeing the island, or ... what? The prospect of Stopelli anywhere near us made my stomach turn, and I had to keep my temper in check. My mind clear.

I needed physical exercise and worked around the cottage and garden, pad-locking the garage, checking the window shutters, and again clearing the snow from the paths. I humped armfuls of wood from the shed to the fires. I noticed that the Old Lady of Criach looked particularly menacing in the gathering darkness, hiding herself well behind ominous black clouds. I checked the rifle and ammunition I kept in the cellar safe then replaced them carefully. I locked up the axe. Rather than pad after me, Bonnie chose to stay close to Annie.

We were silent over dinner. Annie drank too much, but my heart wasn't in alcohol. Long ago I had lost the taste for too much of it. Andy's training and my own sense of survival had taught me how essential it was to act swiftly and with a clear head in any crisis or emergency. And this was the kind of day that climbers and hikers got themselves into trouble. I jumped; given the interruption of telephone calls, I had forgotten to tell Annie about the Israeli boys.

'I ran into friends of yours today. Two lads from Israel ...'

'What?' It was like a yelp. 'And you didn't tell me earlier? That isn't fair. You just didn't want me to know, did you? God, I hate you. Where are they now?'

'In town, staying at the pub.' She rose quickly from the table and ran towards the heavy coats that hung in the hall with the waterproof boots. 'Annie, we can't go out in this weather. It's too dangerous. You'll see them tomorrow.' She pushed me out of her way as she struggled into her heavy jacket.

'Stop interfering! You're just like Grannie, making decisions for me, living my life. Keeping me from my friends. I'm going, and you can't stop me.'

'I can, Annie, and I will.'

'Then I'll walk.' She opened the door and the wind and snow blew inwards, blowing her hair around her face. She hesitated, then stepped outside. I caught her before she reached the gate, and dragged her inside, defending myself from the blows to my face and chest. Once inside, I sat her down and tried to explain how dangerous it was to drive on icy roads at night during storms.

'Oh shut up. I'll walk then. I want to see David ...'

'No. I'll drive you tomorrow.'

'No, tonight.'

There was nothing else for it, but to check the snow chains and drive very slowly to the pub. The conditions were as bad as I'd ever experienced them on Criach, and this, I thought ruefully, was still spring and the storm was just getting started. Sitting on Annie's lap, Bonnie was equally as watchful about driving on the icy, slippery road. The cold had never bothered me, but tonight it was as though we were living inside an iceberg, despite the car's heater at full blast. I wasn't sure if Annie's affection for these boys – or one boy – was such that she was desperate to see them, or whether she was testing her will against mine. If the latter, she had won.

Bad weather meant the pub bar was nearly empty except for a few residential guests. Mariella, David and Ari were sitting in front of the fire drinking hot chocolate, looking warm and comfortable, chatting amiably after, no doubt, a fine meal of Criach produce. In an earlier moment of rashness – or pride or vanity – I had blurted out to these boys that I was Annie's father, and now realised how stupid I had been. Mariella would find out, and have all the confirmation she needed. But I didn't care any more.

When I saw the reaction between Annie and the boys, I knew there was more than a friendship. David rose quickly with a shout of surprise, and opened both arms to her. Ari also rose, and then there was a tangle as they all embraced, talking together, clasping each other tight, until eventually they unwound themselves and sat down in front of the fire. They fired questions at each other without waiting for the answers. I recognised David as a man in love. And why not? In her thick red waterproof jacket, tight black trousers and fur-lined boots, Annie looked gorgeous, animated and smiling her beautiful smile. So different from the angry, wild creature that had flung herself at me barely an hour before. They were a happy trio, laughing and talking, making a lot of noise.

Mariella watched it all with a slight smile. She looked up from her drink and raised her eyebrows at me. Something new to add to her story, I thought. For me, there was nothing else to do but to order a coffee and wait for Annie until she decided to come home. After a few moments, Mariella joined me at the bar.

'A whisky, Duffy?'

'Driving, Mariella. Wise not to take chances.'

'But you've always been a man to take chances,' she said, levering herself up on the bar stool. 'and you took one helluva risk telling these boys you're Annie's father.'

'I told the truth.'

'I know. So I will be honest with you. Yes, I am a journalist and indeed I will write a big story about Stopelli and his crazy idea to come here on some kind of revenge mission. I want to expose to a city that has forgotten that fifteen years ago a good man, Ellery Kendall, was killed because he wanted to stamp out drugs and crime. I have good reason to loathe drugs, Duffy, as you do, because I have seen, as you have, the world of misery they bring. Stopelli got off lightly, and even from prison he worked his contacts to make sure that Sydney's still being taken apart by gangs and dealers. We have a new Premier who promises to crack down on drugs, and who seems serious about using Kendall's old legislation. You and he did an excellent job, and it was a huge loss when your work got parked somewhere in the bowels of State parliament. If I can bring off this story about how dangerous Stopelli and his people still are, how far they will go to achieve their ends, it will give the Premier much-needed ammunition. Bob Connelly, your good mate in Sydney, has told you how ham-strung the police are in many cases. Sydney needs tougher laws, and politicians haven't delivered them. You could help me, because you've a vested interest and you know how these criminals work; for God's sake, you put most of them in gaol, even if they're soon out and about again, dealing in their filthy trade.'

'I've no wish to be involved, Mariella. But I like what you're trying to do.' I looked across and saw Annie talking to David while he held her hands and appeared both amused and resistant to what she was saying. She was talking fast and animatedly, her hair, free of the beanie, was spread over her shoulders and flying about her face. She stopped talking, and raised her eyebrows as though asking a question. He nodded, as if something important had been decided, and then Annie rose and walked towards me, her smile so wide and so like Anna Maria's that my heart actually hurt.

'David and Ari are coming home with us,' she announced breathlessly. There was no point in arguing with her. 'They've got sleeping bags and the pub is too expensive for them. I'll help them collect their things and then we can leave. Back in a minute.' She swept off upstairs with the boys behind her, and as I glanced at Mariella, her eyes followed them with something like affectionate indulgence. Or was it pleasure at hitting the jackpot with a very interesting – incendiary–story?

'Write your big story, Mariella, but I won't have a word said about my daughter in your newspaper. I'm giving you fair warning.'

'I give you my word that I won't print anything about Annie, or your relationship, without your express permission. As far as I am concerned, she is not the story. Unless, of course something bad happens to her, and then you will see fury like you've never seen before.'

'And why would that be, Mariella?'

'Because, James Duffield, I am Anna Maria's sister. Annie is my niece.'

\* \* \*

# CHAPTER TEN

t was a good thing I needed all my wits and concentration to drive home on a perilously icy road and through rain that battered down on the windows and reduced visibility to almost zero. No-one spoke and Bonnie sat between me and Ari, peering through the darkness as though she were the chief navigator. Like her, I wanted to get everyone home, warm and safe and me able to digest this extraordinary information from Mariella Ridge.

Further conversation had been impossible. When Annie re-appeared with the two boys, she had tugged impatiently at my sleeve and urged me to leave immediately, leaving my coffee half-drunk and unpaid for. I left without saying another word to Mariella. It was hard to take in what she had said. Instead, in a kind of numb state, I packed my passengers and their gear into the car, told them to buckle up and prepare for a nightmare drive.

The cottage was still warm and the fire burned behind its safety guard in the sitting room. I made fresh coffee and the boys ate the remains of the curry. Automatically, I went about the business of finding fresh towels and blankets for them, but they were politely independent and set up their own sleeping bags and overnight necessities. Annie was happy and helpful, and as the three of them were clearly in their own world, talking about London and laughing about their bad behaviour in pubs and marathon drinking bouts in cheap hostels, it was best to leave them to their own company, wish them goodnight, and go to bed with Bonnie. The boys had set up their gear in the sitting room, but I suspected that David would find his way up into Annie's bedroom as soon as the lights were out. I didn't want to explore too far how I felt about that. Certainly, these lads were interesting, responsible, and probably trained within an inch of their lives in military arts and staying alive. They looked like they would be useful in a fight. Jesus, Bonnie, I said out loud. Have I been too trusting, letting them in the house?

From my bedroom, I heard below the muffled sounds of chatter, laughter and clinking of glasses, while I lay in bed with Bonnie and thought about Mariella. I had earlier bailed Annie up in the kitchen, as she unscrewed a bottle of my good malt whisky, and asked if she knew of any aunts on her mother's side. She had impatiently shaken her head, and said no, no-one ever spoke about her mother's relations; it was a banned subject. Try as I might, I could not recall Anna Maria talking about a sister called Mariella. I knew she had shared a bedroom with an older sister, but she was never named. In fact, she never ever talked about her family. All I remember from that one visit to the Peroni property, as a young copper, was a lot of raggedy-arsed kids running around the dusty paddocks.

I wanted to talk to Mariella immediately, but I knew the telephone lines were down, there was no mobile signal, and another trip tonight into the village was out of the question. First thing tomorrow morning I would see her and demand explanations. Was this a cruel ruse on her part to get me to talk? If so, she would rue the day. She sounded sincere about stopping drugs in Sydney, but claiming to be related to Annie was surely a step too audacious? Besides, she bore no resemblance to Anna Maria.

Mariella wasn't my only puzzle. Stopelli was in Glasgow and it wouldn't take long for him to reach Criach: a three hour train journey, a short ferry trip. He would know his tracks would be covered by the British police, and was unlikely to be welcomed wherever he went. Was that why he was so transparent in his actions? Or, as Mariella suggested, he was a sick man with nothing to lose whatever acts of bastardry he had up his sleeve.

I was tired; it had been a wearisome day, but before I turned off the light and pulled up the doona, I thought of Feddy and how comforting it had been to have her company in the cottage, not just in bed. I missed her. I eventually fell asleep listening to the cottage closing down for the night, the lights switched off and the old timber rafters creaking against the weight of rain and relentless wind. But not before I heard the soft footfall of two pairs of feet slipping up the stairs and into Annie's bedroom.

\* \* \*

I was awake at six the next morning. Miraculously, the storm had exhausted itself, and although it was pitch black outside, the air was still. Bonnie ran outside but was quickly upstairs and back in bed with me, shaking ice off her fur. There wasn't a sound in the cottage. By another miracle, the phone lines had been restored. I dialled the pub number and waited for Kenny to answer the old black phone that sat on the bar counter. It rang for ages, but he eventually picked up. He sounded irritable, and after some curt comments about the storm and the mess it made with broken branches, he put me through to Mariella Ridge's room. He seemed delighted to be able to wake up a guest at this pagan hour; I guess he felt that while he was up, humping beer kegs and preparing Scottish breakfasts, it was fair that others should share the pleasure. Mariella sounded sleepy and grumpy.

'James Duffield here. We have to talk.'

'Sure, but give a girl a chance to wake up. Where and when?'

'I'll come into the pub. Don't drive anywhere with that car of yours. Say, ten?'

'I'll be here.'

'And Mariella ....' I hesitated, 'you weren't kidding, were you? Was that a joke?'

'No, Duffy. I'm happy to talk to you. On one condition ... ' Now the journalist was speaking. 'you give *me* some information.'

'We'll see.'

By the time I had showered, shaved, dressed, then cooked breakfast and fed bits of bacon to Bonnie, the two lads were up and ready for whatever the day would bring. I remembered that Andy had promised to take them up the Old Lady of Criach when he returned. I poured them coffee and asked what their plans were, apologising that my own commitments made it impossible to join them. They happily replied that they intended walking with Annie in the good weather, climb a few easy tracks until Mr Cameron came back and maybe have a drink or two at the pub later. That sounded like an excellent idea to me, but there was the nagging concern about leaving Annie in the company of strangers. Strangers? One had spent the night in my daughter's bedroom. When Ari left the kitchen, David asked to speak to me in private.

'Sure.'

'We have enjoyed your hospitality, Mr Duffield, and I want you to know that I would not presume to take advantage of that hospitality. Your daughter and I ... well, you may have noticed, we like each other very much. Last night, I went to her bedroom, as she asked, but it was not to ... take advantage of her. I respect her, and you, far too much. But she was a little drunk, and she talked about her past and was upset ... I cannot pretend to know the full story ... but she needed company. I hope you understand, Mr Duffield.'

'The name's Duffy. Yes, David, I do understand. Thanks for explaining. The history of my daughter and me is very complicated, and I'm not sure how much you know. We're still working through it.'

'Cool. I understand. Her mother is dead, and this person who may come to this island is somehow involved, and very dangerous ... .'

'As I say, David, it's a complex story. But tell me this, does Annie use drugs?'

'No. She hates them.'

Annie appeared in the kitchen, wrapped in Feddy's dressing gown. She looked pale and dishevelled, and shivered as she stood in front of the oven and warmed herself, then turned and smiled sleepily at David. Ari re-appeared, and I couldn't help noticing how fresh-faced and healthy these boys looked. They sat down to breakfast, and I discovered there was nothing wrong with their appetites. I made more toast and fried some eggs, tactfully omitting pork sausages and bacon. They talked quietly and politely amongst themselves, and I was reassured that my fears for Annie's safety were groundless.

'I have to go into the village today', I told them. They looked up expectantly, and I noted Annie did not hide her relief, or pleasure, that I was leaving them alone for the day. 'Pack yourself some food and coffee, and enjoy the island. There's some lovely walks around here. Make the most of it, before the weather turns again.' Bonnie and I left them to it, and I drove into the village as fast as safety allowed.

Mariella was sitting alone in the pub lounge, a large mug of coffee in front of her. The room was cold, empty and quiet, the fire as yet unlit, and she sat forward expectantly in a big armchair as I shrugged off my jacket and asked Kenny for a very strong coffee. He good-naturedly reminded me of my unpaid bill of the night before. Sure, sure, I muttered ... As I leant in close, Mariella took a notebook from her bag.

'No recording, Mariella,' I warned. I looked more closely at this woman. Yes, she was definitely Mediterranean, but the sister of Anna Maria? She was older, of course, and maybe at a stretch there was a faint resemblance around the eyes; Mariella was more heavily built, her features less refined. Her face was lined, as though she'd known hard, tough times. There was no sign of her sister's ready smile or laugh, and her dark eyes were guarded, cautious. A little sad. At the sharpness of my tone, she sighed and opened up her handbag to indicate the absence of any recording device, even holding out her arms to suggest she was prepared to submit to a body search. Although I sensed she was mocking me, she looked genuinely compliant; I was still alert. 'That was quite a bombshell you dropped last night. Are you really Anna Maria's sister? I don't recall her mentioning you.'

'Duffy, let's not beat about the bush. I know all about you and my young sister. She was five years younger than me. There were so many kids in my family, and the girls didn't matter as much as the boys. Except for Anna Maria; she was always the favourite, the beautiful one with the sparkling personality, always full of plans and ambitions, always singing. Everyone loved her. For as long as I remember, she wanted to run away from home, find another life for herself, become an opera singer, a rich lady. The day you came to ask questions about our tomato crops, we were terrified of you being a police officer, but I saw how you looked at her, and knew you'd forget about regulations and health rules. She had that effect on people. Nor was I surprised when Anna Maria later snuck out of the house to meet you, and how she sometimes didn't return until morning. She told me everything, partly because she was happy and wanted to share it with me, but also because she had no option because we shared a bedroom the size of a cupboard. I never ratted on her. Not once, in all those years. I was hurt for you when she told me she was going to marry Ellery Kendall, and begged her not to go ahead with such stupidity. I tried to convince her she was wrong, but you know how stubborn she was. Sure, she got her dream; became a lady with designer clothes and fine jewels, but what did she give up? You, for a start. A music career. She abandoned her family, and never told us why. We were heartbroken, and forbidden to use her name.'

'That was tough, Mariella.'

'Yeah. She hurt a lot of people, Duffy. Not just you.'

'I guess she did.'

'No matter how often I warned her it would end in tears, she just wouldn't listen. She was determined to get her own way, no matter the cost. I wasn't surprised when she told me the marriage wasn't everything she wanted. How much she missed you. How she longed for a baby. At the time I was a junior reporter with the *Sydney Mirror* and going nowhere, but through her contacts she got me a job in the parliament house press gallery. I was grateful because I wanted a career, to make something of my life, but not by marrying some rich old guy. By then she knew she was wrong, Duffy. Very wrong. And ... ' Mariella turned away and took a deep breath. 'She paid the price.'

'Why didn't you tell me straight away who you were?'

'My family were devastated when she was killed. We hated the Italian gangs who had done this to her and her husband. Trust me, we never had anything to do with them, kept right away from them. The Peroni family were only trying to make a living the best way we could, for God's sake. You cannot imagine our grief when we were banned from her funeral.'

'I can. I felt the same. But why are you here, and why weren't you prepared to tell me, or Annabelle, who you are?'

'Do you know why I became a crime writer for my paper? I wanted to follow the man, or men, who killed my sister. I was good at my job, I worked hard, and got results. I wanted to know everything about Stopelli and his connections; as I told you, I visited him in gaol. He is seriously dangerous. Clinically mad. When he was released, I knew what he intended to do, because he told me. The other criminal, the despicable little cross-dresser Italian guy who actually did the killing, is still in gaol and festering away, destined for deportation as soon as he's released, if he ever is. He's no problem. But Stopelli is lethal.'

'You still haven't answered my question. Why didn't you tell me you were Anna Maria's sister? And did you know I was Annabelle's father?'

'Yes, I did. When Anna Maria was with me, all she could talk about was how much she wanted a baby, and how it couldn't happen with Ellery. She didn't stop loving you, Duffy, you know that, don't you? – and when she became pregnant, she didn't need to tell me who the father was.'

'You could have told me who you were when you arrived on the island, up-front, no subterfuge. Sure, I understand you're chasing a story, but I'll ask again: why the secrecy?'

'Duffy, you've been away fifteen years. I had no idea what kind of life you led now. You left Sydney with quite a reputation, good and bad. I didn't know how you would react to seeing Annabelle. She's a very rich girl, and vulnerable.' I felt my temper rise at the insinuation, but forced myself to remain calm. 'I didn't want my niece hurt ... again. I wanted to be near, in case ... well, she needed protection. That is, in the event you turned out to be a disappointment. Sorry, but that's how I felt. You're not, by the way ... a disappointment, that is.'

'And were you going to tell Annabelle about your relationship to her mother?' For the first time, Mariella lost her composure. She couldn't speak for a few moments, shaking her head and staring into the embers of last night's fire. 'What's your real motive, Mariella? Are you a journalist, or a caring aunt? I'm still a bit confused about that.'

'Honestly, Duffy, I don't know what to do. Would she want to know? All she's heard from the Kendalls is that her mother was a migrant Italian girl who came from a pretty shabby family who broke laws. Annabelle was denied access to us, so that's all she had to go on.'

'I don't know either if she wants to know you're her aunt,' I said.

'She's been pretty knocked about by people who've lied to her for years. But put that aside, Mariella, and consider this from my point of view: you're a journalist with a helluva story for your readers. It's got the lot: murder, revenge, scandal. No wonder you chased it to the other end of the world. Just too good to pass up.'

Mariella reacted swiftly. She practically spat at me that she had given her word there would be nothing printed about Annabelle without my permission. Her aim was to check me out, protect her niece and expose Stopelli and his criminal drug dealings. Yes, she agreed, she could have splashed her sister's relationship with me on the front pages of the *Sydney Mirror* and exposed what she knew about the Kendall marriage and Annabelle, but who would be most hurt? Her own flesh and blood, her niece. And her sister.

'I loved Anna Maria, Duffy. I miss her.' Tears sparkled in the dark brown eyes, and I felt remorse for my cynicism, but I pressed on. Despite Mariella's obvious sincerity – or was she simply well-informed? – I wanted to be sure of her identity. As though reading my mind, Mariella drew an old dog-eared coloured photograph from her handbag and handed it to me; against the backdrop of the old Peroni house as I last remembered it, were two young, dark-haired girls with their arms around each other's waists, wide smiles to the camera as they posed in frilly dresses. One I recognised immediately as Anna Maria and the other, older, gap-toothed girl was recognisable as Mariella. 'I've had my teeth fixed since then,' Mariella said with a snort and a roll of her eyes, 'but it's me.' I put my doubts aside.

'Did you have anything to do with Annabelle as a baby?'

'No. It was too risky. She rarely left the Kendall house. Anna Maria was terrified about kidnappers. After she was … killed,' Mariella swallowed hard, 'I used to watch my niece sometimes, going to school with her nanny and bodyguard. She never knew. Over the years I saw her growing up. Saw how as a teenager she was going off the rails. I wanted to help, but you know how tight the Kendall compound was. Anyway ...' She fished a tissue from her handbag, and blew her nose. 'All water under the bridge now, of course. My sister is gone, my niece remains. Yes,' she said with a sudden spurt of determination. 'I *will* tell her who I am, when the time is right. In the meantime, let's deal with what we have. I've given you everything I know about Anna Maria and Anna- belle, so how about you keep your side of the bargain and tell me about Stopelli and his mates? Tell me about Sydney in the 70s, you and Ellery, how you tried to bust up those gangs. And, dear God, how did such a tragic lapse of security happen at the Kendall house? All that surveil- lance, all those coppers ... '

'Thanks, Mariella, for the reminder. Look, there's nothing more I can add apart from what was in the newspapers at the time, the court cases, the wall-to-wall press coverage. I left not long afterwards, and haven't been back or even interested myself in anything that's happened since in Sydney, apart from a couple of conversations with Bob Connelly. I'm glad Ellery's work is being recognised. But I have nothing new to add to the whole sorry Kendall saga, or explain, as you so pleasantly remarked, how such a security bungle happened on my watch. Sometimes, often actually, the bad guys win.'

I ordered more coffees and thought for a few minutes as Mariella slowly stirred several teaspoons of sugar into her cup. She knew that Stopelli wanted to harm me, and probably would harm Annabelle just for the hell of her being a Kendall, but how much did he know, or suspect, about her relationship to me? Had Mariella ever raised the subject with him? I bluntly asked her, and she shook her head.

'No, Duffy. I have not told a soul. Not my family, or my husband – who was also a journalist ... '

'Where is he now?'

'He died five years ago. He was a good reporter, Martin Ridge, you might have heard of him." Yes, I had heard of him; he was one of the few reporters in parliament house for whom I had any respect because he was dogged and accurate. "Well, he was covering a story about drug deals in some of Sydney's high schools, wouldn't let it drop. He got on the wrong side of ... well, according to the coroner it was an unfortunate car accident, but I knew better. Do you wonder why I am determined to stop Stopelli? First my sister, and then my husband. I have no children. The Peroni family have never been associated with drugs or organised crime. Yeah, yeah, maybe we still get around some minor laws, but ...' she shrugged, 'that's irrelevant. What *is* relevant is the fact that Stopelli hasn't so far made the connection between you and Annabelle, but she is a Kendall, and that's good enough for him. Make no mistake about his court-room vow to ruin you. Think about the malicious pleasure it would give him to link the two of you. He would regard that as killing – forgive me – two birds with one stone.

'He is here in Scotland, you know.'

'Yes, I know. Your police mates are generous with information about scum like him. Unlike this community, from which I couldn't get one word about you, or about the Australian girl who suddenly and mysteriously appeared and is now living with you. I couldn't get anything either on your girlfriend ... Feddy, isn't it? – and where she fits into the picture.' I didn't try to disguise my anger now, and she put a restraining hand on my arm and smiled. In that instant, I saw a flash of resemblance to Anna Maria, and my heart did a peculiar lurch. 'Calm down. I wouldn't do it, but by Jesus, I'd love to write about the old Sydney copper who established himself on this damned cold but spectacular island ... successful, probably wealthy, a star mountaineer, a hero dragging bodies off mountains, gorgeous girlfriend ... wonderful stuff. In the meantime, I'll settle for some names that didn't hit the press in the 70s, and those who kept themselves out of court. Some background, Duffy, so how about it?'

I talked for about an hour, reluctantly dredging up names and places

I had hoped never to revisit. She took it all down in a notebook in some kind of shorthand. It was old stuff to me, of absolutely no relevance. It was nearly noon when I said I had to leave to check the islanders around the coast to see if there had been any suspicious private boat landings. I would check the ferry to see if Stopelli had dared to arrive. She rose to come with me, but I shook my head. I needed to be alone. I still had to check up on Annabelle and her foreign visitors.

I shook Mariella's hand when I left but she pulled me to her and hugged me. I didn't resist too hard. I liked her, and believed her. Besides, she was part of Anna Maria.

'Your daughter is singing in the pub tonight,' she said.

'I didn't know that.' I paid the bill and gathered up my jacket to leave when Bonnie's excited tail-wagging told me that Andy had arrived. He nodded politely to Mariella, then hurried on to say how he had caught the ferry by the skin of his teeth, was cold and hungry and looking forward to catching up on news. Rubbing his hands together in anticipation of a full Scottish lunch and a large pot of tea, he enquired of Mariella if she had found some warm clothing. She looked embarrassed.

'Aye, our wee lassie is singing here tonight,' Andy went on, 'And by the way, Duffy, no strangers on the ferry. Just give me twenty minutes to finish a wee bite, and we'll catch up with our Israeli boys. I'd promised to show them something of the island.'

I sat down again and waited until he had eaten his lunch. Mariella tried to engage Andy about his work in the Highlands, but as always was reluctant to talk about himself so she switched the conversation to bush-walking in Australia. She didn't have much time for it, she admitted, but found it cleared the head when you wanted to escape life's shite. Andy amiably agreed and continued to enjoy his soup.

I left Mariella and her one-sided conversation to ask Kenny if anybody had booked accommodation by telephone in the past day.

He looked up his book, as always a manky tea towel over his shoulder, pencil behind his ear, and said, aye, he was just telling Andy that some Glasgow hotel had booked a single room for two nights. Name? A Mr Stopelli. So the old swine *was* determined to come to Criach, and definitely without any pretence at disguising who he was. To do what? Rather, how?

After finishing his meal, Andy left his car at the pub and drove with me to the cottage. It gave me a chance to bring him up-to-date with events, especially about the two lads and the revelations of Mariella Ridge. Interesting woman, he remarked, and I glanced at him curiously

'She's a journalist, Andy.'

'Och, mercy, she's a nice enough wee soul. I have a feeling there's more to her than being a tough old reporter.' He glanced up at the mountains. 'There's nothing wrong with a bushwalker.' We rode in silence for some moments, while he studied the white sheep with coloured markings on their back dotted along the hills. Some had meandered along the side of the road, and as we slowed down, he said quietly, 'So, she's your Anna Maria's sister. How d'ye feel about that?'

'Honestly, I don't know. It's hard to get beyond the journalist bit.'

'You will, son. You will.' Within half a mile of the cottage, we caught sight of Annie and the two Israeli boys trudging along the road, heading towards a popular walking track. I stopped the car and Andy leant out the open window and cheerfully called out to them.

'Hello, there! Grand day for a walk. Duffy's a bit busy, so if you'll let me join you, I'll just be borrowing Duffy's gear and be with you in ten minutes. You okay with that, Annie?'

She nodded happily, presumably at the prospect of an afternoon without me, and pointed to her boots. Yes, she was ready for an adventure. Back at the cottage it didn't take long for Andy to organise himself into warmer climbing gear, and then he set off to join the others. We have work to do, I told Bonnie, and although she wagged her tail, the slight sag of her ears told me she wouldn't have minded going with Andy and Annie. They'll come back, I promised her.

Our 'work' entailed driving around the island's coastline, twenty-five miles of craggy coast and coves, sheer cliffs and caves. I wanted to check with the locals to see if they had noticed any private boats off-shore, or seen strangers hanging about. Unlikely, I knew, but if Stopelli was determined to travel to Criach and book himself into Kenny's pub in full view, there was always the possibility he had accomplices working for him, and who were not quite so visible. The old motto: check every contingency.

I withstood the many offers of cups of tea, shortbread and wee drams, and ploughed on. Bonnie loved it. At each cottage, farm and fisherman's shed along the way, I was told there had only been a few familiar hikers, walkers and climbers around. Bad weather, I was repeatedly told. Keeps the tourists away, even the keen ones. And this is spring, they each said with a rueful tilt of the head. Then again, this *was* Criach. The Old Lady was no respecter of seasons.

I felt in my bones I would confront Stopelli that day. Earlier, I had telephoned Roddy at the Grand Central who told me that Stopelli had checked out, leaving behind in storage a large suitcase and was now travelling with a small valise.

'Auld bastard looked like he was off on a nice wee day's outing,' Roddy whispered to me, in between dispensing maps and advice to hotel guests about how best to get to Edinburgh or the Burrell Collection. 'He's on the 12.10 from Central. I seen him get on the train mysel', Duffy, just to make sure.'

'Thanks, mate. Check what's in that bag in storage, would you?'

'I'll do that small thing.'

The Glasgow train would take Stopelli as far as Inverness, then he would have to make his way to Kilsney – a good taxi fare? – and then to the jetty to catch the late ferry to Criach. As I was driving around the island, I knew he was travelling ever closer towards an inevitable confrontation. The day was getting dark, and so was my mood. It was essential to keep control of myself, my wits alert, and impervious to provocation while I worked out what this guy intended to do, and what my response would be. Like all criminals, he would make mistakes. Was I still sharp enough to spot them? I glanced at my watch and decided to end my fruitless circling of the island, and return home before meeting the ferry. I needed to check that Annie was safe with Andy. As I changed gear, and speeded up, Bonnie seemed to agree with that decision.

\* \* \*

# CHAPTER ELEVEN

The ferry should have arrived within the hour, but it was late, Timetables never mattered to Old Hughie. Probably he was enjoying a yarn with his mates on the other side, or the schoolkids were larking around and delaying getting on board. Maybe some sheep or goats were refusing to budge. One never knew what the cargo was. But this time it probably contained a man who was determined to harm me, and my daughter. I couldn't stop him arriving in Criach, but I had to stop his evil intentions.

How did I feel now? Was it like the old stake-outs with Bob Connelly, confident, actually relishing a punch or two? Then I only had myself to think about; this time my thoughts were about Annie as I waited in the car listening to the radio and news from the mainland, fiddling with a mobile phone that never worked. The grey skies were turning dark, the seagulls cried and hovered above, and another storm threatened. When would spring arrive, I asked Bonnie. In her waterproof, wool-lined tartan jacket, it made no difference to her; she loved the snow. I ruffled her fur until she spotted the ferry's lights and sat up straight, those shiny black eyes focussed only on the growing speck amongst the rough, choppy sea. Here we go, sweetheart, I whispered.

God give me the will-power not to kill today.

My shoulders were hunched against the cold, wet wind as I stood on the jetty and watched the old ferry bump itself into position and tie up on the pylons. There weren't many passengers or vehicles on board, but I noticed a solid, smallish man near the exit gate, clad in a thick tweed coat, heavy scarf and a hat with fur ear-flaps. He carried a leather overnight bag, which, as he stepped off the gangplank, I recognised as an expensive Louis Vuitton. He was looking directly towards me. I could not move. Hatred, bile, fury, renewed grief, all rose within me and my hands began to shake. Bonnie gave a low growl, and I snapped my fingers for her to remain quiet and stay beside me. She did as I commanded. Right behind Stopelli I saw Sergeant 'Corky' McCorquodale, doing his best to look other than what he was: a policeman on surveillance duty. He and I nodded discreetly to each other.

'Mr Duffield, we meet again.' Stopelli was now within close range of me, and my hands were clenched. Bonnie fretted beside me, itching to be let loose, but she remained by my side. I stared at this old man, his face sunken and greyish, his lips pinched and blue-ish, but still reeking of evil money and arrogance. That hadn't been rubbed away with his stint in gaol. I ignored the outstretched hand as he said in his still-accented English, 'No man is an island, indeed, Mr Duffield, and here we are, after all these years ...'

It was too much. It was the smile that did it. I couldn't bear another second of this vile old bastard's superciliousness. This was the man who had killed not only Anna Maria and Ellery Kendall, but countless children in Sydney through his drug syndicates and dealers. This was the man who had haunted me for almost two decades with his evil trade, oblivious to the misery he caused. Because of him, Anna Maria had been shot like a rag doll, her beautiful face disfigured. I sprang as though all those years of misery could no longer be contained. My hands lunged towards his throat, my face, I knew, a twisted mass of rage and hatred. Bonnie leapt at him too, growling and, for the first time in my life, I saw her bare her teeth as she sank them into his ankles. He tried to kick her away, but she refused to let go. I felt a solid weight pushing against me, while Bonnie continued to tear and rip at Stopelli's trousers.

'No, Duffy. This is not the way.' Andy forcefully wedged himself between me and Stopelli, his face framed in that expression that did not brook defiance. He was strong, stronger than anyone I knew, and it was impossible to break through that muscle and get to the man I wanted to kill. And probably would have, had he, with Corky behind him, not restrained me.

'Come on now, Duffy, enough of that.' Corky wasn't going to have a premeditated murder on his hands, no matter how provoked. He gestured to the young policeman in plain clothes who was sitting in the unmarked police car, and I saw it slowly driven off the ferry and stop, the passenger door open. Corky signalled for Stopelli to get into the car, and turned to me as I struggled to free myself from Andy's grip. 'Calm down, now. You'll not be getting yersel' into any trouble now. Whatever we may think, this man has served his time. All right? Go and have a wee drink, man, and we'll take care of what's necessary.' I pushed against Corky and Andy, but it was futile. I was strong, but together they were an impenetrable barrier. Bonnie did not stop growling, and I saw with bitter pleasure some bits of merino wool caught between her teeth.

\* \* \*

At home in the cottage, I found Annie wedged between David and Ari on the sofa. She left as soon as I arrived, and went upstairs. I poured myself a whisky and sat down by the fire. I could not speak, I shook, and my heart was beating so fast I feared I would pass out. David sat beside me. He didn't drink, but briefly put his hand on my shoulder and together we silently stared into the fire. How could my island be so defiled by this evil, unspeakably cruel man? How could I sleep under the same sky as him? I covered my eyes with my hand, and Bonnie whimpered and pawed at my legs. It was past her dinner time, but it wasn't hunger that distressed her.

'Duffy, I am here to help,' David said quietly. 'I know what it is like to feel threatened. To have things you love in danger. To feel helpless. But we are never helpless, believe me.'

I looked at this earnest young man, handsome, young, in love. Dangerous to cross. Defending his own tiny country surrounded by enemies who had sworn to blow Israel off the face of the map. I nodded. No, he wasn't helpless. With boys like David, Israel was in safe hands. And, whatever happened on Criach, I would make sure Annie was safe. Andy and Corky would combine to ensure I did nothing stupid, and David and Ari clearly stood between Annie and any danger. But I knew I harboured a need for revenge that blinded me to rules and decency. As Bob Connolly and I used to say in the past: there was more than one way to skin a cat. Or catch the bad guys. How many times had we said that? We'd proved it so many times. The trick was to remain cool, calculating and crafty. Sure, we had taken shortcuts and used unorthodox – probably illegal – methods, but we didn't care as long as we could rid the earth of scum, those who, for thrills, money or plain cruelty, desecrated the lives of innocent souls.

'You're right, David.' I finished my drink and stood up. 'We're not helpless. And, by God, we'll protect what's ours.' I feigned cheerfulness as I switched the conversation. 'Annie's singing in the pub tonight. She needs to earn some money, so let's go and support her. Look after her. Okay?' He nodded. Ari had been sitting quietly in the shadows, listening carefully and I saw him nod in agreement. They were a fine pair to have around in an emergency, I thought.

Stopelli would take every ounce of guile to outwit, whatever he was up to, but he would find no mercy from me. Bonnie sensed my mood as I went upstairs to change. She tripped alongside me. 'It's okay, Bonnie,' I whispered to her. 'Remember how you love chasing rabbits in the fields? How good it feels when you catch them?' She cocked her head at me; 'rabbit' was a word and prey she knew well. 'Well, I'm going to catch a big rat.'

I heard Annie humming in the bathroom, unaware that Stopelli was now on the island. She didn't need to know just yet. She sounded happy, looking forward to the evening with two friends she liked and trusted and doing what she loved – singing and entertaining. It was her night to shine, to show her talents, and I would let nothing spoil it.

I apologised to Bonnie for leaving her home tonight, as the pub on a Saturday night, especially with a 'guest artist' would be crowded, smoky and noisy. She knew there was no point in objecting, so she curled up in her basket and watched us leave the cottage. Her head was on her paws, and her beautiful, intelligent black eyes stared up at me with something like caution. Or was it a warning?

\* \* \*

# CHAPTER TWELVE

As usual on a Saturday night, the pub was busy but tonight it was crammed. Word had got around about the 'wee Ozzie lassie' and there was curiosity as well as the opportunity for some unexpected entertainment on the island. There were a few die-hard tourists and ramblers, but the main crowd consisted of local farmers, fishermen and their wives who enjoyed getting together at the end of a tough week to share a drink and exchange news. Their work was hard, looking after sheep in dismal weather, or setting off long before dawn to trawl for the island's famous fish and seafood. It was smoky and boisterous, and David, Ari, Annie and I wound our way through the crowd to find a table near the fire where Mariella sat nursing a large vodka and tonic. Annie was animated, and I noticed a tinge of rouge on her cheeks, and black mascara on those long, long lashes. Her shiny black hair curled around her shoulders, and she looked young, fresh, beautiful, and in love. I heaved a sigh. Was it possible to shield such a vibrant, defiant young creature from the world of bastards? Her allegiance was with David, not with me. But why would it be otherwise? What was I to her?

My nerves were stretched to snapping point, and my body was taut, ready for trouble from wherever it came. Or so I convinced myself. I looked around the room and assured myself that everyone was known to me, and the few strangers were young tourists that Andy had checked earlier. Kenny told me that Stopelli had signed in at reception earlier and then retired after ordering an evening meal to be served in his room, pleading exhaustion and sore ankles. 'I'm glad yer dug bit the prick,' Kenny had muttered to me as I entered the pub. Stopelli had been rude and dismissive of the hotel staff and their Scottish courtesy, and had made no friends. I noticed the young policeman in plain clothes loitering near the stairs that led upstairs to the guest rooms. He looked keen but inexperienced.

Andy and Corky stood close together, sharing a whisky and talking to each other in low tones, occasionally glancing over at my direction. It would be foolish to cause any disturbance, I knew, for they would be by my side in an instant. It was a hellish situation, and I felt hemmed in, constricted, trapped in a very personal kind of nightmare. Corky had taken me aside earlier and reminded me that while Stopelli was on record as muttering threats to me, there was nothing they could formally charge him with. 'But we're keeping a close eye on him, Duffy.' he said under his breath. 'We've checked his luggage, and there's nothing there to worry about there, apart from a heap of prescription drugs for his bad heart and other complaints. So don't worry, we'll get him off the island and back to the cesspit from whence he came as soon as possible. Strange business, though ... '

After an hour or so of boisterous talking and drinking, Kenny called the crowd to order by banging on his old Celtic drum, the bodhrán he kept underneath the counter of the bar for use when he wanted to get his patrons' attention, or tell us time was up and to get the hell home. There was applause and cheering as Annie picked up her guitar and walked to the make-shift platform.

'Introducing a fine wee Australian singer, ladies and gentlemen,' Kenny boomed, 'Annie Kendall!'

When the din died down, Annie acknowledged her audience with a wide smile, adjusted the microphone, and then quietly began to strum her guitar. From the corner of the room near the stairs, I saw Stopelli appear and move towards the unoccupied end of the bar's service area, the young policeman right behind him. He not so much smiled as smirked as he ordered a drink from Moira, the waitress who came in only on a Saturday night. I half-heard Stopelli order a bottle of French champagne, and then he pointed to Annie. Moira was gone for a few minutes and returned with the bottle from the cellar. She took some time to open the bottle of the expensive wine and poured two glasses.

Buying Annie a drink, indeed! I wasn't having that. I was restrained from lunging towards Stopelli by David's broad shoulders pressing against me, and then I heard Annie sing. Like everyone else in that room, I was captured by the sweetness of a song I didn't know, something about Scotland's past and its longing for independence. Everyone in the pub became quiet, moved by the words, the voice, the melody, and the heart-felt yearning behind it. Before the applause died down at its end, Annie swung into another song, this time a cheerful, bawdy ballad, the chorus of which her audience knew well and joined in with gusto. She was, I had to admit, one hell of an entertainer. I glanced over at Andy, who smiled back and raised his glass first at me, and then at Annie.

Stopelli remained at the end of the bar, removed from the crowd, and I loathed his smug, confident expression. He hadn't come to the Highlands for amateur hour, of that I was certain. David and Ari stood close together, but David edged closer to me, as if to say, we're here. Nothing can happen. No harm will come to Annie, or you. But was that true? Why was I so nervous, apart from the fact that the man I detested most in the world, and whom I wanted to see dead, was within striking distance of me and the daughter I loved? I was overwrought, I knew, but something nagged at me. Doubts. Inadequacies. I remembered the intricacies of the security in place for her mother ... and that had gone wrong. What had I missed this time?

Mariella sat beside me, on her third vodka, flushed and visibly moved by Annie's singing. At one point of the performance, she placed her hand on mine and smiled, tears in her eyes. There was a flash of the Peroni resemblance, as well as the look of a very proud aunt. Annie launched into another song, and this time Jimmy the postman pulled out his bagpipes and was warming up with gusto, while Old Hughie began drumming the table with drumsticks in perfect time to the music. Kenny was keeping the beat by banging on his bodhrán, Moira was jigging about behind the bar. The place was in an uproar of music, singing, clapping and cheering. Annie sang and laughed, encouraging her audience to join her, her own voice surging above everyone else with her clear, sparkling, soaring notes, full of fun and melody. She was having the time of her life, sure of her control of the audience, knowing she sang with an instinct for capturing the emotions of her audience.

Her mother had never sung like this; it was usually snatches of arias from operas or musical shows, softly sung when she thought she was alone, or to please me. No, Annie was unafraid to let her talent rip. On stage, there was a brief spell while she acknowledged the applause, her hair flying, and laughing as she bent down to accept the glass of champagne from Moira. She took a long, thirsty sip. I glanced at the gesture, then at Stopelli, and my heart stood still. His face showed malevolent pleasure as he half-smiled and watched the girl on the stage drink from the glass, saw her frown as though she didn't much like the taste and then take another sip. I heard the scream within my head. No! No!

I was off my seat and lunging towards the stage, pushing everyone aside. I snatched the glass from her fingers, but some liquid splashed across her mouth. 'Corky,' I yelled, 'This is poison! For God's sake, stop him!' I gestured towards Stopelli and everyone stared at me, shocked. I knew I looked demented as I held the unfinished wine away from Annie and handed it to Corky, then punched my way towards Stopelli. Andy stopped me, but this time my strength was greater. I grabbed Stopelli by the collar and shoved him up against the wall, my fist ready to smash into his face. The gasps from the crowd would not have stopped me, but the thud from the stage did. I turned around to find Annie crumpled on the floor, her face strained and her hand at her mouth. Her guitar was flung to the floor, and she was having some kind of seizure. Oh, Jesus. I dropped Stopelli and flung him in the direction of Corky and Andy. muttering something like, lock the bastard up before I kill him, and flew towards Annie.

David and Mariella beat me to her. She was in trouble, I could see, trying to catch her breath, her pallor chalk-white. David checked her heart and got her to her feet, urging her to remain conscious. Ari was beside him, and they exchanged a glance that made me feel sick. 'We must get her to hospital, Duffy,' said David. 'I mean, now!' Desperately, I looked around the crowd for Old Hughie, but he shook his head. There was no way we could get to the mainland tonight; the weather had turned and the combination of a black night, wind and snow meant it was impossible to manoeuvre the old ferry across a stretch of sea in turmoil. The phone lines were down. Even if it could fly, it would take too long to get the emergency helicopter from the mainland to the island. I pleaded with Old Hughie, but he shook his head, and said he would kill everyone if he tried. Mariella was screaming at him. 'Please, Hughie ...'

David carried Annie to my car, all the time talking to her and imploring her to remain awake, to keep moving. 'I am a doctor, Duffy,' he said to me, 'and Ari is a pharmacist. We know of drugs like this, and I can smell it – a high potency drug. We must get it out of her system as soon as we can. And keep her conscious.' Andy was at my side, his face pale and anguished. David turned to him and spoke very slowly. 'You must somehow contact the hospital and have an ambulance waiting. Ask them to prepare for a drug overdose – probably a combination of fentanyl, heroin, and other unknown opiate drugs.

We need intravenous naloxone ... '

'Sure, sure ... just bring her back safely. Duffy, don't worry about Bonnie ... ' I didn't hear any more. Old Hughie was grim-faced as he prepared to tackle the crossing in weather that taunted the finest mariner. Once on board, I held Annie's head in my hands and begged her to stay awake, to talk to me, to live. I had left the pub without a jacket, but I hardly felt the cold or biting rain until Mariella draped an old oilskin coat of Old Hughie's around my shoulders.

The crossing was a test of Old Hughie's skill, a battle against the elements that had sprung up in defiance of a pleasant day. The waves were high, the gale as wild as I had ever known it, and the rain pelted in our faces. The old boat bucked and weaved. At the other end, Andy had worked a miracle, and we saw the lights of an ambulance waiting for us on the Kilsney jetty. My heart began to beat again. I barely thanked Old Hughie as we leapt off the ferry before it tied up at the wharf and the para-medics took over. I held Annie's cold hands during the short ambulance trip to the town-centre hospital. I felt faint with relief when I saw the doctors and nurses waiting outside for us. They began their work immediately, wheeling Annie away from me and out of sight.

I have no idea how long I sat with Mariella in the waiting room, clenching and unclenching my fists and swearing under my breath. The bastard. He had done it again. He had beaten me. I could not speak, or accept the food and coffee that was offered to us during those long hours of waiting. I knew one thing: if Annie died, there was no point in me continuing to live. Mariella sat white-faced, clutching her rosary beads and mouthing endless prayers. David and Ari worked with the local doctors, who welcomed their advice and assistance, having little experience of this kind of drug-induced emergency. I heard David explain to them that it was a criminal act; the young woman had unknowingly been given a potentially lethal cocktail of drugs, the strength of which would have been fatal had she ingested more than she did.

There were streaks of dawn in the dark sky when David came to me in the waiting room. 'She will be alright, Duffy. With these good doctors, we managed to get most of the toxins out of her system in time. And fortunately you stopped her before she drank any more. That saved her life. She is weak and unwell, but in time will recover. We will get her home, because there is little else they can do for her here. Ari has the appropriate medication now, and we can care for her. She needs rest, warmth and peace. Let's give her a few more hours, and then we will wrap her up and take her home where she belongs. We will look after her. Hey, Duffy ... ' I clasped the boy in my arms and wept against his shoulder.

Old Hughie had not budged from the ferry from the night before. It was very late in the afternoon when the ambulance delivered us back to the Kilsney jetty, Annie wrapped in so many blankets that it was difficult to discern a human body within. She was awake, but drowsy. We were despatched with medications and innumerable instructions to look after her, to which David and Ari nodded. Yes, yes, they knew ... Mariella sat beside her niece, stroking her face, and pushing back the strands of damp hair that crossed her face. From time to time, she tugged at her rosary beads. The ferry ride home was quiet, the weather now spent and gloomy, as though to reflect the moods of the passengers on Old Hughie's ferry. When we reached Criach, Andy was waiting for us on the jetty, the car's engine running and the heater at full blast to keep the interior warm. Bonnie was inside, her two front paws on the steering wheel, and when she was let loose she sped towards me almost on her belly with relief to see me and Annie, her tail a blur of fur. As I left the ferry, I clasped Old Hughie's hands, but couldn't find the words to thank him. He nodded, and flung the ropes over the pylons. 'Look after yon wee lassie, Duffy. Make the auld swine pay.'

I had every intention of doing that.

\* \* \*

Annie was sleepy, and had no strength to put up any resistance when David carried her upstairs to her bedroom and tucked her tightly under a thick, warm, doona. Very professionally, looking every inch the earnest young doctor, he checked her blood pressure, pulse, heart and eyes, and nodded to Ari after saying something in their own language. 'What?' I demanded anxiously, 'what are you saying?'

'I was saying, Duffy, that Annie is very lucky. That particular combination of poison – it is virtually unknown on the market – is lethal. It is good you acted as quickly as you did. Come, Annie has been given a sedative, and we must keep her quiet and rested. She will be fine, but I will check every half-hour or so. You need a stiff drink and some food, Duffy, and perhaps some rest yourself.'

'I won't rest, David, until Stopelli is behind bars again or dead.'

Bonnie refused to leave Annie's side, so we left her there, the bedroom door open in case Annie called out. Downstairs, Mariella sipped from a large glass of whisky while she jotted some notes into a notepad. She could write what she liked, I thought. I didn't care any more. Nothing mattered except Annie's survival. Andy arrived, and I tried to thank him for his help in miraculously getting word to the hospital, and for looking after Bonnie while I was away, but neither of us found any words and we stopped trying. A shared whisky would speak for us.

'The glass and liquid have been sent to the mainland for analysis, Duffy,' he said gruffly, at last. 'And a police ferry was supposed to come today to collect Stopelli, but was delayed by some emergency, so we've got him for another night. Don't worry ... ' he put his hand on my arm as he saw my agitated reaction, 'He's locked up in the cellar pub, which is securely bolted and padlocked.'

'Are you sure, Andy? He's a slippery bastard.'

'Corky and the other officer are staying at the pub overnight. Try and relax, man. You've been through a lot, and you need a bit of a rest. Annie will be fine.'

'Will she, Andy?'

How could I relax knowing that man was alive and on my island? Did he really expect to get away with trying to murder Annabelle? And if he had succeeded in making it look like an accidental drug overdose, no doubt I was next on his murderous menu. Corky had discovered how he had hidden the drugs. The sheer brazenness of hiding them within prescription capsules that escaped scrutiny was breath-taking. Simple, clever, almost successful. He was known to be a sick man, and, if Mariella was right, he had nothing to lose if he got caught. I was conflicted: all I wanted to do was to sit with Annie and make sure she breathed. That, and smash Stopelli into a helpless pulp.

When she finished writing in her notebook, Mariella made coffee and said she was going to cook some pasta; something to do, anything, she said, to take her mind off other things. Besides, we must all be starving. Andy declined the invitation to stay on and share the meal, saying he wanted to get back to the pub to double-check with Corky that everything was locked up, with no chance that Stopelli could escape his temporary prison. I could see he was worried. For me, for Annie. I want the man off the island and dealt with, he said, as he left.

I ate but did not taste Mariella's pasta, then went upstairs to see Annie and Bonnie. They were both sleeping, Bonnie having worked her head near the pillow and was resting under Annie's arm. What have you done to her, Bonnie seemed to say in reproach as she glanced up at me, and I wondered the same thing. What danger had I allowed my daughter to stumble into? It was no good David saying I had saved her life by stopping her from drinking any more of whatever it was Stopelli had used; the truth was that it was because of me that she was in danger in the first place. Mariella quietly came up behind me and stood beside me.

'He would have tried to harm her wherever he found her, here or in Australia,' she said gently. 'When he got out of gaol, he had people trying to find her. And you. He told me all this. Why do you think I came to Criach? A story, sure, but I needed to warn you.' She leant her head against my shoulder. 'Like David said, Duffy, you saved her life. And Stopelli won't get away with this. He's sick, so take heart from knowing he won't be long for this world, one way or another.'

'You're dead right about that, Mariella.' I kissed Annie's cheek, indicated to Bonnie that I needed her and she was beside me in an instant. 'We have work to do, girl.'

\* \* \*

# CHAPTER THIRTEEN

Despite the lack of sleep, I felt wide-awake. I changed into my mountain-climbing gear, picked up my helmet and boots and crampons – I anticipated a lot of snow on the mountain and would need their grip – and shouted to Mariella and the boys that I was going out for a while. David was beside me immediately.

'I'm going into town, David.'

'I will come with you,' he said firmly.

'No, I must go alone. This has nothing to do with you, David. I am grateful for what you and Ari have done for Annie, but I cannot involve you. It's my fight, my family.'

'Duffy, I know there are things that are not my business, that Annie is angry with you, is feeling lost and alone, and all those things you must work out with her. You love her, and so do I. She nearly died last night, and this man who harmed her cannot be allowed to hurt her again ...'

I hesitated. Did this boy guess what was on my mind? I thought so, perhaps because he would have done the same in my situation. I studied him closely; he was strong, tough, with cool nerves. And he could keep his mouth shut. Perhaps it would be good to have his company.

'Let's go, son. Put this gear on.'

Outside, the wind had abated. Later into the night, it would blow up with greater intensity but for now it was clear but bitterly cold. Neither David nor I spoke on the way to the village. Being a Sunday night, the front bar of the pub was closed, but it was easy enough to slip in the back way while the few hotel guests were in the front room. No doubt Andy and Corky were together, or perhaps they and the young policeman had gone to bed early, having made sure Stopelli was locked up in the next best thing to a cell the island could provide, the basement cellar. But the copper in me knew it should have been guarded; then again, for my purposes, I was glad it wasn't. I indicated to David the stairs to the cellar and he slid silently behind me and followed me down into the darkness. It was a long time since I had picked a lock, and it took several attempts before the padlock opened with a slight spring.

Stopelli sat on a make-shift bed, a tray of uneaten sandwiches and a pot of cold tea beside him. At first, when he heard the door open he looked relieved, but his face quickly turned to fear when he saw me. He had every reason. David pressed against me to stop me from hauling the man up against the stone wall and battering him with every ounce of my strength. I was forced back. I let David fling the extra set of protective clothing and boots we had brought, and indicated to Stopelli to put them on. There was a struggle, but he got the message when David shoved him back on the bed and silently gestured to get them on quickly. I felt only loathing and determination.

It was equally easy to get out of the pub without being seen, Stopelli's mouth being covered by David's gloved hand, and my car was parked way down the road and out of sight of anyone glancing out of the window. I drove quickly from the village and headed for a favourite parking spot of climbers who preferred the gentler slopes. Our jaunt would start there, but I knew where to find the peaks that suddenly became sheer and unpredictable, listed as dangerous in the guide books and marked on the site with skulls and cross-bones as an extra deterrent. These were not peaks for beginners or amateur adventurers. As I pushed him forward, Stopelli began to protest, whimper, shout out, but apart from him, David and me, there was no other human life close enough to hear. Stopelli's voice disappeared into the slopes of The Old Lady of Criach.

'I am an old man, you fool,' he shouted at me, looking slightly foolish in his orange helmet. His accent had become thick. 'you can't prove a thing. The girl was an addict ...' I pushed him hard and furiously in the direction of the path marked with skull and cross-bones. He wore sufficient clothing to ensure he was warmly dressed, but it wouldn't take long for an old, sick, unfit man to succumb to the bitter elements and fatigue. I wanted to shout back at him that he was an evil excuse for a man who created misery wherever he went, but I remained silent. He wasn't worth the words, and, in any case, they would hardly be heard against the rising wind. Bonnie, who was normally keen to trot beside me on any kind of mountain expedition, tonight seemed strangely reluctant and stopped frequently to look up at me, and then back towards the path that meant home. I urged her on.

As we trudged up the mountain, Stopelli was slow and clumsy. The cold, thin air bothered him, as I knew it would, and his breathing was laboured. I tried not to care as I pushed him forward and upwards. David was a natural sportsman and his long legs covered the distance as quickly and as sure-footedly as a trained athlete or mountain-goat. 'I have long wanted to climb mountains like this,' he shouted to me at one stage. 'I have spent too long in the desert, in classrooms and in hospitals, in the sun.'

'It hasn't done you any harm,' I mouthed against the rising wind, admiring his stamina and the straight back despite the punishing conditions. No wonder Annie loved him. My heart softened when I thought of her; my clever, gifted, lonely Annie. I prayed she would fully recover, in heart and body, and allow herself to fit in where she was loved, cared for, safe. Please God, let it be with me. I'd be happy to share her with David.

Stopelli doubled up and began to gasp for breath. 'You're going to kill me, aren't you? In cold blood ...'

'Why not? It didn't bother you when you ordered the killing of the Kendalls. Or when Annabelle Kendall was nearly killed last night. Don't ask me for sympathy, you criminal waste of air.' I doubt if he heard a word, and I knew it was dangerous to let my anger get the better of me. I had to remain disciplined, focussed, in control of the dangerous situation I had put us in.

David marched some distance ahead and waited for me to catch up. I saw again how hesitant Bonnie was, and how, for once, she was not enjoying this mission. She constantly stopped and looked back at the paths we had taken, as though wishing to be home. Probably with Annie. Stopelli dropped to the ground, panting and cursing. A searing wind had blown up, and we stopped under a sheltered ledge to rest. An hour later we had made little progress. The storm was getting wilder and I doubted if Stopelli could go much further. The damp cold and unremitting gale would creep into the marrow of his old bones. Good.

I glanced at David and saw him shivering. I felt a reluctant pity for these sun-saturated people who came from countries that knew only warmth. It had taken me years to get used to this kind of cold, and learn how to equip myself to combat it. I was the only one with skill and experience to survive on this mountain in the weather that engulfed us, and I felt no particular thrill at holding their lives, or deaths, in my hands. Strangely, I felt as though The Old Lady of Criach was waiting to see what I would do next; she certainly was helping with the foul weather, but she was capable of worse. I found another shelter and dug my ice-pick into the ground.

The snow was now falling lightly and the tracks beneath our feet were slippery and icing over. There was a silvery tinge to the mountains around us, and our breath condensed in front of our faces, despite our coverings. The temperature was dropping fast, but just for the moment we were out of the wind. From my pack, I took out a flask of hot coffee. It was a familiar gesture of comradeship, one that Andy and I had shared many times as we climbed together. Tonight was not such an occasion. My hand shook slightly as I handed the flask to David. Did he know I was on my favourite mountain, where I had spent many happy, hilarious, exciting hours with good companions? Where life was good? Where life was precious?

The rules of mountain rescue were inviolate: Andy had trained me, over long, exacting years, to save lives, not destroy them. I remembered how proud I was to be invited to join the regional rescue team, after years of gruelling instruction and encouragement from him and his mates. It had been a coup because I had to wait to be accepted, once I proved to hard-headed Scots mountain rescuers I could do the job as a trusted team-member.

'You are the leader, Duffy,' David breathed into my ear. 'But this man can't take much more.' His young eyes behind the balaclava and goggles were glowing from exertion, exhilarated and challenged. But he was cold and shivering, and perhaps wavering in his ability to keep going. He had no idea what I planned. Kill the man? Leave him here? Or frighten him? In truth, anger and craving for revenge had temporarily obliterated any rational thoughts. I wanted to harm this old man who had made my life a misery, but in that moment, looking into David's brown eyes, seeking my leadership and trusting my authority, I knew what I had to do.

Stopelli coughed and bent over, pleading with me to get him off the damned mountain. He cursed in Italian. Beneath his thick woollen hat and helmet, he looked grey and exhausted, and wouldn't last much longer. David sank down against a rock; he was beginning to flag.

'You're mad, Duffield. What's the point of killing me? You won't get away with it, and you'll only ruin your own life ... and his.' He pointed at David. 'Okay, you did put me away for fifteen years, and every day I thought about blowing you away ...' He coughed again. 'Just to amuse myself, to pass away the boring blasted hours. And when I got out, I only wanted to see what kind of life you had while I rotted away. Sure, I wanted to destroy you. Show you I still had the power to wreck your life, the way you wrecked mine.' I only heard snippets of what he was saying, as the wind whipped the hoarse and patchy words away, but I guessed much of what he raved about. Crude, malicious revenge. But what about my own revenge? Was that right?

'And what do you call poisoning a young kid? Another folly? Just another feel-good murder?' I grabbed his jacket, but David's restraining gesture was quick. 'A man in your condition wouldn't last five minutes on this mountain if I leave you. You could try and make it to the bottom, but your odds are poor. In fact, I'd say the chance of falling over the side of a cliff are pretty good. Broken back, broken legs, smashed head ... last year we found a bloke who had done just that ... with his brains in his helmet.' I turned to David and shrugged. 'Come on, time to go home.' Stopelli scrabbled to his feet, but I pushed him back on his haunches. 'But I haven't finished with you yet. Before we go, tell me how you managed your grubby deals from prison? Who helped you? Spill your guts, or I'll leave you here to freeze and rot.'

Stopelli was alarmed, but refused to speak. When I indicated to David that he and I should start our descent, he started blubbering and spewing out names and places. Mariella would have her story, and I bent down to listen carefully, to hear every word and memorise the names and places he was spitting out. Protected against the wind, I switched on the mini-recorder I carried in my jacket and pressed it close to his mouth. Eventually, he ran out of names, and energy. Repulsed, I put my arm out to help the old swine stand up, but I hadn't yet finished. I enjoyed seeing his terror and his desperation.

'How does it feel to feel frightened, to know you can be killed ... just like that?' I snapped my gloved fingers, my mouth unpleasantly close to his face so he would hear every word. 'To feel powerless? No, I won't kill you, you sad old piece of rubbish. Time will do that. I just wanted to see you to suffer. And break up your filthy business.'

My fury and craving for vengeance were spent; at that moment all I wanted was to get down off that mountain and be home with Annie and Bonnie. I wanted my old life back again, writing my stupid novels, fishing and bird-watching with Andy; climbing for pleasure, eating good food, and drinking fine whisky in Kenny's front bar. I wanted everything that was ordinary and safe. I wanted to save lives, not destroy them. I wanted Feddy close to me, in my bed. Above all else, I wanted Annie in my life and everything surrounding her to be good and decent. Uncomplicated, honest, safe. I wanted no more of this world of killing and plotting, of drugs and deals, and people who smirked as they planned your death or those you cared about. David put his hand on my shoulder, and signalled downwards. Yes, yes, I nodded, it was definitely time to get down off this mountain. Bonnie began to bark. What the hell was I doing, I thought. It was madness to think that the sins and horrors of the past could be wiped out in one night, by one act of revenge. I couldn't kill Stopelli. Why should I expect the Old Lady of Criach to do my dirty work? The game was over. My head was clear.

'Time to go,' I said. 'All of us.'

I heard shouts from below and I strained through the dark to locate the source, and saw two vague moving pin-points of light, torches, moving up the track we had taken. Whoever held those lights was making good time, even in the snow and wind, and there was only one person I knew who was that good. Andy Cameron. Bonnie barked wildly and ran towards the lights. I cupped my hands around my mouth and shouted down to him. He yelled back at me, and then appeared out of the swirling snow, almost unrecognisable in his layers of heavy clothing against the darkness. My torch begun to flicker.

'Your battery's running out,' he snapped as he came closer, indicating my fading torch. I always suspected that if Andy hit you, it would be like being struck by a sledgehammer, and I found out how true that was. He hammered me against a rock, his eyes blazing with anger.

'What the hell are you doing? For God's sake, get everyone down and safe.'

'I wanted to scare him. I wouldn't leave anyone ... yeah, I thought about it, but I couldn't do it when it came to the crunch ...' I shouted above the wind, but wasn't sure if Andy heard me, or believed me.

'Well, you cut it a bit fine.'

Andy's anger was fearsome, and when he released me and pushed me towards the downward track, Bonnie seemed relieved to turn and lead us home. Andy pulled Stopelli to his feet and wedged himself between him and me, but neither of us saw the quick movement of Stopelli's heavy boot as he kicked at Bonnie. She yelped in pain and surprise, and before we could stop him, he gave her another kick that sent her flying over the precipice. To this day her scream haunts me.

I doubt if Andy had ever heard the expletives that erupted from my mouth as I saw Bonnie lying lifeless twenty feet below us, her blood already staining the snow. In my panic to get to her, I moved without thinking, without care, too quickly, but Andy held me back. 'Careful, this way ... ' In the seconds before he unravelled the ropes around his waist, he turned to Stopelli and swung such a fierce blow that the old man lay flat on his back in the snow, groaning, blood seeping from his nose. Andy's voice was calm as he resumed untying ropes and shouted back to David, 'Help needed here!' He clipped ropes to my harness and dropped me over the ledge, easing me slowly downwards towards Bonnie.

She was alive, but bleeding from a jagged cut to her head above her left eye. She was wet and lifeless as I gathered her up and pushed her inside my jacket, zippering it up as best I could to keep her warm and secure as Andy and David pulled me up the cliff-face. Back on the path, I shook with shock and fury, but Andy kept me moving homewards. Only the sheer discipline of hard training and the desperate urge to get my dog to a vet moved my feet. Uncharacteristically, almost forgetting the rules of survival, I hurried, made mistakes and stumbled, and each time Andy corrected me and forced me to concentrate on moving with care. Stopelli was half-conscious, and was half-carried, half-dragged down the slopes. His face was a mess from Andy's blow. Staying close, Andy checked that David was alert and able to keep moving. I had known and worked with Andy for thirteen years, but I had never seen him so angrily concentrated on getting everyone down his mountain to safety as I did that night.

Andy's mood did not change when we reached ground level. His car was in the parking lot beside mine, and he roughly shoved Stopelli in the back seat with David and turned on the engine and the heater. 'I'll get you and David home with Bonnie, Duffy. Leave your car here and pick it up later. Main thing is to get this ... ' he looked at Stopelli in disgust, 'locked up, and Bonnie seen to.' He again looked at Stopelli, now unconscious with the exertions of the gruelling past few hours. His face was covered in blood. This was an Andy I did not know; every time I had seen him in action, sometimes under great provocation, he was calm, measured, reasonable, his Inverness accent never betraying anger. He had safely seen us down the mountain and treacherous conditions, but his anger was at boiling point, his face white with a rage he struggled to contain.

When we reached the cottage, Andy dropped David, Bonnie and

me off and then sped away with Stopelli towards the village. Inside, David took Bonnie from me and examined the wound on her head in front of the fire, and under the lights. He looked worried as he parted the fur and saw the extent of her injury. I could see white scraps of bone.

Mariella appeared to see what the commotion was about. She drew back and uttered an Italian swear word when she saw Bonnie's wet, blood-stained body, but quickly busied herself by finding blankets and boiling water. The rosary beads came out again as she stared at the inert bundle of black and white fur, the closed eyes and lolling tongue. With impressive efficiency, David and Ari put together hot water, disinfectant and cloths and bathed the ragged edges of skin and bone above Bonnie's eye. They glanced at each other. 'What?' I snapped, 'what is it? Will she live?' David said nothing, left the room and returned with a small pack, an emergency first-aid kid, and drew out a needle and what looked like fine string. He cut around the wound with scissors to remove as much fur as he could, then poured antiseptic over the gash.

'I have to do this, Duffy, to stop the bleeding. Look away, it will not be pretty. Perhaps you could hold her, in case she wakes up ... '

The dog I had grown to love lay motionless in my arms and I winced as each stitch pierced her flesh. Stay sleeping, I begged her, but please stay alive. When David finished, Mariella put a pot of coffee beside us, and some whisky, as we sat in front of the fire, Bonnie covered with her favourite rugs, a bandage over her head. We remained like that for the rest of the night, David checking her heart, me stroking her and whispering words only Bonnie understood. It was pale daylight when we saw the first indications of her awakening, of coming around from unconsciousness. Please God, let her live, I thought, again and again. What had a small dog to do all with this horror that's come to our island?

There was a movement from the stairs, and Mariella, David, Ari and I looked up to see Annie standing there, wrapped in a blanket.

Her face was white and questioning, but then it crumpled with distress when she saw the blood-stained bandages on Bonnie's head. Oh, no, she whispered. In a stride and dropping the blanket, she was on her knees and gently hugging the limp, furry body. No, no, no, not Bon Bon, she kept saying, her voice ragged with tears. Bonnie lifted her head slowly, and licked Annie's hand. On her knees, Annie turned to me, her arms outstretched. She held on to me as she cried convulsively, loudly, huge tears dropping from her face onto my shirt. I held her close and buried my face in her hair, feeling how tense she was, how convulsed with pain and grief. Bonnie struggled weakly to her feet and leant against us before she flopped back onto her basket.

'It's okay, Annie. Everything will be fine. Bonnie will be fine ... ' She sobbed as if her heart was breaking, and maybe it was. She cried for everything that had gone wrong in her life, and all the losses, betrayal and dishonesty she had known. For knowing that someone, whom she had never harmed in her life, had tried to kill her. For the father who had abandoned her. For my many failures that denied her a normal family life. The last straw would be losing a dog she'd come to love. 'You're safe, sweetheart, you're safe ...' I glanced at David, and he nodded. But of course, he said silently. She will always be safe with us. Annie bent her head over Bonnie and wept.

That was the sad, emotional scene that greeted Andy when he entered the cottage not long afterwards. He was still white-faced and tense, but purposeful. He dumped his boots and gear in the hall and bent over Bonnie, who raised a small wag at his presence, which made him smile slightly with relief. David gave him the thumbs up. 'The vet will be here soon,' Andy said, with a stifled catch in his voice, 'but is she okay?'

'Yes, Andy, but she needs antibiotics and an x-ray. I have done my best.'

'You're good lads,' he said. 'Stopelli is back in his cellar, this time with handcuffs and a guard outside the door. When the weather clears, Corky will take him back to the mainland, although the man doesn't look so healthy to me. I think he'll be in the hospital very soon. Bad heart and all that ... and I wouldn't be surprised if he's broken his jaw as well.' He let the words drift over us, unconcerned. Then he took the sobbing Annie and held her gently, his face a picture of raw tenderness and love.

'You're home, lassie. Cry all you want; you've got every reason. But you're safe with us. You're with family.'

* * *

*When you come out of this storm, you won't be the same person who walked in. That's what this storm's all about.*

*Kafka on the Shore,*
Haruki Murakami, 2002

# PART THREE
## TWO YEARS LATER

still look back on the spring of 1994 with a cold chill around my heart.

Bonnie survived, although for months afterwards she was slower than usual and hesitant about going up the mountains with Andy and me, but eventually her spirit and confidence returned. In my lighter moments, I accused her of spinning out her convalescence so she could continue to enjoy the finest steak the butcher had in his shop, but in truth I would have stolen sturgeon from the Queen if Bonnie wanted it. As she healed, she shared her time equally between me and Annie.

All our visitors returned home. Mariella flew back to Sydney to publish her story, and said she hoped we would meet again. 'Come and meet my family, Duffy,' she said. 'we're doing quite well these days.' David and Ari returned to Israel and what promises were made between David and Annie, I never knew, but suspected the problem of wrong countries, wrong religion, played heavily in their farewell. She was sad and dry-eyed as she waved David and Ari off on the ferry. I hugged them like sons and made them promise they would return for some decent mountaineering and hospitality. 'I owe you so much,' I told them, and they promised they would visit Criach again. Andy said he would keep his pledge to take them up The Old Lady of Criach, this time, he said, with a warning directed at me, 'the safe, proper way.'

Andy went back to bringing his tourists to Criach when the spring eventually arrived, and we saw a lot of each other at the cottage when he came to see Annie. He brought her wild flowers and heather from the glens, and the cassettes she ordered from an Inverness music shop. We had a brief awkward conversation about Stopelli and my madness on the mountain; it was important to me that he knew, in the end, I couldn't leave an old man to die on the mountain, no matter how tempting or how despised he was. I think he believed me. The subject was never raised again, nor was the question of him flattening Stopelli and breaking his jaw ('aw, come on, Duffy, he deserved it; ye cannie kick a wee dog').

I learnt that Andy understood the lure of revenge. With an uncharacteristic large whisky, and an expression of ineffable sadness on his face, he spoke, as he had never before, about losing his wife and child. Isabel was a fine athlete, a fit walker and climber, he began. The pregnancy was healthy, normal, until she was taken to hospital when she went into early labour and suffered complications. The doctor was late, and arrived drunk. Isabel died and the baby, Hamish, a day later.

'I knew black burning hatred. But the thing is,' he said in a quiet voice. 'The man wasn't fit for his job. The nurses told me it wasn't the first time he had come to work so drunk he couldn't do his job properly.' There was a long silence. 'But even though I made sure the man was struck off and never practised again, it didn't bring my family back. They were gone. I'd lost the only woman I'll ever love, and a wee soul who should be here with me today, climbing mountains.' His sigh was deep and painful. 'I hated every minute of it, all that publicity, the courts, the bad memories, but it was the right thing to do. I couldn't let that happen to anyone else.' The right thing to do: that was how Andy lived his life.

And I had to find the right thing to do about my daughter. . .

\* \* \*

Stopelli had been taken to Glasgow and charged with possession of a lethal drug with intent to harm, his face bearing the deep fingernail scratches left over from Mariella when in a crazed fury she attacked him as he stepped into a police vehicle; very little effort was made to stop her, just as I noted earlier that medical attention was slow to materialise to tend his broken jaw. His court case never came up because he collapsed in a Glasgow prison cell and was taken to hospital with pneumonia where he died alone a week later in a public ward. I was pleased to hear it. His body was never claimed, presumably because his terrified criminal network knew it was now unwise to associate themselves with their *patrone*. I was adamant he would not be buried in Scotland and suggested his body be delivered to the Italian Embassy in London, or even the Vatican. It mattered little to me, so long as his remains were far, far away from Criach and Scotland.

Armed with taped evidence, which was very poor quality, given the background noises, but mostly able to be transcribed – together with material found in Stopelli's suitcase still held at the Grand Central in Glasgow, including a notebook bulging with names, contacts, codes and dates – Mariella wrote her long 'sensational exclusive' piece for the *Sydney Mirror*. It was serialised over several days and secured her reputation as Sydney's top, best-paid, investigative crime journalist. She added names and information I had given her as background about the undercover crime problems in Sydney in the 1970s. Whether it provided solace or not, I have no idea, but amongst a swag of papers she found evidence of her husband's criminal 'disposal' which contradicted the coroner's report.

In her tight, journalistic style, but with some literary flourishes thrown in for effect, she described 'an idyllic Scottish island, so far hidden from crime and corruption as was possible to imagine until a former Sydney drug dealer and gaol-bird arrived with vengeance in his heart.' She described in detail the whole, sordid events of 1979 and the Kendall murders, and how, when released from prison, Stopelli vowed to continue his history of destruction and violence.

She outlined the gist of Ellery's legislation, blasted successive State governments for ignoring it, and appealed to the present government to take up unfinished business and honour the Kendall legacy. Of Annie she said nothing. Of me, she said only that I had retired from police work, and now only wrote novels about crime which were now televised and popular. 'But he still has the capacity to strike fear into criminals or those who threaten harm to his community or anyone he cares about.'

She won a top journalists' award for her investigative work, and Bob Connolly was unusually lyrical in his praise for her courage and the tough, no-nonsense stance she took in badgering the government into action. 'I know you hate the press, Duffy, but this one's working with us. She knows her stuff, although I suspect your paw prints are behind a lot of it.'

Mariella kept in touch with Andy when she left the island. When I dropped her off at Glasgow airport, she told me how much she was attracted to the taciturn Highlander. 'Imagine that,' she said, 'I never thought I could feel that way after my husband ....' What could I say? Probably what I should have said – but never would – to the many women who found Andy Cameron's simple charm irresistible, his company amusing and his protective nature endearing: what he once told me one Hogmanay, when sentimentality tugs at the stoutest Scottish male heart, 'I made a wedding vow once, laddie, and that'll do me fine for a lifetime.'

\* \* \*

During all the farewells, the taking of police statements, the transporting of people to the ferry or airport, the only person who mattered to me was Annie. She suffered some kind of quiet breakdown which was dreadful to watch. It began on the night when Bonnie was injured, whimpering in pain, and with Annie ill, inconsolable and weeping for hours. I'm not sure it was the right thing to do, given the trauma and deception Annie had so far endured, but Mariella took her aside and told her they were related; that she was, in fact, her aunt, her mother's sister. Annie's eyes turned huge with disbelief; there was no pleasure or excitement in hearing about her new-found aunt. 'So many lies,' she whispered. 'Lies, lies, when does it end?' She left Mariella and walked upstairs to her bedroom, and quietly shut the door. There was silence.

'Leave her be,' Andy said to me and David. 'There's only so much a soul can take.'

When she re-appeared some hours later, she asked everyone to leave. Just go home, she said, go back to where you belong and leave me alone. Her eyes and voice were flat, exhausted, and the expression on her face suggested that something very bleak and despairing was haunting her. David tried to talk to her, but she shook her head and pushed him aside. Firmly, Andy told everyone it was time to pack up and do as Annie wanted, to give her space and privacy. Thank you, Andy, were the only other words she uttered. As I was already home, I took comfort from not being so similarly dismissed.

Andy was the last to leave, and Annie wept against his shoulder while I stood by, helpless. In the silence that followed when he left, the house was cold and unfriendly; even Bonnie whimpered and tried to creep upstairs to be with Annie. I held her back, stroking her fur; I had two broken creatures in my home, both because of me.

In the days, weeks, months that followed, Annie remained pale and subdued and we rarely spoke beyond what was necessary. She had no energy or fight left, and an awful apathy took hold of her. Our only common interest and point of affection was Bonnie. Thankfully, Annie still had a good appetite and I liked cooking for her. I noted what she liked, and when all else failed, I fried up batches of chips which she ate with mounds of tomato sauce. She drank some wine and whisky, and slept a lot. The only time she half-smiled was when Bonnie lay across her lap, enjoying potato crisps and kisses.

As if to make up for the cruel winter and false spring, Criach turned on a rare gorgeous summer. The days were long, almost free of rain and very clear, the sky as blue as a blue-bell, the glens a lovely hazy heather purple. Tourists came and spent their money in the distillery, the village pub and shops, or camped, walked or climbed. The mountains still kept their ring of snow at the apex, but they looked majestic and inviting. The Old Lady of Criach retained her granite-hard haughtiness. The old girl was so inviting in good weather that Andy and I and our team were often called out to retrieve idiots who underestimated her come-hither perils, or they had unwisely overestimated their stamina or skill. It was a risky combination, and no matter how often we cautioned the amateur climber – and sometimes even the not-so-amateur – there was always someone who chose risk over sound advice. To be fair, it wasn't hard to be deceived by the Old Lady's capricious nature. Neither Andy nor I ever took her for granted.

Annie had never shown any curiosity or interest in mountain rescue work, or asked why Andy and I sometimes disappeared for hours when the emergency call went up, or spent long days and nights on the mountains, laden with gear, battling hostile weather and conditions. Until, that is, I came home one July night after a long, difficult recovery. Bonnie and I were exhausted and dehydrated; she gulped water from her bowl, and I stood at the kitchen sink holding a large glass of cold water. I sensed Annie behind me. As I had learnt to do, I did not press her for conversation.

'Was it bad?'

'Yup.'

She didn't need to know it was a young Japanese couple on their honeymoon, or that the helicopter medical crew doubted the husband would recover from his wounds, or, if he did, he would be a paraplegic.

Annie would see it all on television later in the night, anyway; it was the sort of dramatic and emotive story the press thrived on, especially when summer news was slow. Andy and I had seen the young couple in the pub the day before, both diminutive figures, speaking very little English, and noted they were properly prepared with their brand-new designer mountain climbing gear and expensive cameras. To all our cautions they nodded enthusiastically if slightly non-comprehendingly. Andy and I could do no more; we glanced at each other and exchanged the same thought: inexperienced but keen to get as many photographs as they could to record their dream holiday. We figured they wouldn't venture too far or too high, but, two hours into their climb, they strayed into narrow pathways, and the man lost his footing when he stepped back to take a photograph of his wife against a steep cliff. He plunged backwards and down twenty feet onto a craggy stone boulder, landing on his back with no snow to cushion the fall. When I later restrained the woman as she cried hysterically into my jacket, it was like comforting a small child.

'You're tired,' Annie said. 'Let me make dinner.'

'To tell the truth, Annie, I'm knackered. A bath, and then bed.'

'I'll bring it up to you. Beans on toast okay?'

It was a welcome gesture from a girl who had barely spoken to me for weeks, and despite my bone tiredness and aching limbs, my spirits lifted. I kissed her lightly on the cheek as I left the kitchen, relieved that she didn't recoil or blast me with expletives. 'Thank you.' With that small kindness, my daughter was getting better. *We* were getting better together.

She never sang again at the pub, and whenever we had a meal there, despite Kenny's anguished protests and apologies, I made sure she drank only from bottles of beer or wine that were opened in front of us. I was desperate to keep her safe, but knew I had to curb my excessive and unwelcome over-protection. I wanted to give her everything she needed in order to recover. I opened a bank account in her name, with a credit card to be charged to me, then agonised every day knowing she now had the means to leave the island any time she wanted. When I saw her playing on the old, badly out-of-tune piano that had come with the cottage, I arranged for a piano tuner to come from Edinburgh to restore it as best he could. Although she said nothing, it pleased Annie. I watched her as she played, picking out tunes, often with Bonnie at her feet, but most often she sat outside in the garden playing her guitar, breaking off now and then to jot down notes in a scruffy exercise book she carried around with her. I assumed she was writing songs, but I observed the rules: I never asked, and she never told.

Apart from Andy, we had few visitors. Agnes from the village came every week to clean the cottage; she was a nice Highland soul who chatted, sang and hummed as she flicked her feather duster about the place, always with a nearby cup of tea. I noticed Annie was intrigued and often stopped to listen. One day she asked Agnes about her songs. Where had they come from?

'Och, I don't know, lass, it's just auld songs I heard as a wee girl.'

'They're nice. Will you teach me the words and melodies?'

Every week from then on, Annie followed Agnes around the cottage as she sang, jotting notes in her book, sometimes stopping for translations or meanings. It was strange to observe her being so polite, but it was heartening to see her interested in talking to another human, no matter what the topic. And this one clearly captivated her. When Agnes left, Annie spent hours at the piano or with her guitar, picking out the remembered tunes. Scribbling in her book; in a world of her own.

When the gorgeous weather continued, it was clear that Annie's wardrobe didn't extend to summer clothes. She came along with me one day on a shopping trip to Kilsney, darting in and out of various shops and re-appearing with bags of clothes. She bought a new leather collar for Bonnie, and had the tag inscripted, 'Bon Bon'. When she reached her credit card limit, she asked for my card. I didn't care about money, and urged her to buy whatever she needed or wanted. Anything to see her interested and looked after.

Some weeks following that expedition, and fully expecting a sharp rebuff, I asked if she wanted to travel to Glasgow with me for the book signing of my newly-published book. It was nothing more than a publicity stunt, an aspect I hated about my work, but I was under an obligation from my agent and publisher to undergo the ordeal of sitting in a Glasgow bookshop and signing books for those interested enough to buy a copy. There was usually a good turn-out, especially since earlier books had been turned into a television series, and the book-shop welcomed the publicity. As well, it could be a laugh, as most Glaswegians liked to have a 'wee bit blether' when they were in the shop. Nonetheless, I was always glad to return home, having talked more in one day than I normally would in a week.

Annie considered the prospect of a long car journey with me, and possibly an overnight stay, then said, okay, but not with any great enthusiasm. She had no intention, she stressed, of standing in line to see me sign a book and write some stupid, meaningless comment on the inside. But yes, she would like to get to the Glasgow music shops and summer sales. We left very early, leaving Bonnie with Old Fergus, and barely exchanged a word until we reached the city centre. There, she effortlessly slid amongst the friendly crowd, and was soon chatting to shoppers, or women in the sweetie shops in a broad Glasgow accent that matched their own. I also saw how she slipped notes and food to beggars in the street, and stayed behind to chat to them when I moved on.

Late in the afternoon, my obligations fulfilled, we caught up for a drink at the Grand Central. I didn't mention that I had spotted her peering in the window of the bookshop earlier that day. Or that when

I next looked up, she had vanished. Now, in the hotel's upstairs, over-priced, cocktail lounge we watched in silence the activity below on the train station's concourse: the busy flower and gift shops, the food outlets crammed with customers, the timetables flashing up on broad screens, passengers setting off with suitcases on their way to summer holidays, or returning home with nary a tan or money in their wallets. There were some American and European tourists, but most were local commuters returning from work, heads down. Maybe they'd slip into a pub for a quick beer before they headed home.

Annie and I watched in companionable silence, glasses in hand, until a sharp burst of laughter from a nearby table caught our attention. A group of pretty city girls, one with some kind of frilly tulle and tiara affair clipped to her hair, was drinking champagne and coloured cock-tails decorated with tiny paper umbrellas; they were loud and happily drunk, obviously celebrating the upcoming wedding of one of their group. From time to time, they glanced over at Annie and me, and whispered together. Not being entirely discreet or quiet about their curiosity, they clearly wondered what our relationship was. I wanted to boast that this lovely girl with the long dark hair, in the ragged jeans and denim jacket, was my daughter.

Watching the girls and their easy companionship made me think about something that had often crossed my mind, but had not dared to raise with Annie. Why did she never talk about friends in Sydney? On our second drink, I put this to her. Unsurprisingly, she shrugged, and deliberately and noisily slurped her kir royale through a straw. I waited, not expecting a response, and was surprised when she eventually began to talk.

'Nuh. Not big on friends. Either they called me names at school or sucked up to me because I was rich and they wanted something. Mostly they were stuck-up private school girls, groomed for marriage and rich husbands. Not my bag. I preferred to be alone, not bother with them.'

I reminded her about the 'bad crowd' Coralyn mentioned in her letter. Again the shrug. 'Did it mainly to annoy Grannie. They were fun at first, but, honestly, all they did was copy someone else's cults and fads. Boring. Not an original thought among them.'

'No friends at all?'

'Well … ' She stopped suddenly, and that ended that conversation. I knew she was lying, but who, and where, were her friends? People who cared about her? Those who would be worried that she had, to all intents and purposes, just disappeared? She neither wrote nor received letters, not even from David. Experience told me it was pointless to pursue the issue.

The young women at the next table were now on their third bottle of champagne and rounds of cocktails and the laughter level was rising to raucous. The girl with the mock tiara nearly fell off her seat as she leant across and asked, in a broad Glasgow accent, if we were celebrating something special.

It took but a second. Annie leant towards the girls, and in the same broad accent whispered confidentially, 'It's my grandpa's birthday, and matron's let him out for the day for a wee treat.'

Smiling the sweetest smile I had ever seen from her, Annie raised her glass in my direction. The girls shrieked with laughter. He's nae bad for an auld man, the tiara girl quipped, and Annie joined in their hilarity, snorting with amusement. The noise was such that any response from me would be unheard. In any case, what else could I do but roll my eyes and pretend offence? Annie beckoned the waiter and ordered drinks for everyone on her grandpa's tab, her shoulders still shaking with laughter.

Nothing was said about the incident on the drive home – we decided to return home that night, as it was still light – and I didn't interrupt her while she listened to music on her earphones, shopping bags and music tapes jumbled around her feet. Unexpectedly, she began to chat as we neared home and the waiting ferry. 'Glasgow's a great, gritty town,' she said. 'I love it. You always get a laugh. D'you know, of all the places I busked, Glasgow was the most generous?' It can be tough town, I wanted to say, remembering my early days with Grannie McPhedron and my epic drinking in city bars, but I didn't want to disrupt the unaccustomed friendliness. 'You really nail that Inspector Galvanney in your books, you know.' After a moment's silence, she added, 'He's *dead* Glaswegian.' I could have purred with pride at such unexpected praise from a girl who professed never to have read my books, but I said nothing apart from a muttered thanks. 'Yeah, you're not bad,' she murmured thoughtfully, then fell asleep.

Some days after our shopping trip to Glasgow she joined me in the garden as I chopped wood. It was a task I liked, and it kept me fit. Annie sat with Bonnie on the old wooden bench and watched me sweat, shading her eyes against the sun, her long tanned legs stretched out in front of her. Her pencil and notebook were nearby, but she seemed distracted by something beyond her own musical musings. I waited for her to speak, not breaking my rhythm as I splintered the wood and made a neat pile. Following the rules, she had to be the one to break the silence.

'You know women flirt with you, don't you?'

'Never noticed.'

'They do. Those girls in Glasgow were dying to crack on to you. I heard what they were saying: good-looking guy, no wedding ring, and all that. It's the same everywhere we go. The women in the village fuss over you, and want to marry you off to their daughters. You never respond. Why is that? Devoted to your Feddy?'

'I never think about it. But yes, I am fond of Feddy.'

I wasn't being honest with her. Of course I knew when women flirted with me. I'd always noticed details about people. It made me a good detective. But I never wanted any other woman when Anna

222

Maria was alive, and after her death I closed my heart to any romantic entanglement. Years ago, Feddy had caught me off-guard when I was in London to sign over the television rights to my books; she was gorgeous, vivacious, interested in my work, and I was excited, slightly drunk and unexpectedly flush with cash. I allowed myself to be flattered, taken to dinner and eventually to her flash Kensington bedroom. Afterwards, I felt guilty and ashamed and fled home immediately afterwards to the safety of Criach. I felt unfaithful to Anna Maria, and I willed away the uncomfortable self-disgust by furiously writing, editing, or chopping wood. It was good that as soon as I was home, I was called out to find a missing a wee girl who had strayed from her tourist parents. It wasn't difficult, but it took my mind off London. Andy asked about my trip, and I just nodded. We never raised the subject again. .

When Feddy rang a month later with the implausible pretext of 'being near' the Scottish border on some kind of business, I felt very uncomfortable. She had some ideas about promoting my new book and the later television series, she said, but I brushed her off. It was ungracious, I know, but I still felt a cad after our liaison in London and my hasty retreat with the crudest of farewells. No, I knew I couldn't face her. Even then I knew she wanted more from me than I could offer.

Undeterred, she rang again two months later. This time she was more blunt; she was in London and had been re-reading my books and enjoying them. Perhaps she could drive up and spend the weekend in Criach, getting to familiarise herself with the Scottish background? She promised not to be a nuisance, but needed to get to know the author and his world before she worked with the publishers and the television people. I wasn't keen, but wasn't sure how I could dissuade her. Publicity and women were far beyond my range of comfort. I promised to think about it, but an insistent phone call from my agent and the television people a few days later made me realise there was no way I could refuse. I booked Feddy a room at the pub, but when I met her at the ferry with her glamorous clothes and expensive luggage, it was clear she had no intention of staying in a country pub without an ensuite and five star facilities.

My cottage hardly boasted a five-star rating, but Feddy seemed delighted with it. 'This is very romantic,' she said. Bonnie was polite, but reserved. It was late afternoon, and the lamps and open fires had worked their cosy magic on a dull, misty day.

'Wait for the winter,' I warned.

'I look forward to it,' she said, with a smile I could only describe as 'winsome'.

For three days, she filled my cottage with unaccustomed laughter, perfume and the wonderful food she brought from London and prepared with little fuss on the old stove. She appeared to be genuinely interested in the Highland life and my books, and by the second evening it seemed churlish to turn her away from my bedroom. The following morning, when she pressed the issue of me coming to London to stay with her, I had to tell her as gently as I could that I was a solitary creature with nothing to offer a woman like her. I meant it then, and repeated it every time afterwards when she came to visit. I was so sure of myself, but not so much now.

So yes, Annie, I wanted to say, of course I notice women. But, apart from Feddy, that is as far as it goes. She was silent for a while, as though considering something that puzzled her, and watched as I stood up and stretched my back.

'You're not a shagger, then?' It was a statement, not a question.

'No, Annie, I'm not. Never have been.'

She gave a kind of harrumph, and went inside to put the kettle on. She came out a few minutes later with two mugs of tea, chocolate biscuits gripped between her teeth. As she handed the tea to me, she muttered, 'Yeah, I sorta understand now.' I wasn't quite sure what she meant, but felt it might have been another small victory. The rest of the afternoon was spent in mutual silence.

But it was Andy who worked the miracle and brought the life and love back into that girl's heart and mind. She watched us go off to the mountains for work, or simply for a day of climbing and trekking fun, and never questioned why we did it, or what propelled us to put our lives at risk. It was a particularly lovely sunny day when Andy suggested to her that she might care to join us on an easy walk up The Old Lady. I said nothing, and kept in the background. At first, she shook her head, but then after a few moments' thought, nodded, and went off to find her boots.

She was now physically fit and strong, and strode alongside us, with Andy typically watching his protégé carefully, but deliberately not offering assistance so as to let her find her own rhythm and capability. When we stopped to rest, he chose a safe ledge where we could look down on the most beautiful part of the island and beyond; just as I had done those many years ago when I saw the view for the first time, Annie took a deep breath in wonder at how high we were, how superbly majestic the mountains around us looked, from a distance how peaceful the glens and streams were, how tiny the houses and barns, the sheep and cattle mere white and brown dots, with the sea and mainland beyond a vague hazy blue outline in the distance. We were but mites on the back of a giant. She drank the coffee, ate the sandwiches, said nothing, and stared below as though in a trance or a reverie that excluded everyone around her. I knew the feeling.

That began our shared love of the mountains. I bought her the best equipment available, and she often joined Andy and me on the slopes, proving to be courageous with heights and a quick learner. Neither Andy nor I let her become too adventurous, but we approved of how she learnt to become a team member, taking a hand when it was offered in help, or offering her own where it was needed. Her body, always lithe, became tough and streamlined, and her olive skin even browner.

She learnt to joke with us on the slopes, and the day she made it to the top of The Old Lady, sweaty, grubby, and jumping for joy at her achievement, she turned and hugged Andy, and then, with perhaps the slightest hesitation, flung her arms around me.

Only very occasionally, usually after dinner and over a few glasses of wine, she talked about her life in Sydney. She loved Grannie Coralyn, she said, but she was always strict and too protective, which was fine when she was younger, but when she got older, she felt trapped. And there was no way out, no-one to talk to. So much was expected of her. So much was assumed. 'So, like Feddy, I rebelled.' The Kendall family she dismissed with a sneer. 'I knew there was something different about me. The kids at school whispered behind my back and called me Orphan Annie; some didn't like me because my skin was different from theirs, and called me other names ... ' She sighed. 'And mostly they all had mothers and fathers who came along to prize nights and recitals and things. Grannie always came, of course, but more as a duty. She was treated like a duchess because the school needed her donations. Sometimes my nanny would come ... but that wasn't the same. In fact, it was worse. I just felt so *different*.'

'Do you remember anything about your mother?' I asked her once. She thought for a while, staring ahead and out at the garden with its flowers and cabbages, as though she was conjuring up as many scraps and bits of baby memories as she could. Her mind was tumbling around and reaching out for those memories.

'I remember her perfume, how her skin felt and smelt. How pretty she looked when she came to say goodnight before going out somewhere. How she hugged. All shiny and smiley and noisy. Yeah, I remember her laughing and singing ... ' There were tears in her eyes, and if she had been looking in my direction, she would have seen a shine in mine. 'I don't have any photographs of us together. Grannie Coralyn had lots of her and Ellery together, all dressed up for some posh ditzy ball or party ... '

'I have photographs,' I said impulsively. 'Would you like to see them?'

For the next hour or so I showed her the snaps I had of Anna Maria, some of us together when we had asked some stranger to capture us as a couple, arms around each other, laughing, kissing, horsing around, casually dressed in bathers or shorts; sometimes she stood alone, laughing, in short sun dresses with halter tops. Annie studied them carefully and handed them back with a sad smile.

'She was lovely. And she looks like great fun. You look good together. It must have been awful to lose her. I mean, first to Ellery and then ...'

'It was more than awful to lose her, Annie. She was my life.'

'Still is, I think. After all these years, you've built a shrine around her memory. And you've cut yourself off from everything, and I don't mean physically. Criach is fabulous, but I've seen how you distance yourself from people. You don't let anyone get close, apart from Andy, and poor old Feddy ...'

'I don't want to distance myself from you, Annie.'

'You managed it well enough for eighteen years,' she snapped, and I winced. 'But that's old news. Feddy deserves more.'

'Of course she does. But I have never led her on. The truth is, it's hard to forget your mother, Annie, and what she meant to me. Or how life could have been different for the three of us.'

'You know what, James ...' It was the first time she had used my name. How did she know that was what Anna Maria always called me? 'Shrines are meant for the dead, not the living.' Her voice was quiet, but emphatic.

I gathered up the photographs and left her. We were on shaky ground, and I didn't want to lose any of the tentative good feelings built up over the past weeks. But of course she was right. Apart from Andy and Grannie McPhedron, I hadn't let anyone into my life since Anna Maria's death. Feddy put up with the fragments I offered, and

I knew it was cruel and selfish.

Annie followed me into my bedroom while I locked away the photographs alongside Anna Maria's old perfume bottle and Ellery's book of war-time poems.

'I'm sorry if that hurt.'

'That's OK. What would you like for dinner?'

'Don't change the subject. You know, that night when I was on the ferry going to hospital ...' She closed her eyes as if to either conjure the image, or block it from memory. 'I heard my mother's voice, very clearly ... she had a slight accent. Stay with your father, she said, over and over again. Stay with James. Look after him. Please, for me ...'

'I'll take Bonnie for a walk, and then get dinner going,' I said, in a voice that sounded vaguely like my own.      We never returned to that conversation.

As July went into August, Annie spent more days away from the cottage. She took long walks with Bonnie around the island, stopping at farms to talk to the crofters and fishermen. She easily made friends, for she was young and pretty, loved animals and keen to help out with chores wherever she went. Everyone remembered the plucky young singer who nearly died on their island, and in their gruff way, the Criach people wanted to atone for what they saw as an affront to their Scottish hospitality. She rode their horses, and was often seen galloping along the beach, hair flying behind her, with Bonnie racing alongside and looking every bit as happy as the rider. Sometimes she packed sandwiches and a flask, and spent the day on the beach, swimming in the safer, shallower parts of the still-freezing ocean, returning home tired, sun-burnt and starving.

Often she spent time with Old Hughie on his ferry, helping to collect fares and learning how to handle both the eccentric old vessel and its master. She discovered in him a gold-mine of myths, legends and stories about the island because neither he, nor his predecessors, had ever left it. Annie came home with her exercise book damp and crumpled, but she looked satisfied with her day's activities, even if it was full of stories of 'pushy tourists', most of whom she wished would fall overboard and never be rescued. Somehow, she always knew when Andy was due to visit. She waited at the jetty for him, and blew kisses as the ferry neared land.

But relations between us were still strained. I worried about the lack of young people on the island. Young Lachlan with the clapped-out motor cycle pestered her with invitations of day trips to the mainland or nearby islands, but he came up against a cold block of ice. Poor, lazy Lachlan had little to occupy him and persisted in slicking back his hair and pretending to be Marlon Brando from the film *The Wild One*, or a spiv, although his only dare-devil exploit to date was skiving off without paying Kenny for a beer in the pub. Whenever Annie heard his motorbike struggling up the road, she yelled, 'Quick, quick, tell him I'm not here.'

'I'm not telling lies, Annie,' I would shout back at her disappearing back. I felt sorry for Lachlan, for I knew from my experience with bored Sydney and Glasgow kids how they could slide off into bad habits and dangerous company if not kept busy. 'Find a job, Lockie, or help your dad with the sheep and fencing,' I told him once.

'D'ye reckon Annie would be impressed, like?'

'Probably not, but your father would be.'

The long summer days went by peacefully enough. I taught Annie to drive properly, and for fun we competed to see who jogged the fastest and longest along the coastline. She was mischievous and playful when the mood struck her, as I found out when I sat down at my computer to complete a chapter about Galvanney's exploits, to find she had been there before me, changing the plot to have the tough but prudish Presbyterian Glasgow detective dancing in night clubs with exotic young pole-dancers and with a vocabulary to bring a blush to a

Glasgow dock-worker. 'Oh, no, Annie, not the pole-dancing again!' I would roar with confected rage. As I deleted her text, I could hear the chuckles upstairs.

These moments were few and far between. I constantly asked Andy if we should do more for her, but he was adamant that only time and kindness would restore her confidence and faith in the human race again. No more strangers in her life, he insisted. No professional meddlers. But, he assured me, I was doing a good job. Look how far she has come. I wasn't so sure, but it certainly wasn't for the lack of trying or care on my part.

Despite her work on the farms, her fondness for animals, the long walks with Bonnie, and the occasional joke at my expense, I knew Annie remained inwardly troubled by doubts and nightmares I couldn't make disappear. The worst times were when she was scared and relived the horror of the night she sang in the pub, or when she had asthma attacks. Many nights Bonnie and I sat with her downstairs when she was reluctant to climb the stairs to her bedroom, and I lit every lamp and made us late-night suppers of hot chocolate and toasted cheese sandwiches.

Those nights were long, and becoming less often. We often didn't speak until the sky lightened and her fears subsided. There were times when she slipped into sleep on the sofa, Bonnie's head on her lap, the pair of them snoring in unison. Seeing her face in repose, the likeness to her mother was stark, and my thoughts strayed to Sydney days. Perhaps that is why, as I watched her sleep, my own exhaustion eventually drifting into slumber, I had the strangest, most comforting feeling that Anna Maria was close, holding us fast in her embrace. Good God, I thought, I have lived too long in Scotland; I'm as bad as the villagers with their myths, spirits and 'ghosties'. But it was a world where I liked to linger.

I was astonished to receive a letter one day from Sydney lawyers, saying they acted for the estate of the late Mrs Coralyn Kendall and advising that I was a beneficiary of her will – with the proviso that it be used to assist in the care of her granddaughter, Annabelle Louisa Kendall – and if I cared to get in touch with them, with proof of identity, they would forward a cheque to a Scottish bank of my choosing. That night over dinner, I mentioned this to Annie. She shrugged and dismissed the subject as being of no importance or interest to her. But a matter that *was* of concern to her – or should have been – was her own substantial inheritance, particularly now with Coralyn's death, and I asked her what she intended to do about it. Again she shrugged, and dipped her chips in a pool of tomato sauce.

'Why? Sick of paying my bills?' she snapped nastily. We were back where we started, but this time I couldn't remain silent. I was hurt and very angry. Apart from the incident with my dented car, I had never lost patience with her. Nor had I, by word or deed, given any indication that I begrudged her anything, whether it was money, possessions or my time. I wouldn't let this go unchallenged.

'That was uncalled for, Annie,' I said quietly, but there was a hard edge to my voice, and no mistaking my fury. To her credit, she looked ashamed and blinked uncomfortably. After a few moments of strained silence, she lifted her head and looked directly at me. Her cheeks were flushed pink with shame or embarrassment, and there was a trace of tears in her eyes.

'I apologise. You're right, it was wrong of me to say that. I didn't mean it. You have been ... good to me. I'm very sorry, James.' She gulped. 'Will you forgive me?' '

'Of course.'

I let the conversation go, and vowed never to raise the subject of her inheritance again. It was Annie who brought it up some weeks later. Since the night of our tiff she had been deep in thought and moody about something, but I knew better than to pry. Andy, on the other hand, whisked her away for lunch in the village one day and brought her back very late in the afternoon, both obviously having had a fine time drinking and talking about matters that excluded me. I didn't mind; when she came home, Annie seemed more settled. Resolute, I thought. But about what? I didn't have to wait long to find out.

'I've decided to go back to Australia,' she told me the next morning at breakfast, fondling Bonnie and feeding her toast. My heart sank. 'You're right, I must sort out this inheritance business once and for all. I'll have to risk getting arrested for the shop-lifting caper. Honestly, it was just a couple of hundred dollars from Coralyn's purse, and a few crappy clothes from a shop I probably own anyway.'

I wondered how she felt about going back to Australia: was she pleased to return home, or glad to leave Criach? Whatever it was, I couldn't hold her back. She was spirited and confident, physically strong, and the bouts of asthma and anxiety had lessened after she took up rock and mountain climbing. I looked at her now; she was tanned and healthy, her skin and hair glowing. She still drank but, like me, for pleasure. Was I about to lose her, now? Now that we had formed a kind of bond? Or was I kidding myself that our months together meant anything to her?

'The shop-lifting charge has been lifted,' I said. 'but Bonnie will miss you. Where will you stay?' There was the usual shrug in response. 'You don't like your cousins.'

'Hate them.' She pretended to study the garden outside the window for what seemed like ages, and then said in a small, hesitant voice, 'Will you come with me?'

I was so astonished I dropped some cutlery on the floor. Of course I would go with her, not, I rushed to tell her, that I could take part in discussions about her inheritance, but I would make sure she had the best lawyers in Sydney to protect her interests. My mind raced. Bonnie had to be billeted with Andy, but neither would mind. Money: the lawyer from Sydney had verified that Coralyn left me $250,000 which was now deposited in the Bank of Scotland in Glasgow; that had made me look carefully at the state of my finances to discover I was, well, if not wealthy, certainly not skint. Money for the first time in my life was no problem. In fact, even without Coralyn's benevolence, good old Inspector Galvanney had fattened my wallet nicely.

'When do you plan on leaving, Annie?'

'Soon. Let's get the bloody thing over and done with.'

I couldn't contain my joy – there was no other word–at these developments and I whistled as I got ready for bed that night. I explained to Bonnie that I would have to leave her for a longer time than usual, but for good reasons. Her eyes never left mine for a moment, and I think that, while her ears sagged, she licked my hands to indicate she understood and was pleased for me.

\* \* \*

Annie didn't believe in hanging about once she made a decision. Within three weeks of her deciding to return to Australia, we stood together on the jetty with our suitcases and waited for Old Hughie to set sail on the first leg of our long journey. Andy came to say goodbye with Bonnie at his side, who struggled against her lead, so rarely had it been used. He was forced to clip it on when she desperately tried to follow me onto the ferry. She whined, barked and struggled, and I had to harden my heart against her misery. Andy hugged Annie hard and wished her safe journey. 'You do what you planned, lassie, and it'll all work out the way you want. God speed, both of you.' He turned and gave me one of his big, hard bear-hugs. 'Well done, lad,' he whispered.

We stood on the deck and waved goodbye to Andy and Bonnie as the old ferry ploughed its way through the blue, choppy sea. I heard Bonnie barking long after we left the shore. To take my mind off that separation, I asked Annie a question that had bothered me since she made her decision to return to Sydney.

'Why do you want me to come with you, Annie?'

She slipped her arm through mine and pressed in close. I smelt the youthful scent of good health, light perfume and shampoo as her hair whipped across my face. Underneath her coat, she felt firm and strong, and as she looked up at me, her dark eyes danced with fun, the beginning of a dazzling smile against her tanned face. So many times she tormented me with her striking resemblance to Anna Maria, but at that moment she was Annabelle, our daughter. She was her own person, a precious individual, certainly no replica of her mother. I raised my eyebrows, waiting for her reply.

'I like having a dad,' she said, and after a moment's teasing hesitating, added mischievously, 'I like having *you* as my dad.'

At that moment, I probably wouldn't have needed a Jumbo jet to take us to Australia. I felt I could fly there unaided, without wings. I kissed her cheek.

'Not as much as I like having you as my daughter.'

* * *

Bob Connelly met us at Sydney airport and hurried us through passport control and customs. He looked heavier, older, but more in command than I had ever seen him. High rank and authority suited him. As arranged, Annie returned to her grandmother's apartment in Elizabeth Bay, which had been kept open and cared for by the old husband-and-wife retainers who acted as housekeepers to Coralyn. It now belonged to Annie, together with a portfolio of properties at this stage she could only guess at. I watched her disappear behind the apartment's security doors and knew she was struggling with memories. But I couldn't help her with this; I wanted to be with her, but I knew only she could tackle her old demons and those familiar surroundings that held no particular warmth for her. I had no place in that world.

Bob dropped me off at a nearby serviced flat he had rented for me and I waited for the inevitable telephone call. Within an hour, and as I anticipated, Annie rang, her voice slightly shaky, and asked me to come and collect her. I caught a taxi and was there within ten minutes. She was standing outside the apartment.

'It's just too much,' she whispered, as she stepped into the taxi and sat close to me. 'I wish I was with you. Grannie's gone, but nothing's changed. Not a thing. It's all so ... sad.'

'What do you want to do?'

Food, as always, came to our rescue. She directed me to a favourite seafood restaurant overlooking the harbour, and we sat under coloured umbrellas while I ordered the wine she liked. She was quiet and reflective, but soon perked up when the wine and food arrived. She began to laugh when I described the run-down flat Bob had rented for me. Knobs fell off things, and nothing worked.

'We'll find you something better, James,' she said, "as posh as you like.' As she tossed back her head and laughed, I could not help but wonder if Criach had lost her to Sydney. The late afternoon air was warm, the restaurant busy and vibrant, the seafood good, the wine cold and the service fast, friendly and casual. Music played in the background. We were surrounded by tourists and a mixture of accents and languages, there were sober-suited city office types alongside well-dressed women with diet salads and bottles of sweet white wine. Together, we looked beyond the dazzling blue harbour with its ferries and pleasure boats going about their business, the Bridge and the never-ending lines of cars, and I saw the fatigue and anxiety slipping away from Annie. She was home now in familiar surroundings, and I saw her confidence returning.

I had to admit it was good to be back in Sydney, exhilarating. I remembered how the city always throbbed with life and a holiday atmosphere. The push and shove of pedestrians, the tourists and commuters at the ferry terminals, the cafés and restaurants filled with noisy patrons. The sun shone, the people smiled. My mobile phone worked. My clothes were light and comfortable. After so many years of semi-solitude, used to the soft, musical lilt of the Highlanders, I found at first the noise and clatter of crowded spaces unsettling, but soon surrendered to the sun and sound of people enjoying themselves. I let it, and Annie's chatter, wrap around me.

I dropped Annie back at the Kendall apartment, and she promised she could endure staying there until she found her own home. I knew she would be fine; she was strong and resilient and after a good sleep would be ready to tackle whatever lay in front of her. If not, I was nearby. I yawned; a good sleep was needed all round.

Late next morning, Bob met us in the foyer of a smart international city hotel and ran through the arrangements made to finalise Annie's legal business. True to his word, he had contacted Coralyn's family lawyers on Annie's behalf and negotiated appointments to meet them and to finalise her affairs. I was uncomfortable about hearing any aspect of Annie's inheritance, but she insisted I stay and listen. 'Mrs Kendall – Coralyn – had the best lawyers in town,' Bob said over his fourth coffee of the day, 'pricey, but they say it's not a complicated affair; Annie's legacy from her parents and grandmother was left in a trust fund until she turned eighteen, which she is now, and therefore able to claim it in its entirety, including her mother's jewellery which is held in a bank safe. I doubt the Kendall family – particularly the cousins – have grounds to contest the will, but you never know. Anyway, Annie, you'll be in good hands.'

Despite Bob's optimism, the legalities took much longer than expected. Not that there were complications, I gathered, or any objections from the Kendalls thus far, but the estates were complex and wide-ranging. I never enquired into the extent of the wealth or properties, but could hazard a guess. It was substantial. Annie was always busy during the day, but when we met up at night for a meal, she talked about everything except what she and her lawyers had agreed that day. That was the way I liked it.

I had a lot of free time while Annie was busy, and caught up with old police mates. I joked and drank with them, and shared their jubilation that the old Police Commissioner was gone and replaced by someone younger, less bureaucratic, and who had fought his way up to leadership from cadetship and the rough, rowdy Sydney streets. A good bloke, it was declared. But it should've been you, they decided. I ignored the comment and ordered another round.

They were different guys now, I thought. They were in senior ranks and serious about their work, carefully monitoring their beer intake. They were curious about the lack of police presence around my islands. No need, I told them. They were good-naturedly interested in my life in Scotland and keen to let me know they had either read the books, or seen the Galvanney television series. 'Big shot now, eh, mate?' one said as he punched me on the chest. 'Good on you, mate!. You'd be good for a few quid, eh?' It felt good to be back in their easy, bantering company, but their interest soon turned to what they liked and knew best: police work and cracking crime. 'Hey, great story from that Mariella Ridge woman in the *Sydney Mirror*. About time Stopelli and his gang got busted for good. Jesus, mate, that must have brought back a memory or two. How'd she get him to talk? Deathbed confessions, maybe?' I shrugged. Who knows? Probably. Maybe. I teased them about how easy their jobs were now, what with computers, DNA, CCTV footage, mobile phones. Not like the old days, I said, when we ran about looking for public phone boxes, typing with carbon copies on clapped-out typewriters, and got by on instinct, plain dogged coppering. And luck. With maybe a bit of physical persuasion thrown in.

It was only when Bob and I were alone did I tell him how I had bailed Stopelli up the mountain and was tempted to kill the vicious old thug, but couldn't. How I wanted to make him suffer. How fear and a temperature below freezing had done the job for me, because I knew he would soon die of pneumonia or complications from an existing heart condition. Bob cringed when I described how he had kicked Bonnie off the cliff, and she nearly died. As always, he listened quietly, nodding, hand wrapped around a glass of beer. 'Good work, boss,' he said. 'glad the bastard's off this mortal coil. Bit of help from you didn't hurt, neither.'

I found the days long, sunny and pleasant, but there were tasks I wasn't looking forward to. Before I left Scotland, my agent had arranged for me to promote my books, and I now faced a line-up of radio, newspaper and television interviews. I didn't want to go anywhere near the media, but as it was part of my contract there was no option but to turn up and answer questions about Criach, my 'productive process' – I sat down at my desk and wrote, I replied – and had I ever imagined a cranky old Glasgow police character would capture such popularity overseas? No, was the simple reply to that. One television interviewer introduced me as the policeman who had botched the Kendall security and fled the country for the wilds and safety of Scotland, and I seethed with fury. With difficulty, through clenched teeth, I answered the questions about my books, but when he returned to the Kendalls and the viciousness of the crime, I snapped. Nothing to say. All over. Leave the Kendall family in peace. When the television lights went out, I sprang out my chair.

'Try that again, mate, and you'll be sorry,' I said, and stormed out the studio, scrubbing at the filthy make-up off my face.

To calm down, I headed for a nearby pub. God, I missed Criach. If it hadn't been for Annie, I would have left that afternoon. So far, even though journalists had twigged to the fact that Annabelle Kendall was back in Sydney to claim the Kendall fortune, 'after a long overseas holiday', she managed to avoid press intrusion. I suspected Bob's firm but friendly hand behind her unavailability. When I was with her, I kept an eye on who came near her, although I learnt early that she was more than capable of looking after herself, and not shy in deploying a blistering vocabulary.

One day during a lull in her legal 'conferences', Annie surprised me by announcing she wanted to meet the Peroni family. I admitted I too was curious, and remembered Mariella's invitation to visit them. I had seen jars of their tomato sauces displayed in supermarkets and wondered if they were still operating without a licence from their ramshackle property. Not that it mattered to me. Annie insisted I go along with her and Mariella.

Annie didn't say what had piqued her interest in her mother's family, but I imagine being with lawyers all day discussing the Kendall family and her mother's charitable foundations, it was inevitable that Anna Maria would start to take shape and emerge from the shadows; hollow spaces would be filled in. Meeting the large Peroni family – her grandparents, aunts, uncles and cousins – was a significant factor in that process. It was a good decision, a brave one, although I wondered how the Peronis would respond to a granddaughter thought lost to them. How would Annie react to finding herself part of a large Italian family? And would they remember the policeman who had seduced their daughter, but didn't marry her?

With Mariella at the wheel of her sturdy SUV, we set out the next Saturday morning for the two-hour journey beyond the city and into the western suburbs. Annie seemed tense and said very little. I noticed with a tiny heart-skip that she wore a pair of gold hoop earrings with a diamond sparkle which had once belonged to her mother. I knew this, because they had been a present from me.

We sped along the Parramatta Road and Annie now began to ask questions about the Peroni family. Mariella was happy to answer, and for the rest of the journey she talked animatedly about the young Italian migrant couple who arrived in Sydney in the 1950s without money and only a few English words. They had no relatives for support and took any jobs they could find, saving every penny until they had enough to buy cheap land many, many miles from the centre of the city. At first they grew tomatoes and sold them by the side of the road. As good gardeners, they soon provided vegetables to local shops and restaurants and set up stalls in farmers' markets. Over the years, the business grew, as did their family. Seven children, Mariella exclaimed. 'Anna Maria was the youngest, and the prettiest, the favourite. She had to work in the gardens like all of us, but she was different. Always restless ...' There was a strained silence for a while, until she could take up the story again.

'Many migrants came to Australia, Greeks and Italians, and Australians were travelling overseas and returning home with new ideas about the world, about food, about different cultures. Multiculturalism was the buzz word. My parents borrowed money to buy more land to increase their plantings and employ more people. Tomatoes, olives, lemons, everywhere! Too many to sell on the side of the road, or flog to restaurants and markets, so we made sauce. Lots of it! Then we borrowed more money to build an industrial kitchen and equipment to cope with the volume and to turn out fancy labels. My God, my family worked! It paid off. The Peroni sauces–ha!–home-grown and 100 per cent Italian! – suddenly became very popular, and a great money-spinner.' Mariella laughed at the memory. 'We advertised the sauce as a "family secret" never to be divulged, but it's only tomatoes – grow 'em, boil 'em, bit of olive oil and whatever herbs you've got on hand, that's it ... dear God, how many years did I do that before I escaped to the city?'

With a slight falter in her voice, she said how good it was to show the world how her family had prospered in Australia through hard work, good decisions and obeying, well, most of the laws. 'Respect for us is important,' she said firmly, 'and we have that now. We worked together as a family, except for ... ' There was another uncomfortable silence, and she swallowed hard. She could say no more.

And then suddenly we were there. We turned off the main road and drove through an open ornamental gate and onto a wide, white-gravelled drive lined with olive trees. The Peroni family's prosperity was now on full display as their huge house, *La Dolce Vita*, came into view. I took a deep breath and watched Annie closely, and saw her eyes widen in amazement. We turned into another set of tall, electronically-secured wrought-iron gates, but not before I noted the expensive, sophisticated burglar-alarm systems. Before us was a sweeping, round lawn, around which olive and lemon trees flourished, interspersed with marble statues, fountains, and terracotta pots of herbs and flowers. Two large flag poles flew the Australian and Italian flags side by side. Annie blinked. I guess she had never seen anything quite so flashily ornamental. From the huge, two-storied house of red brick, red geraniums tumbled from every window. The effect was grand, gaudy and eccentric. Annie's eyes widened even further.

'Wow!'

As soon as the car stopped in front of the covered marble entrance, the huge, brilliantly-coloured glass-fronted and oak front doors flew open and bodies seemed to fly out onto the verandah and down the steps to engulf Annie and Mariella in hugs, tears, and exclamations in rapid Italian. I counted at least twenty people – Mariella's brothers and sisters and their spouses and countless babies and children. Papa Peroni held back, but Mama Peroni cried volubly and held up her arms: 'Mary and Joseph, will you look at this – it is my Anna Maria, all over again – but so tall!' She began to cry.

'No, mama, this is our *Annabelle.*' Mariella chided gently, as she wrapped her arms around her mother and kissed her on both cheeks. 'Of course she is a Peroni, the daughter of our Anna Maria, but she is unique, special. She is herself.'

How right she was; Annabelle *was* very much her own person, something I had learnt to accept. While she was the image of her late mother – with her height and temper my only contribution – this vibrant, beautiful girl was no copy or shadow.

'And do you remember James Duffield, mama?' I offered my hand, but I was grasped and hugged so fiercely I struggled to breathe. Mama Peroni smelt of warm bread and basil, her skin brown and lined from hard hours in the sun. She nodded and wiped away her tears. Of course, of course, she said. The boy with the beautiful eyes. My Anna Maria, such a silly girl …. to leave him. She hurried off indoors, saying we must eat, and she must get the food ready. First, papa, the drinks …

When the excitement eventually died down, we spent the afternoon seated at a very long, white-table-clothed table in the lush garden under a huge olive tree, eating pizza, barbecued pork, salami, prawns, salads, bread, tomatoes, olives, prosciutto and pasta, drinking grappa, prosecco and coffee. It was endless. Italian music was played through speakers hooked up on the veranda. The conversation was rapid, in both English and Italian, voices overlapping, and we were urged to eat, eat … there were a few references to Anna Maria, but were quickly passed over and more food was produced. At the point at which I thought I was about to explode, Papa Peroni offered to show me around the vegetable gardens and the processing plant, while Annie was happy to stay behind with Mama Peroni, Mariella and the rest of the crowd, eating cakes and chocolates. She seemed comfortable and at ease, surrounded by a newly-discovered enormous and voluble family. Already, she seemed to have won their hearts.

Papa Peroni told me how proud he and his children were of what they had achieved. 'But *mama mia*, how many years did it take?' He shook his head, and I noticed how bent he was, how his hands were still strong but brown and scarred, 'But now we have a good life. Maybe some people still think of us as migrant gardeners, but, hey, do I care?

We have the last laugh. I am a big millionaire now!' He chuckled. We were standing under an olive tree, and as he fingered the fruit affectionately, his lined, sun-battered face became sad and thoughtful. 'A good life, yes, but I miss my little Anna Maria. You came to our house all those years ago, and I thank you for ignoring our ... not knowing the laws ... but I knew what you and my daughter were up to. Why you not marry her? I know you are the papa of my beautiful granddaughter. But at least you have brought her back to us.' Tears came into his eyes, and I had to look away. 'My heart it still breaks. No papa at her wedding .. no family at her funeral ... how could that be?' I had no answer to give him that meant any sense any more.

I saw that Annie was tipsy on grappa when we returned to the house. Mama Peroni was showing her photographs of Anna Maria as a baby and a young child. 'We not have any of her as a woman, a married lady,' she said sadly, wiping her eyes with her apron. "maybe a few from the newspapers ... such a beautiful lady ...' It wasn't a surprise to me, given the amount of wine she had drunk and the emotion of the day, that Annie suddenly burst into tears. I was on the verge of emotional overload myself. Mama Peroni gathered Annie up in her ample arms and bosom.

As the afternoon turned into early evening, twinkling lights began to automatically turn on around us – in the trees, inside the house, on the veranda, along the drive – until it looked like we were in some festival fair ground. Despite the invitations to stay for an evening meal and a party – stay the night! – I knew it was time to return to the city. Annie glanced at the photographs spread on the table in front of her, and quietly asked if she may take a few home. Take, take, Mama Peroni said, and thrust a handful at her. We left *The Dolce Vita* laden with photographs, bottles of sauce and grappa, the latter I suspected home-grown in quantities well outside the legal limit, but what the hell?

'Come back, come back, my beautiful girl, Annabelle,' called Mama Peroni as we left.

'I will,' Annie replied. I knew the tone; determination.

* * *

I loved being with Annie in Sydney, but inevitably my thoughts returned to going home. After five weeks I found the media interviews, the drinks and parties in fabulous harbour mansions beginning to pall. It was an easy life. Money was no problem. The sun shone, and storms were few. All around me, pretty Sydney girls flirted in their short dresses, long brown legs and high-heeled sandals, full of fun and bubbly wine. I still enjoyed the luxury of a mobile phone that worked, even if it was hard to raise anyone on Criach. It was fun to risk a dive in the warm Bondi surf and hope the sharks stayed away. I liked the feel of light clothing and shorts and sun on my face, but I missed my home, my wood pile and the cold, clean air of Criach. I missed my mountains. I had spent a few days in the Mount Kosciuszko area, climbing and walking with good, keen climbers. The views were stunning, the comradeship of fellow mountaineers familiar and hospitable, but found it all too easy. I missed the challenge of the Old Lady. Most of all I missed Bonnie and Andy. And, I finally had to admit, there was someone else I missed.

Premier Roland Perritt insisted on a meeting with an 'important proposition' to put to me. I had a fair idea what that would be, but duly suited up and met him in his office in parliament house. Over a whisky in the late afternoon, against a magnificent backdrop of yachts, sailing boats and ferries in the harbour, he quizzed me about whether I *really* wanted to return to Scotland. How could I leave all this? His arm swept over the view from his window. This is where it's *at,* he grinned. Politics had made him more confident, able to afford better suits. He looked groomed and shiny, pleased with himself, bravado hiding the fear of every politician that power and privilege could be swept away at the whim of his own party or the mood of the electorate. On the second whisky, I knew the 'proposition' was about to be revealed: a well-paid, top position on his staff. Influence, he declared, that most could only dream about. How to tell him I wasn't seduced by the privileged Sydney life-style or the trappings of political power? I knew what I wanted. I promised to think about his very generous offer, thanked him, left his office and never gave it another thought.

\* \* \*

I later met Annie at her favourite harbour bar. Despite her once telling me she had no friends, I found her sitting with two very attractive and lively girls about her own age. They were introduced to me as Kylie and Holly, and to them I was simply James. They nodded briefly and politely, shook hands, and then returned to their questioning of Annie about where she had been for the past six months. What had she done? Had she been singing? Making money? With a boy? – go on, tell us. To all the rapid-fire questions, the only information Annie offered – with a wink at me – was that she had been on a gorgeous island.

Their questions going nowhere, the girls changed the topic. Sitting back and listening to them, I learnt that they had busked with Annie in the city streets, late at night, outside railway stations and restaurants. How Annie had managed to avoid Coralyn's vigilance to escape to the city and perform in public for the pure hell and devilment of it, just because she enjoyed being free from constant vigilance and earning her own money. Holly and Kylie, on the other hand, looked as if they worked as buskers pretty well full time because they needed the income. From their clothes and accents, these were not girls from private schools, the eastern suburbs, or from homes with country and harbourside estates. But they shared a lot of interests. The three of them chattered and giggled about music, boy musicians, the best new places to hang out or busk, and occasionally exploded into laughter as they remembered past adventures and escapades, and Annie's near discoveries as she smuggled herself back inside the Kendall house. I bought them food to soak up the alcohol, and left them to it.

I strolled down Rushcutters Bay without consciously knowing why I was drawn there. Soon I found myself in a tree-lined avenue facing a small white house which was shrouded with trees and behind a high security fence. Opposite the house was a bus shelter, and I sat down in the shade and stared across at the pretty, private place where Anna Maria and I used to meet all those years ago. It hadn't changed. If it hadn't already been sold, it was probably now part of Annie's portfolio of assets. Should I tell her what it meant to me? Could I buy it myself? But why? My life was in Scotland.

That little house contained so much heartache and pleasure. How did I feel, looking at it now from the outside, when so many years had gone by? Still sad and nostalgic, of course. But the rawness was gone, and I could remember Anna Maria without misery and guilt. When the sun suddenly dipped behind a cloud, the air felt still and cool. I felt Anna Maria's presence around me, and, God help me, I felt Grannie McPhedron urging me to let the spirits in. I began to talk to Anna Maria inside my head. *Am I doing the right thing, my love? You are still so much a part of me, how can I let you go? Thank God you live on through our beautiful daughter. You would be proud of her. And you might even be proud of me. I hope so.* There was a slight breeze and the trees that hid the house behind the high fence seemed to shiver and turn their leaves outwards to show a silvery side. Maybe they were shaking their leaves at me. Or was it the whisky and wine I had drunk earlier? No, there was no mistaking Anna Maria's sweet, slightly accented voice in my ear. It was very clear, soft and insistent, as near to me as if we were sitting close together on that bus shelter bench. *It is okay, James, dear boy. It is right for you to be happy. I know you will care for our daughter. You will care for each other. But be with your new love, and cherish her the way you cherished me. You must forgive me, and forgive yourself. I loved you with all my heart, but I made a mistake and caused you, and so many people, such unhappiness. For my sake, enjoy your life. Let people love you, James. And never forget that you were the one, and only, love in my life.*

And then she was gone. The breeze dropped and the trees fell silent. I felt lightheaded, calmed, as though I was emotionally washed clean by a bracing cold shower. With one last look at the little house, I hailed the approaching bus as if in a trance, got on, paid the fare, sat and watched the clean, sun-washed streets go by until we reached the city. I found Annie and her girlfriends still laughing, still talking at high speed. I must have been smiling the entire time.

'Hi, James, you look happy,' Annie said when she saw me.

Thank you, Anna Maria, I thought. Thank you for this glorious girl. And thank you for coming into my life one more time. Not so much to say goodbye, but to give me your blessing.

\* \* \*

I was keen now to return home, but I couldn't leave Annie until her legal affairs were settled. Most of the Kendall property assets, including Coralyn's harbourside apartment were to be sold, and Annie had to find a place to live. We spent days driving around in her new, revved-up Mini Cooper sports car looking at houses and flats along the eastern suburbs harbour. She was fun as she kept up a running commentary on what she liked and what she most definitely loathed. She fell in love with a two-storied white building that, to me, looked like a larger version of the house Anna Maria and I had secretly shared. 'I kinda like this place, James,' Annie said. 'It seems familiar somehow.' The view was spectacular, the interior cool and modern, and it was only a few steps from the boutiques and cafés where she liked to shop and spend her money. The security was good. She was a rich, beautiful girl with valuable possessions, and would be pursued by many boys, but she was still chary of strangers, unknown pubs and bottles of drinks she hadn't seen opened herself. I encouraged her caution; I was her father, but still a copper.

Annie's life would be lived as a wealthy Sydney girl with huge responsibilities in managing her assets and investments. She would have masses of professional help and people would be drawn to her for many reasons, including money and romance. So how did I fit into her life? When I returned to Scotland, would she forget me, Criach, Andy and Bonnie? Would I lose her? And what about David in Israel? She never mentioned him. Whatever she decided, I couldn't – wouldn't – let her disappear from my life.

There was also the question of our relationship. I was aware of whispers about our arrival together in Sydney, and our being seen so frequently together. In time the truth would spread through the gossipy eastern suburbs, but until then we avoided the subject even if it one day had to be faced. When I did eventually mention it, she shrugged, and muttered something like she 'really didn't give an (inaudible) about what people thought.' We let it go at that, although she later added that she would never shame or embarrass the memory of Ellery Kendall or her mother. Although we didn't resolve the situation, for the time being that was good enough for me. If Annie didn't care, then I certainly didn't.

It was time to go home when Annie said her affairs were nearly completed. She had moved into her new house, with Kyle and Holly as flatmates, and hired a housekeeper and gardener. As I well knew, housework was not a strong suit of my daughter. When I told her I had booked my return journey home, I suggested we have a farewell dinner with Bob. We chose a small Italian restaurant in Paddington, and as it was a hot, humid night we sat outdoors. I was anxious to get this conversation over with. Annie looked dazzling in a short white linen dress with a halter top, her skin brown and flawless, her face open and affectionate, wearing her favourite hoop earrings. She was the image of her mother at that age. How could I leave her? I felt the next few minutes were about to alter the direction of my life. She ordered food for us in what sounded like pretty good Italian.

'I'm taking lessons, and the Peroni family is helping,' she explained. She bit into a grissini and put her hand over mine. 'James, I know you have to go home ... '

'Yeah, but I will never be far away.'

Thankfully, the wine arrived and drinks were poured. The waiter was keenly interested in catching Annie's attention, and spilled more wine on the table than in our glasses. Bob started to protest, but I silently urged him to remain silent. The tension was killing me. Annie drank her wine and peered into my face.

'Of course you must go home to Bon Bon. She will be fretting. I miss her terribly, so tell her I will come soon ... and often, to see her and Andy. To climb our mountain ... it's as much my home now as yours. I've promised David I will visit Israel one day to see ... well, just to see him.' She blushed and gulped at her wine. 'Honestly, James, you and I won't ever be apart for long. You're too much fun to have around.'

I felt dizzy with relief. Then she told me about her plans for the future, and what she intended to do with her fortune. As I listened, I realised it was *exactly* the right thing for her to do. In essence, a substantial proportion of her assets, shares, properties and investments were being converted into a not-for-profit charity to be called the Ellery and Anna Maria Kendall Foundation (The Kendall Foundation) that would continue the aims and ambitions of the original Kendalls. In this way, she would pay tribute to the man she once thought was her father, the mother she knew for such a short time, and a grandmother who loved her and cared for her. They had all worked hard for Sydney's underprivileged and desperate people, the not-so-lucky ones, and who deserved to be remembered, she said.

'And it will be a tightly-run, no-nonsense affair,' Bob broke in to say, 'as Annie has appointed me as chairman.' An excellent choice; for the diligent, hard-working, loyal Bob, there was no such thing as retirement. I could rest easy knowing he would protect her interests.

'You'll be a director, James,' she turned to me. 'so you'll need to come back once a year for the annual meeting. Mariella is the other director. My Kendall cousins can go to hell, and screech all they like, because I know they've been very well looked after in Grandma's will. My new foundation is ready to be incorporated as soon as we find premises and staff. Sadly, from what I'm told, we won't have any problem finding business.'

She looked very pleased with herself, and at that moment my heart almost burst with relief. With a slight crack in my voice, I managed to say how brilliant she was, and how proud her mother and Ellery would be of her.

'Do you really think so?' Her voice was soft and wistful. 'I wish I'd known her, both of them, but for their memory this must be done. It is the right thing to do.'

'Did you talk to Andy about this?'

'Of course.'

When she left to go to the bathroom, every eye in the restaurant followed her. Bob inclined his head to me and whispered. 'My God, Duffy, she's a chip off the old block. Never saw any likeness to you when I first met her, but, by the living bejesus, she is definitely your kid. You should have seen her today, dressed in those ripped jeans of hers and an old tee-shirt, while the Kendall people filed in with their flash Savile Row suits and snappy Italian leather shoes. She heard them witter on about fairness, their share of her legacy, how unbefitting, not really Australian, how ... I don't know, some other bullshit that went on for some time, until she held up her hand, and then let rip. And by "let rip", Duffy, I mean, she let them have it, all guns blazing. Her money, she said, her idea, her tribute to her grandmother, Ellery and Anna Maria, and if they'd care to challenge her, well, by all means, to go ahead. She'd welcome it. And if they raised one word about her being an Italian, a bastard, a wog, an outsider, she'd have them in court so fast their ears would ring, for some kind of ethnic discrimination. Beautiful to watch, Duffy, bloody beautiful. At the end of the tirade, she said, quite pleasantly, "Now fuck off." Bob and I laughed out loud in that familiar, remembered, shared comradeship. 'And don't worry about her money, Duffy. Even with the money poured into the foundation, she's more than comfortable.'

\* \* \*

The time had come to leave Sydney. I felt a combination of melancholy and exhilaration; sadness at leaving Annie and happy to be returning home to Scotland. At the airport, Annie hugged me hard before I walked through to the waiting Qantas jet, and she repeatedly promised to return to Criach soon. 'I mean it, James,' she said as she adjusted my jacket collar. 'you're a great dad, I love you, and you're never going to escape again.'

We had that morning visited the cemetery to see the graves of Coralyn, Ellery and Anna Maria. Annie left a big expensive pot-plant on her mother's grave ('I can't bear the thought of flowers dying on a grave,' she had said) and I laid some violets alongside. I didn't like to tell her that her plant would probably be nicked before the day was out; she didn't need to hear that. Without Coralyn's vigilance and instructions about regularly clearing the family plot of unwanted 'debris and rubbish', the Peroni family had now laid plastic flowers and framed photographs over Anna Maria's grave. It looked cared for in an eccentric sort of way. Annie cried silent tears as she drew her hand over the inscription of her mother's name and the dates of her short life.

'How I wish, James ... how I wish ... ' She could say no more. I held her close, and whispered back that I wished the same thing. But Anna Maria had chosen her life, had made a mistake, and the consequences couldn't be wiped out. She had brought affection and purpose into a grieving man's life, and learnt a bitter lesson that while enjoying the soft, privileged life of the wealthy, it couldn't fill a hole in her heart. Or guarantee her safety. The latter still hurt, because I had failed her. We had shared so much love, sadness, regrets, heartaches and secrets, and in the end, grief. But she had left the most prized possession of all, our daughter.

'She wants you to be happy, Annie.'

'You too, James. She wouldn't mind about Feddy ... so, please, no more shrines.'

I gazed down at her dark brown eyes, so full of light and hope. So like her mother and yet, so individual. She and her mother were right: the time had come to shed the painful memories of the past, to let them go.

'Time to go, honey, or I'll miss my plane.'

Sydney Harbour was beautiful as I flew over in the late afternoon sun. Annie would return to her new house in Elizabeth Bay and establish her new life. Bob would look after her, but I missed her already. It's a hellish thing, I thought, as the stewardess in the flash business-class cabin offered me a selection of fine food and drinks, to have your heart split in two places. Annie would keep her promise to come back to Criach, Andy, Bonnie and 'her home, her mountain', but until she did, I knew I would miss having her jog beside me, or grasping her hand as she struggled to reach a higher, difficult part of The Old Lady. You haven't lost her, I consoled myself. Not again.

I settled down in the comfortable cabin seat and sipped my drink.

The pretty stewardess hovered, enquiring with a cute smile and wide blue eyes whether I wanted anything to eat, or something more to drink. Was there anything more she could do to make the flight more comfortable? I shook my head. Perhaps women flirted with me, but I could only think of the woman who had waited on the sidelines for too long, and so patiently. As the jet headed towards London, and before I fell into a deep sleep, I knew there was one more thing I had to do, and then my circle was complete.

\* \* \*

Feddy and I were married six months later. When I landed at Heathrow, with unoriginal gifts of duty-free perfumes and Hermès silk scarves in my bag, I took a taxi to Kensington and hoped like hell that she would be home. The gods were kind to me, and she opened the door within a minute of my rapping at the fancy brass doorbell. Feddy was wearing tight, slim trousers and a loose shirt, her feet bare, a pencil behind her ear, long blonde hair tied back in a pony-tail; her expression was momentarily one of irritation, as if she was ready to swat off an unwelcome visitor. Then her eyes widened, and with a squeal of recognition, leapt into my arms. Had I not braced myself and held her tightly, we both would have collapsed in a tangle on her immaculate white-washed steps.

'I knew you'd come back, I just knew it ...' she shrieked, and then I kissed her. 'Quickly, quickly, come inside ... before you disappear ....'

Feddy's apartment has three floors of rooms, and we made love in every one of them, in the bedrooms, in the bathrooms, and in the hallway. This time, for me, there was no guilt, no need to be guarded, and no presence to remind me that I was unfaithful to an old memory. We ended up that night in the bath in the huge, marble-tiled *en suite* adjoining her bedroom. We drank champagne surrounded by candles, and I told her everything that had happened since she left Criach. I found myself struggling for words a couple of times, but she listened quietly, sometimes nodding in understanding, and when I could say no more, she took over.

'You're jet-lagged and exhausted, sweetie. Time for some food and then bed. Tomorrow we can talk some more.'

'Feddy, when you left Criach, you stopped me from saying something. Why?'

She stepped out of the bath and wrapped a huge white towel around herself, then sat on the edge of the bath and held my face in both her hands.

'You were going to say you loved me, Duffy. It was a kind of love, but you were still unsure. You have no idea how much I have wanted to hear you say that. But at that time, you were grateful, anxious, confused, trying to work out which way your life was heading. The timing was all wrong. You needed to sort everything out, get your head clear, your daughter safe and settled, and then, when all that was done, you would know for sure how you felt about me. You couldn't do it any other way, knowing you.'

'You're right, of course. I was in a mess. And it was hellish, but everything worked out better than I ever imagined. Now I *do* know how I feel about you. I've missed you, and love you very much, Feddy. I can hardly believe you want to see me, because I've been cruel to you ... '

'No, just defensive. I kinda knew you would come back to me. Instinct and hope, I guess, but ...' she sighed, 'it was a long, long wait. The number of times I wanted to pick up the phone, catch a train, jump in the car. I saw you on television the night you and Andy rescued that poor Japanese couple, and you looked so handsome but worn out. It took all my willpower not to telephone you, talk to you. And here you are. God, I love you, James Duffield.'

'Will you forgive me?

'Nothing to forgive.'

'So will you marry me?'

'Sure will, Mr Thistle Man.'

'And live in Criach?'

'Anywhere.'

There. I had done it. And it felt good. Feddy organised a party to celebrate our engagement – what I believe was called a 'Feddy Finds her Fella' occasion, with perhaps another 'f' in there somewhere – and although I wasn't particularly anxious to meet the English gentry or eccentric show-biz people who populated her life, I went along with the idea. Once they arrived though, all I could think about was the inspiration they provided for my Galvanney books: bankers, horse breeders, advertising people, actors, chefs, models, writers and dress designers. No journalists or politicians. They were long-time friends and clients who probably owed a lot to Feddy because of her loyalty or marketing skills, but I saw it went beyond that; they adored her. They were not so eager to meet this 'bad guy' who had led her a merry dance for the past few years. They inspected and approved the pink Argyle diamond ring that had once belonged to Feddy's mother, and which was now redesigned to her own taste. Throughout the night Feddy was, well, Feddy: fun, generous, affectionate, concerned to see her guests happy, fed and cared for. We drifted together automatically throughout the evening, our bodies close, unashamedly kissing and temporarily excluding everyone else.

Most had visited Australia, but few had ventured north to Scotland. They were flatteringly interested in my books and television series, and intrigued about living on an island without basic facilities (to them, that meant restaurants, theatres and airport), and where you risked being snowed in and lost to civilisation until the weather thawed. A television sports presenter, wearing a large tartan bow tie in my honour, asked if 'One played tennis in this little island of yours?' I helped myself to another glass of champagne from the passing waiter, and assured him that yes, we did indeed play tennis. A lot. In the snow. In our kilts. He harrumphed, 'jolly good', and wandered over to the buffet table to gorge on oysters and rare roast beef.

I was bailed up by Coco, a gorgeous-looking fashion model from the Caribbean – who was also Feddy's personal assistant when work was slow on the cat-walk – who asked me why I had taken so long to propose to Feddy, considering, as she saw it, I had been a total cad. It's a long, complicated story, I began to say, but guessed this wasn't the time or place to tell a girl who was tipsy and wobbling about on impossibly high heels. I stopped talking. She looked at me with an eyebrow arched, waiting for me to continue.

'I love her, Coco.'

'You'd better, Mr Scottish Mystery Man.'

Coco's sharpness brought me up with a start. There was no doubt in my mind that I loved Feddy and wanted her in my life, but could that be enough for her? I looked around the beautifully-lit and furnished room, and felt a sudden chill of vulnerability, uncertainty. Feddy was so at home in her elegant home and designer clothes, surrounded by smart, successful, interesting people. Was it fair to ask her to live in a small, old-fashioned cottage, cut off from boutiques, the opera, museums, fine food and old friends? What about her business? Could I live in London? Sure, I could write wherever I had a computer and a desk, but I couldn't live without my island, Andy or Bonnie. Maybe I was still jet-lagged, or had drunk too much, or perhaps the enormity and consequences of marriage to Feddy had just hit home. She was giving up too much. I felt the fun go out of the room.

The party ended well past midnight, and Feddy and I fell into bed, slightly drunk and very sleepy. My strange reflective mood had not dissipated. She pressed in close to me, her arm crossed over my chest. The doubts had crept in and stayed. I knew I was selfish, stuck in my ways, and whatever I could offer Feddy wouldn't match what she already had. Her life was so different from mine. How could I have thought otherwise?

Feddy was half-asleep and I studied her face in repose. She was lovely, and, free of make-up and jewellery, looked young, trusting and vulnerable. She half-opened her eyes, and frowned drowsily.

'Don't you dare have second thoughts, Mr Thistle Man.'

'I never want to hurt you again, Feddy, but can I offer you enough ...?'

'Log cabin in the wilds of Scotland, you mean?' She snuggled in closer. 'The answer is yes. You give me everything I want, sweetie. We'll make plans for a life that suits us, however that works out. Maybe a second house in Scotland nearer Glasgow or Edinburgh. Who knows? We'll work it out. I'll keep my flat here in London for visits. Delegate more at work. Maybe even sell the business. I'm ready for the life of a Highland married lady.'

'Are you sure?'

'James Duffield, listen to me,' she raised herself up on her elbow and stared down at me crossly. 'Look, I've had a lot of time to think about this, and yes, I'm sure. I know your heart lies in the Highlands, with Andy and your dog, and I will never take them away from you. It's who you are.'

'You're absolutely sure?'

'Uh huh. Do you know what your problem is? You're still having trouble letting me love you. You're a dear, loyal soul who loves not often but when you do, it's for keeps. That's the kind of man I've always wanted. I loved you the moment I met you, did you know that? And I haven't stopped. Never will. An old cottage and a snow storm won't stop me. And this,' she extended her arm around her beautifully-furnished bedroom with exotic rugs, flowers and fine paintings, 'I've lived with it all my life, and it never brought me much happiness.' She sat up straight, and now looked slightly indignant. 'Besides, can you honestly see me with any of those chaps you met tonight? Great friends and colleagues ... but husbands? Hardly!' She laughed, but then became serious. 'I told you once I was prepared to accept any part of your life you offered me. I can't quite believe it, but now I have the whole James Duffield, and I will love every minute. Never doubt it.'

It was very late, we had drunk too much and were exhausted but it was the sweetest love we had ever made, and I felt my confidence return that our lives together would work out. My doubts, my cold feet, disappeared. I loved this woman, and, by God, I would make sure I kept her, whatever it took. I didn't have to give up my island or cottage. It was a question of compromise, and sharing. I was bad at that, but I could learn. Annie had taught me that.

My remaining time in London with Feddy was fun, filled with visits to art galleries and museums, sharing meals in smart restaurants, talking about things that involved my past that I had never shared with anyone, eating in sleazy little bistros with unexpectedly delicious food; Feddy making me laugh and disturbed in turns by her tales of exploits in Paris. But the pull of a furry black and white face was too much to resist any longer, even against Feddy's fabulous cooking and her huge, warm, comfortable bed, well-stocked bar of champagne, liquors and fine malt whisky. She understood my need to return home, and helped me pack, drove me to Kings Cross Station and promised to join me in Criach as soon as she dealt with some neglected office work.

'You're absolutely sure about all this, Mr Thistle Man?' she asked, more playfully than plaintively, and I hugged her hard. 'This is what you want?'

'Yup.'

I blew her a kiss as the train left the station. As I stowed my luggage, I heard Scottish voices all around me, people like me who were returning home. Already it was strange without Feddy beside me, but my mind was clear of doubts and worries: I was going home to my old life, but it would be a shared life now. For so many years I had sought solace in silence and isolation, but now I felt only a sense of quiet contentment at the prospect of Feddy and Annie in my life.

When Old Hughie pulled into the jetty at Kilsney, he had Bonnie by his side. I whistled, and Bonnie worked herself into frenzy as she dived at me, her tail wagging at impossible speed, and, as always when she was excited beyond containment, she lay flat on the ground and showed me her belly, then leapt up and jumped into my arms. I nuzzled her soft fur and promised never to leave her for so long again. As we ploughed through the waves on the way across to Criach, I took a deep breath and stared at the yonder crags and caves and the rugged coastline I loved so much. At the twinkling lights that were beginning to appear in the gloaming. Seagulls circled and squabbled, and high above in the distance I could make out the magnificent wing-span of an eagle. Even the moody Old Lady of Criach seemed to welcome me home with some warmth. I saw Andy waiting at the jetty, waving, his strong, solid figure set against the stiff breeze, his ginger hair flying. Now I was home.

It was good to sit with Andy in the pub over a slow whisky, and hear that nothing much had changed in my absence. Kenny still grumbled at the bar and served the same ramblers, climbers, farmers and their dogs. Outside, the weather was turning icy, and it promised to be another severe winter. Andy knew of Annie's philanthropy and I recalled how the pair of them had spent hours together in private talks. She'll be back, he assured me. You know the lure of yon old mountain. Surprisingly, he ventured to say that he knew I'd always marry Feddy, when my 'heart was ready'. I was keen to find out how busy the rescue team had been. Not very, he said, and for hours we talked about a promising new team member, new equipment, and fresh rumblings about the possibility of a connecting bridge from Criach to the mainland to attract more tourists. It will come to nothing, he said, and I knew that if Andy thought his island was about to be over-run by too many unwelcome tourists and day-trippers, there was no chance of a bridge. Later, as we shared a meal of fish he had caught earlier in in the day, Bonnie lying under the table with her head on my lap, he told me his real news.

'I'm giving up the tourist business, Duffy.' I knew he was too young and far too active to retire so I waited for him to explain. With winter coming on, and the closure of his coach company, he had finally accepted the job of senior ranger for the Scottish north-western island region. It had always been on offer to him, and I was delighted he had now accepted it. Not only would he be based in Criach and near his mountains, but he could indulge – with authority – his zeal for protecting the environment and his beloved birds and animals. Great stuff, I told him. It would be good to have him nearby more often, living in his wee cabin by the shore. Getting around the islands with old boats that were unreliable and hardly able to withstand the winter storms, though, was a serious issue and a perennial problem. Still, if anyone could fix it, it was Andy Cameron.

A very tanned Annie returned to Criach a few months later, via Tel Aviv, tight-lipped but thoughtful when the subject of David came up. Over the months she stayed, she told Andy and me what she intended to give to the island, on condition that the donor remains anonymous. She offered Old Hughie a new ferry, which he declined, and accepted instead the offer of finance to update, paint and repair his old one. He was gruffly thrilled with his smart, faster new ferry and immediately raised the fares. If it hadn't already been called *The Criach*, he would have named it *The Annie*, he told us, but he felt it was bad luck to change a boat's name.

*The Annie* was a name that was conferred on a brand new fast speedboat that arrived in Criach from Glasgow. It was sleek and impressive, designed and equipped to handle the most hazardous weather conditions that Scotland could serve up, and able to zip easily and rapidly amongst the islands scattered around the western coast. According to its specifications, we read, it accommodated a crew of four, and could be handled by one operator in any emergency. 'Look,' Andy said with a grin, 'it says here it's essential for rescue and assistance on lonely islands. Just the very dab for us, Duffy.' He had called it a 'wonderful surprise', but he couldn't kid me; I knew that he and Annie had been up to their ears in its selection and delivery.

Everyone in Criach and the nearby islands came out to welcome *The Annie,* and to take part in its christening. Annie wanted the vessel called *The Bon Bon* but reluctantly agreed to *The Annie* and launched it with a bottle of local whisky (it was actually tea in an old whisky bottle; I'm not wasting good whisky, she had said) with raucous roars and applause from the crowd. After much cheering and handshaking under coloured bunting and Scotland's Saltire flag, *The Annie* was formally handed over to Andy by the ship-builder who had had sailed her up from the Clyde River. Looking very smart in his ranger's uniform, Andy was now 'Captain Andy'.

It was a tremendous gift worth millions of pounds, and of course the islanders knew it had come from Annie, the rich girl from Australia who turned out to be 'Duffy's wee girl'. We all remembered the terrible night in Kenny's pub when she collapsed, and how close she had come to death. And how Old Hughie – in the absence of any other means of crossing the sea in a wild and dangerous storm – had battled and coaxed his old ferry to get her safely to the mainland. The story had already melded into the island's mythology. Pray God, with this new fast and modern speedboat, such a night would never happen again.

Breaking free from the curious crowd, Andy offered to give Annie, Feddy and me 'a burl' around the island to show off the speed of his fabulous new boat. So we clambered aboard, and, with our faces to the wind, our life-vests firmly strapped around our chests, hair flying, we scudded through the waves with effortless ease, flying past what looked like an approving Old Lady of Criach and some of the smaller islands around her. Annie nudged me, grinned, and playfully shouted above the engine noise that she was happy to buy me a new Land Rover to replace the one she had damaged. I, not-so-playfully, refused. She roared with laughter, and pressed close to me.

\* \* \*

Feddy came to live with me a few weeks after I left her in London, and almost overnight my spare, masculine cottage became a different place. Newly-painted, it looked clean and bright, atmospheric with colourful new lamps, cushions and rugs. It took almost the entire male population of Criach to get a new oversized bed up the stairs and into our bedroom; covered with Scottish heritage quilts and oversized pillows, to me it was the most welcome sight in the cottage at the end of the day. The kitchen was modernised as much as possible, but the old wood stove was retained, Feddy declaring it as good an oven as she'd ever worked with. Old Hughie was kept busy with daily off-loads of Feddy's boxes and purchases from the mainland, or those sent up from London.

Feddy and I were married on a sunny spring day in May. Criach folks forgave the fact my bride was English, and adopted the attitude, 'well, if that daft Jamie Duffield wants a wee English wifie, so long as she doesn't take him away over the border, she'll be good enough for us.' For the occasion, Feddy bought me a kilt with every accessory – sporran, dirk and long tartan socks – and ignored my protests about the indignity of wearing a skirt. I'm an Australian, I protested. No, you're not, she replied, you're every bit a Scot.

The service was held at the local (and only) Presbyterian church, with the reception at the parish hall next door. On the day, they overflowed with every villager, invited or not, dressed in their best clothes and tartan outfits. Bob Connelly and his wife arrived in Criach a few days earlier, laden with Australian wine, and booked into Kenny's crammed hotel. A formal typewritten letter grandly headed, 'From the Premier of New South Wales, The Hon Roland Perritt MP' arrived via Bob, congratulating me and Feddy on our 'happy occasion'. Underneath was a personal handwritten scrawl saying if I ever changed my mind about coming back to Sydney, the job was still waiting for me. I screwed it up and flung it in the fire. I enjoyed watching the flames turning it into ash.

David and Ari sent their best wishes, and said how sorry they were that their hospital and military duties meant they couldn't leave Tel Aviv. Mariella unexpectedly made the journey and brought with her many crates of Peroni sauces and grappa. She looked a different, happier woman from the one who had arrived two years earlier. Lots of bush-walking, she explained to Andy. Feddy's closest London friends had hired a yacht with a butler and captain and anchored off the coast, praying the weather held as none had any real sailing experience, and most declared themselves sea-sick before the vessel even moved. They arrived in their smart new sailing clothes, took over the pub, politely declined invitations to walk, climb or swim and spent their time drinking, playing pranks on each other and raising the revenue of the village by many thousands of pounds. At night they returned to their brilliantly-lit yacht for more drinking and eating, emerging late the next morning for a repeat of the previous day's activities. My old adversary, Coco, was among them, looking dazzling and exotic, forever with a glass of champagne in her hand. She bowled me up one afternoon.

'And so, Mr Thistle Man, you've kept your promise.'

'I have indeed.'

She stood back and surveyed me, then smiled a forgiving, gorgeous smile and hugged me. 'Life's just too short for sadness,' she whispered in my ear.

On the day, as the bridesmaid she shimmied to the church in a figure-hugging pale blue satin dress which had every male Criach bloke slack-jawed with admiration. The other London guests appeared in formal wedding gear, with top hats and outrageous hats, prepared, if necessary, to frog-march a reluctant groom up the aisle. There was no risk of that, I assured them.

Annie had pinned a big tartan bow around Bonnie's head, while she herself had outdone herself in the tartan department: tartan dress, tartan shoes.

But no-one could outshine Feddy. She looked exquisite in a long white dress with a sort of flower headdress interwoven through her long, curly hair. She held a bouquet of red roses and white heather tied with tartan ribbon. After the church service, we walked hand-in-hand to the nearby parish hall under clouds of confetti and rose petals, surrounded by pipers and guests who were keen to get to the entertainment part of the proceedings. Feddy threw her bouquet to Coco who caught it with cat-like agility.

The London guests mixed cheerfully with the Criach families and joined in the Scottish dancing with verve if not comprehension. Feddy danced with every man in the room, while I was swept onto the dance floor by every able-bodied Criach girl and woman; the champagne flowed, the whisky disappeared, and the never-ending feast of lamb, salmon, potatoes, endless salads and shortbread was constantly replaced. The locally-made wedding cake was a tower of white icing and streams of tartan ribbon.

The pipers, drummers and fiddlers, 'gave it laldy' as the Glasgow expression had it, Kenny pounded on his bodhrán, and the noise could be heard across the fields and up the mountains. 'The Old Lady of Criach will be tappin' her wee cold feet tonight,' one of the farmers told me with a deadly serious face, 'she'll be enjoying hersel' fer a change.' The eating, drinking, speeches and Scottish reels went on until the wee hours of the morning. Never had I ever seen such a swirl of tartans, such cheerful conviviality amongst such ill-assorted people, or the consumption of so much food and drink.

Naturally Andy was my best man, and a fine Highland figure he made in his full Cameron Clan kilt regalia. His speech was gracious and witty, and everyone laughed and interrupted rudely. I blushed, and Feddy giggled. If I didn't know him better, I would have sworn he was very drunk. We had wisely taken the precaution of placing a ban on hikers and climbers for two days, as we anticipated there wouldn't be a sober soul on the island in the event of a mountain emergency. The ferry, despite grumblings from tourists banked up on the other side, was declared 'out of order' for the weekend. 'Like the notice says,' Old Hughie muttered, pipe firmly between his teeth, a whisky to hand as his feet tapped out the beat of the pipes and drums, 'conditions of carriage apply.'

For me, the best speech of the night came from my daughter, who half-way through the night bounded up onto the make-shift stage, holding high her long tartan frock, Bonnie at her heels, and called for a toast to 'the best dad in the world.' With a signal to the musicians, she launched into songs that were crazy, sad, mad, and jubilant, which had her audience swinging and singing. Her months with me had birthed a swag of songs that captured her thoughts about love, friendship, loneliness, betrayal, belonging, and Scotland – all that life had thrown at her. We applauded until our hands stung and felt raw, and one of the London guys who was a top music agent later asked Annie if she would consider making records.

Neither Feddy nor I was sure how we got home to the cottage after our wedding, or, indeed, where all the guests found beds, or who they shared them with. The lovely Caribbean Coco was intent on spending the night with Andy and a bottle of champagne, but I could have warned her there was no chance of that happening. He was a wizard at avoiding unwelcome confrontations. 'They're very pushy, these London lassies,' he muttered as he set off home in the dark, slightly unsteady but with his kilt swinging to an impressive tempo.

The sky was streaked with disappearing stars when I carried my bride over the threshold of my (now, our) cottage, while Bonnie ran ahead to her basket, exhausted and full-bellied. She sniffed the air curiously a few times, then curled herself into a furry black and white comma in front of the fireplace, nose tucked under her tail, and fell asleep. Everything was right with her world. If I was happy with Feddy, so was she.

'I have something for you, Mrs Thistle Man', I whispered to Feddy. I certainly hope so, her eyes responded with a twinkle. I left her making coffee in the kitchen as she stepped out of her long gown. The laundry door was closed, and I hoped my surprise was still inside, safe, if maybe a little lonely and fretful. Inside was a box lined with woolly blankets, from which came a tiny squeak of protest. Bonnie's mother had been up to her old wanton ways again, and Bonnie now had a half-brother. The tiny face looked up at me, glad to see a friendly human after being locked away for hours in a strange place, and struggled to reach me. Come on, wee thing, I whispered to the pup, first a pee, and then meet your family.

Feddy was now in her underwear and pouring coffee into wedding-present Scottish pottery mugs when I returned to the kitchen. We certainly didn't need it, but she poured two, final, glasses of Drambuie. Glancing up at me and the blanket-covered bundle in my arms, she put the coffee pot on the table and came closer, squinting curiously.

'Your wedding present,' I said. The little black and white pup, so like Bonnie at nine weeks old, struggled to get to Feddy. This I know to be true: pups know the magic formula to make you fall in love, and this little fellow was a true magician. Feddy took a deep breath, then held the tiny creature up to her face, letting its legs dangle. She looked across at me with eyes shiny with tenderness. Yup, I said. This little boy's yours.

'He's a Bobby', she said emphatically. 'That's his name.' He was gently crushed between us as she hugged me, and whispered that she loved her wedding present. Bonnie, woken by the commotion and the smell of another animal in close proximity, came to sniff out the proceedings. She did so with a proprietorial air, snuffling at Bobby until she was satisfied that he represented no danger to her property or my affections, and went back to sleep in her basket.

\* \* \*

The four of us settled into life on Criach. I learnt that Feddy really *did* understand how the island was buried deep in my heart and soul. In time, it worked that same alchemy on her as it had with me and Annie. Nothing could replace the peace I found there, the balm of silence, or the gratitude I felt for a mountain that had restored me physically and mentally.

Those first days in Criach after the wedding, and our week long honeymoon around the Highlands staying in cosy bed-and-breakfast places, taking long walks amongst the heather and glens, are imprinted on my memory as the happiest I had known since the innocent, early days with Anna Maria. I couldn't forget her, of course, but she no longer was with me as a dark, sad shadow. No longer a shrine that excluded the living; now she moved lightly between us.

Before she returned to Sydney, Annie framed some of the photographs of her mother that the Peroni family had given her, together with some of us together. It was good to see I wasn't cut out of the pictures, and shared an equal place on Annie's dressing table with her other knick-knacks. In the centre was her mother's empty perfume bottle. I was sad to see her leave, but I knew she had a good life to go back to in Sydney with friends and her foundation. Her bedroom was always kept ready for her return, and Bonnie sometimes escaped for peace from the pup to snooze on her bed, and, like me, wishing she would soon come home again.

But Annie was never away for long. The agent who had been so impressed with her music at the wedding, turned out to be serious about Annie's talent, and he and Feddy finally persuaded her to go to London to record some of her songs. With marketing and promotion to a specific audience, they sold quite well. Again after some persuasion, she was contracted to perform in a few Scottish country towns, and then, when they were sell-outs, in Glasgow and Edinburgh venues. She paid for her two flatmates, Kylie and Holly, to come to Scotland as her back-up singers. They arrived squealing and diving into the whisky. I was astonished when she contacted Lachlan from the village and put a proposal to him that involved being her 'roadie bodyguard'. Barely days afterwards the phone call, Lachlan arrived in Scotland prepared to start immediately and take his new job very seriously indeed. Surprisingly, he turned out to be a very good 'roadie'.

The whole gig thing was out of our league, but Andy, Feddy and I travelled to support Annie when she performed anywhere in Scotland, sitting in the front row clapping like seals whenever she and her two-girl back-up appeared. The three girls were outrageous in their wee short kilts, but were great, instinctive musicians. The audience loved them, and hooted and hollered in appreciation after each set. After the shows, we all crowded into nearby pubs to make a lot of noise, fend off admirers, eat pizza and drink pints of beer. Lachlan was fiercely protective of 'his lassies', and nobody bothered them while he was nearby. It turned out he was so impressive at his job that when Annie returned to Australia, he was invited to join a promising London band as their bodyguard. The last I heard he was hooning around London on a Harley Davison.

Annie could have made a name for herself as a folk singer – or singer of any kind of music, really – and agents were keen to promote her, but after the first forays in sell-out concerts in country towns and then Glasgow and Edinburgh, she decided she would play only to raise money for Scottish charities, animal welfare and the upkeep of the Criach speedboat. Her heart was not in public acclaim, or in the exhausting travel and public exposure that being on the road involved. She preferred to write her songs or perform for small groups where she felt comfortable, but most of all she wanted to tell stories through her music. With Feddy's encouragement and contacts, she formed her own company ('Bon Bon's World'), hired a manager whom she trusted, and sold the rights to her songs and music to other musicians.

In Australia, one of Annie's anti-war songs became a hit and was played frequently on Anzac Day. I recognised the inspiration for the ballad that lamented lost war-time youths on battle fields, for lives that war had stolen all too brutally soon and for those who were left behind to lament and live with sorrow. The song's bitter sweet reprise about longing for home while far away in a foreign country was simple and profound. It wasn't cheap, tawdry sentimentalism. It was mellow, its melody crafted brilliantly, but sharp with rebuke for those careless with political power. I recognised that much of the ideas behind it came from Ellery Kendall's war-time poetry book.

I know Annabelle Kendall is a Sydney girl, sharp and sassy, but I know her also as a Criach girl who rides horses like the wind, and scales mountains like a mountain goat. Who arrives here with a back-pack and claims her bedroom, bringing stories of Bob and the Ellery Foundation, and sometimes bitter, scathing remarks about the Kendall cousins who have discovered the truth about her biological father, and fulminate about court cases and challenging wills, but who wisely do nothing about it. She is keen to be filled in about village gossip, and to share a beer with Old Hughie and Andy. She is bossy, and demands I cook her lots of chips; and still stuffs Bonnie with potato crisps.

But what of David? Although Annie loved him, and wrote beautiful songs in Yiddish, David was implacable that marriage was impossible. He is a child of Israel and the Jewish religion and that excluded Annie. He would not marry a gentile against the wishes of his Orthodox Jewish family, even if Annie were prepared to convert. As intermittent bombing and terrorist acts were broadcast from Tel Aviv or elsewhere in Israel, Annie confided to me her fears that David, although a doctor, would be caught in the crossfire. But, she said, I must be brave. I cannot walk away from fear. If I cannot be his wife, he deserves my courage as a friend. For the first time, she admitted how helpless and heart-broken she felt against his intransigence. 'You just can't fight it, can you, James?' she said sadly

Our son, Alexander Andrew – wee Sandy – was born a year later on Criach and Andy took the role as godfather very seriously. Annie feigned jealousy about a step-brother but her visits to Criach increased. God knows I was a mess when I first saw my wee son, but my throat still tightens when I recall the day he was born, when Andy picked him up and held him close to his chest. I had never seen Andy so emotional before. The wee soul with the corn-coloured hair brought back to him so many sad memories. But there was also the happier prospect of Uncle Andy teaching him all those things that he had longed to teach his own son, spending time on mountains and the ocean, fishing, walking, explaining about animals and birds. About the right thing to do. He would probably be a better dad than me, but I felt no scrap of jealousy, only gratefulness.

I stopped writing novels about Galvanney, simply because I felt the television series was making him a caricature of the character. I turned to other stories about Scotland, mysteries and who-dunnits, set in picturesque villages and often with strong female characters who evaded traps and capture and solved cases. I introduced love interests. It was all a lark, really, and so easy to do. I was often asked to write a novel set in Australia, but I never considered it. Truth be told, I loved Australia but never really understood it. Not the way I understood Scotland and its people, or my own particular place in it.

With the baby and Annie's visits we were cramped for space and a decision had to be made about whether to extend the cottage or find a bigger house. In the end, we decided to do both, mainly because Feddy knew I could never give up the cottage. So we negotiated to buy the stones that lay around the dilapidated old castle and used them to build two downstairs bedrooms and studies for Feddy and me. At every step of the renovations, we stressed to the workmen how the character of the original cottage had to remain intact. As island men, they understood.

Communication still remained difficult in Criach, and inevitably it proved impossible for Feddy to maintain her marketing business from afar. After much discussion and travelling around the areas we liked, we bought an old, run-down stone house with spectacular views overlooking Loch Lomond. Feddy – with her team of architects and designers, who were devoted both to her and her cooking – converted it into a beautiful, modern home. Over time, though, her visits to London decreased and eventually she wound down her business commitments altogether. We enjoyed commuting between our two houses, but it was always with a light heart that I returned home to Criach.

The Criach villagers became used to the English 'Mrs D' and liked the way she often helped Kenny out in the hotel when he was short of staff, even if she struck fear in the kitchen hands when she flipped pans and sliced potatoes with lethal knives at breakneck speed. 'You think *I'm* a tough boss?' she would yell at them, 'Boys, you ain't been where I've cooked!' At home she baked and cooked her delicious meals, always making extra to deliver to any elderly or sick villagers; she substantially boosted the takings of the tourist shop and distillery with clever marketing advice. She talked about opening up a cookery school on the island, dedicated to Scottish cooking, and already the plans were on her desk. Although often exhausted by day's end, she was never too tired to let me show how much I love her.

As promised, I returned to Australia to attend Annie's first board meeting and found the foundation working well. She had an excellent team around her, headed by the now-retired Bob who ran the show like a grandfatherly tyrant. I was again on the first plane available when news reached me by phone from a panic-stricken Annie that bushfires in New South Wales were running out of control, and the Peroni property was under threat of destruction within days. She and I worked alongside the guys from the emergency fire service and the Peroni family when the fires did hit their land. It was gruelling, hot work but eventually we tamed what could have been a total wipe-out of everything they had worked for. After those two days of battling smoke and fire, with no sleep and snatched food, Annie and I lay flat on our backs on the wet lawn leading up to the Peroni house. Although badly singed, it was saved. The gardens were gone, but they would regenerate. We were exhausted, filthy, covered in grit and ash, and shared a bottle of water.

'You're one fierce fighter, dad,' she commented wearily.

'You're not a bad warrior yourself, sweetheart.'

Dad. Husband. No-one needed to remind me how lucky I was. My life came down to this: so long as I could write my mad novels, had Feddy, the baby and the two dogs nearby, I had every reason to be grateful for my second chance at life. Criach and my cottage no longer offered me silent solace and a sanctuary; they were now places of laughter and love. It meant as much to Annie as to me. There is a special space in her heart for that wee dog who loved her the moment she stumbled into the cottage, drunk, disorientated, hateful and hating. Feddy from choice has become a fine Highland woman. We all love Bobby, but he leads a different life from Bonnie. He wears the designer dog-jackets Feddy buys him, and has regular shampoos and haircuts, and hates the active outdoor life that Bonnie craves. Not for him a brisk trot up a steep mountain sniffing out injured climbers, or a determined chase for a rabbit or hare. He prefers to be with Feddy, lounging in his basket in the kitchen while she works, or strolling with her to the village café for shopping and plaudits about how handsome he is.

The gods have been kind to me. Two years on from Annie's arrival in Criach, and having since gone through emotional storms to match those Criach and the Old Lady herself could throw up, I am a happy man. To a point. I soon discovered that loving people has its own perils; I worry about my family all the time, fretting that they are safe and free from harm. I miss Annie when she is in Sydney, and curse the poor connections that often make it impossible to talk to her by phone or internet. God knows, my island isn't perfect.

I think about all this as I walk to the village. I hold Feddy's hand, and wee Sandy is strapped to my chest in his tartan cocoon, while Bonnie and Bobby caper alongside us. Annie is home, and now chucking stones into the sea. My family is complete. We will soon meet Andy at the pub for lunch; wee Sandy will nestle into his arms and be told about the future pleasures of climbing mountains and spectacular views from heights that will take his breath away. And as for the wee birds and animals ... the world, Uncle Andy promises, is full of wonder.

I glance up at the Old Lady of Criach. Her sharp edges seem to be softer as she looks down on us, at what must look like a picture of domestic perfection. The clouds around her peaks are wispy, friendly, and she has temporarily hidden those jagged talons with the capacity to destroy anything that mocks her authority. I offer a silent thanks to the old black mountain that took me to her heart and gave me a life of contentment I never thought possible, or deserved. I am grateful to her for taking Annie into her care and bringing my troubled daughter back to life, and into my world. And for welcoming my wife. I thank Andy,

Grannie McPhedron and Feddy for teaching me what generosity and courage is all about, and how it's possible – against life's cruelties – to slide away from the edge of darkness and despair. Away from the urge to live and seek solace from a life of silence and isolation.

From the mist and clouds of the mountains that surrounded us, I heard the familiar, accented voice of Anna Maria: *this is how your life should be, dear James. Cherish it. Never let it go. And love with all your heart.* She heard my promise.

It suddenly began to rain and we ran for shelter. As always, the Old Lady of Criach was having the final word.

THE END

·

# ABOUT THE AUTHOR

Kim Murray was born in Scotland and retains an affection for Scottish people and its culture, particularly that of the Highlands.

She spent many years working in the corridors of Parliament House in Canberra with politicians and leaders, campaigning, constantly travelling throughout Australia, and on overseas delegations. Later at university, she converted this knowledge and experience into a PhD thesis on politics, and subsequently enjoyed tutoring young students on the 'the art of compromise'.

Kim now lives in Adelaide, writes, and dabbles in broadcasting. She lives with her rebellious, but beautiful, brown poodle, Wee Geordie McKay.

# ACKNOWLEDGEMENTS

*The Solace of Silence* was conceived many years ago, and along the way it has taken many routes and different plot turns. Although the island and its characters are fictional, the essence of the Scottish nature never changed. I am grateful for that Scottish heritage.

My sisters, Eileen Brooks and Mabel Reid, were very helpful in proof-reading and offering suggestions. I am particularly indebted to my brother, John Murray, for his specialised police knowledge. Old friends like Jan Coles, Donna Jacobsen, Betty Ann Daly, Rosemary McKay, and Suzanne Kaspryzak were always available for ideas, encouragement and copious champagne when literary imagination fled. For which I thank them.

The godmother of *Solace of Silence* has to be Christine Lister. A wise and clever writer, she understands the pitfalls of the loneliness of writing, and has kept the goal firmly in mind, and me focussed on the task of bringing *Solace* to a wider reading audience. For her kindness and care, there are no adequate words to express my appreciation.

To all the dogs I have loved over the decades, I thank for the insights, fun, and unconditional love they always gave; in some way, each of them has become a part of the little mongrel so beloved of our hero in *Solace*.

www.ingramcontent.com/pod-product-compliance
Lightning Source LLC
Chambersburg PA
CBHW070547120726
47909CB00007B/2264